Published by: Cornwall Writers
Text Design by: Tracey Dockree
Cover Design by: Lucy H Smith
ISBN: 978-1-8380932-2-8
Distributed by:
Cornwall Writers
Princes House
Princes Street
Truro
Cornwall TR1 2ES

Scan QR code below for Content Warnings

Cornwall Writers

Cornwall: Secret & Hidden

A Collection of Short Stories and Other Scribbles

CORNWALL
SECRET AND HIDDEN
A COLLECTION OF
SHORT STORIES

CORNWALL
WRITERS

Cornwall Writers Short Story Project

Cornwall Writers is a community of writerly friends committed to honing our writing and editing skills and learning how to publish, market and sell books.

This is our second anthology of short stories. The first, *Cornwall: Misfits, Curiosities and Legends*, was published in September 2020. We so enjoyed the process, that we started writing stories for this anthology straight away.

Like the first anthology, our focus is on Cornwall, and this time the stories seek out the secret and hidden aspects of life in our county.

We hope you enjoy our stories as much as we did putting them together.

Cornwall Writers

Cornwall: Secret & Hidden

Short Stories and Other Scribbles

Biographies *page 347*

Story Sketch Credits:

The Triumph of Goliathia Tremayne

by Catherine Leyshon

Goliathia Tremayne lived in a shack fashioned from bits of corrugated iron, railway sleepers, and the mast of a ship in a thorny, gorsey hollow half way up Carn Brea. Her best friend Jason lived in the yard, in a homemade tent the size of a coffin. On Wednesday nights, Goliathia would polish her teeth with the corner of her towel and walk down the hill with Jason to watch Benny Hill at Mother's in Camborne. The rest of the week, she guarded the stolen motorbikes her father had hidden down the mineshaft twenty-five paces to the southwest of the shack. Twenty-five of Goliathia's paces equalled forty of the ordinary souls over whom she towered, filling the space meant for the sky. On rainy days, of which there were many, she wrapped herself in a tarpaulin and stamped through the mizzle to check the shaft. On good days, when the gorse covering the shaft's entrance popped and cracked and smelt of suntan lotion, she sat like a boulder with Jason in the bushes nearby, and they talked.

'What's it like up close, then, the sea?' she would ask. From where they sat, it was just another piece of the sky, ironed flat against the horizon.

Jason was considered an authority on the matter. Whilst neither of them had ever been to a beach, he was a mere fourteen generations downstream of a Spanish captain who had waded ashore and kissed the sand at Housel Bay, his ship no more than a pile of matchwood in the waves. Jason's eyes were as dark as the deepest mine, but liquid and earnest, like a seal pup's.

'The sea's a mirror for the sky, but bright white at the edges. It climbs over itself. Sometimes it comes, then it goes.'

'What about the sand?'

'It's a powder, like flour, only yellow.'

Then there would be a pause before Jason made his oft-repeated promise to the woman who took up as much room in his dreams as she did in the world.

'I'll take you to the beach. We'll go on the bus.'

And Goliathia Tremayne would sigh and say, 'But who will look after the motorbikes? Besides, Father's going to take me when he comes back here to live.'

Sharky Tremayne had lurched into fatherhood with his customary haphazardness. An arsonist of the heart, he briefly lit up Marigold Polglase, Cornwall's strongest woman, who had run away from the circus when it pitched up at Pool Market. Sharky wooed her with his talk of the easy money to be made fencing stolen motorbikes. He had a penchant for Oxford bags, tight fitting shirts, silk scarves and a white homburg.

An exotic bird like Sharky could not be caged in Camborne for long. Shortly after Marigold had parted her colossal legs and given issue to Goliathia, Sharky found he had a pressing engagement up country. His appearances became both infrequent and fleeting.

Goliathia, christened Gloria, grew and grew. Seams strained, blouses were short waisted, shoes pinched, skirts rapidly became indecent. And yet the girl remained oblivious to the way the world saw her until the Trevithick Day parade, 1977. The lower junior class paired up for the march, spick and span, high polish on shoes, and ironed shirts. The fragrance of carbolic soap and Vosene wafted in the air.

Sharky was there for once. Jason was off school with chickenpox but had sneaked out to watch, heartsore to see his best friend's giant hand crowded into David Teague's sticky little mitt, teacher's orders. David was permanently snotty, dragging the thick green stream back into his head with a vehement sniff, only for it to begin its journey across his lip once again. If it reached his mouth, he slurped it in like a fluorescent slug.

Eamon Turnpenny was MC that day, a local boy briefly made good on the telly doing Midlands Today up country, with his voice like butter and honey. He was now bitter and broken and permanently inebriated. Not ten minutes before he took to the microphone, he had been telling the Mayor his version of his tragic undoing at the hands of a beauty pageant contestant in Coventry, who had been all silly plaits and shy thighs and giggling mouth.

The sky suggested a shower to come. He had left his coat in the pub with his glasses in the pocket. His notes bucked and flapped in the spiteful April wind. Just a list of names, floating on a sea of gin.

'David Teague and...' Eamon peered - booze soaked and sweaty - at the boy and the improbable girl giant, and stopped. 'David and...' he began again, his thoughts spinning away on the wind.

'...Goliathia!' roared a voice from the crowd.

It was the laughing that brought the young girl suddenly to a sense of herself, as if she had landed in her body from the sky. Jason, scab-laden and itchy at the front of the crowd, saw the humiliation plunge through his friend like molten lava, mottling her face and neck ruby red. She squeezed David Teague's hand fit to snap. Her real name was destitute, exiled. Goliathia stuck like a barnacle, like a manacle. She disliked anyone who held the name in their mouth with relish like a ripe plum, as if they knew something about her. She was constantly turning away from their stares and grins. Only Jason kept Gloria, her true name, on his lips and in his heart.

Each time Sharky deigned to return during Goliathia's childhood years, it was on a different motorbike. He might appear while she was standing with Jason in the school yard waiting for the bell. Or she might come downstairs in the morning and find Sharky at the kitchen table saying, 'Lovely crib, Mother,' as if he lived there all the time and had every right to be stuffing his face with saffron buns.

'Don't mutt about, Goliathia,' Mother would say, her face as pink as a boiled ham. 'Get your coat on and help Father.'

So the girl would polish every inch of the metal carapace of whatever motorbike Sharky had ridden in on. She would buff their leather seats and black their tyres. As night fell, she would pick up a tarpaulin and the coil of heavy rope that weighed more than Sharky, and troop up Carn Brea while Sharky rode to where the track ended in a riot of gorse and bracken. Sharky would go ahead with a lantern, and Goliathia would carry the motorbike like a corpse through the undergrowth to the shaft, huffing with the effort, for Sharky could not countenance a scratch on a petrol tank or gearbox. Then she would go back for the tarp and the rope.

Together they would swaddle the bounty tight against the salt in the wind and the rot of age, preserving its future worth. Finally, Goliathia, starlit and magnificent, would pull the torrent of her chestnut hair into a bun, bend to the rope, take up the slack, brace her legs, dig the heels of her school shoes into the earth and inch the parcel down as if it was full of eggs. Sharky would lean in with his lantern, suck his teeth, and wince each time the package kissed the walls of the shaft, as if a wound was inflicted on him personally. When the cargo landed like a feather on the motorbike in the pile below it, Goliathia would shake free Sharky's clever knot and haul up the rope. She would look down at her raw, hemp-scorched hands on the ends of her quivering arms.

'Shall you take me to the beach tomorrow, Father?' she would pant.

'Back off up country tomorrow, my bird,' Sharky would always reply.

After a few years, when the last motorbike Sharky stole was lowered lovingly into the dark, he rocked back on his heels and contemplated the future. The chasm was as full as Sharky dared, a precarious tower of sheathed machines, their liquids and juices gently congealing, their roaring and racing but a distant memory. He needed a custodian for his ill-gotten, subterranean hoard that had been lost so long no one was still looking for them. Each year in the mine, their vintage matured, like wine in a cave.

Sharky looked up at his accomplice daughter and said, 'Haven't you just left school? You're a bit old to still be living at home. I've got a job for you.'

And thus, instead of immediately scuttling away up country, he set Goliathia up in the shack forty average paces north east of the shaft. Indentured to the bikes, but free at last of Camborne and folk who stared, she moved out of Mother's with two plastic bags of stuff and a moth eaten candlewick bedspread the colour of bile.

The next day, Jason walked up from Camborne, a bolt of waxed canvas under his arm. Whilst Goliathia watched from the shack door, he carefully built his body-shaped tent in the yard. He was as full of the yearnings of unrequited love for a good woman as any man had a right to be.

Thus the mineshaft had gulped Sharky's treasure, but eventually he sought requital from the gorse-shrouded gash, taking the bikes away to sell. Accordingly, Goliathia was frequently summoned at night from the shack to stand astride the shaft's earthy flange and lower Sharky into the dense black cleft whilst she waited with the rope cinching her waist. A proud sweat beaded her flawless skin. She set her granite eyes on the distant line where the lights on the coast blinked out and the midnight blue velvet of the sea began, broken only by the winking lights of a lone ship. She thought about the day when the last motorbike would hatch from its tarpaulin shell, and Sharky, lacking any further reason to go up country to either steal or sell, would return for good. She would find him on the settee with Mother every Wednesday night when she walked down the hill with Jason to watch Benny Hill. And they'd all go to the beach every single Sunday afternoon.

But when she confided to Jason the yearning that such thoughts induced, whilst they sat on a log outside the shack sharing cornflakes from the box, he barked a short incredulous laugh.

'Don't you remember the one time he hung around more than a day?'

She did, of course. Trevithick Day parade, 1977. Lower junior class, David Teague's snot. Her naming day.

'I wanted to be paired up with you,' Goliathia said.

'I had chickenpox. You got David Teague.'

The memory ticked over. An inebriated host, a stumble on the names, a shout from the crowd for a cheap laugh. David and Goliathia.

'That was your dad. I was standing next to him.'

The poxy boy had glared up at Sharky - who was busy hooting delightedly at his own wit - and willed his scabs to jump ship and infect the man, along with every other known disease.

In Goliathia's head, the cellulose of memory unravelled into an untidy, uncertain, disorderly snake.

'A man capable of that is capable of anything,' Jason ruminated. 'He'll take the last bike, and he'll go.'

Goliathia shook her head to return to her mind the certainty that her father loved her. Then she banished Jason's version of Trevithick Day, and Jason with it.

'You don't know anything. And why are you still living in my yard in your stupid tent?' she asked.

Thus, Jason was cut adrift. He packed up his tent and was gone in a day. If he could have held his broken heart in his hands, he would have flung it down the mine to bounce and jangle against Sharky's metal corpses.

Lead nestled in Goliathia's gut for, with each new withdrawal from the mine's deep bank, she began to realise the truth of Jason's words. But she'd sent him down the hill and couldn't work her way around the mountain of pride and stubbornness to ask him to come back.

The moment of Sharky's disappearance from her life drew nearer. One day he would tie the last motorcycle to the end of the rope, have her haul it up and carry it to the track, where he would mount the machine and roar off. Goliathia carried this fear as it blossomed and burgeoned in every waking moment.

One July dawn, dense with mizzle, Sharky arrived on foot to extract the last of his bounty. Goliathia, keeping a lonely vigil over the final bike, got to her feet and uncoiled the rope. Sharky was a trivial weight as she lowered him into the earth and waited, the distant sea, the fog and the sky one shifting grey shroud. A tug on the rope from below and she set her shoulders, took a breath and pulled, hand-over-hand, her clothes steaming with the effort, until the mine disgorged the last motorbike, still swaddled in its tarp, a gift fifteen years in the making.

Goliathia untucked a corner and threw back the wrapping. The blue petrol tank flashed like a kingfisher. She remembered this bike, the first in and the last out. A '63 Triumph T120R Bonneville. It reminded her of all Sharky's broken promises. She stood it up on its wheels and ran her hand over the saddle.

'Send down the rope, my bird,' came Sharky's distant voice, muffled by subterranea.

Goliathia hesitated, her right hand on the brake, her left hand smoothing over the bright gleam of the petrol tank.

'Shall we go to the beach now, Father?' she asked.

'Back off up country tomorrow, my bird,' he called from below. 'Lower the bleddy rope now, Goliathia.'

There was no stopping Goliathia now. She pushed the bike to the track and stepped astride it, put her left foot on the gear changer and her right hand on the throttle. She felt the visceral thrill of perfect body geometry, a moment in which something finally fits just right. The kickstarter yielded at once to her boot, and the engine roared into life like a dragon.

As she sat for a moment, relishing the sound, a figure started to assemble in the gloom. Jason, minutely beaded in starlight where the mist caught on his jacket and hair, stood before her.

'So the last bike is out,' he said. 'I just came to see if you're alright.' He looked around. 'Where's your old man?'

'I left him down the mine.'

'Forever?'

'Dunno yet.'

Jason shook his head and couldn't help but smile the smile he kept specially for her. 'You're a wonder, Gloria Tremayne.'

He turned to set off back down the track.

'I'm sorry, Jason,' Goliathia said suddenly. 'Don't go.'

Nothing further was required.

Jason got on the bike behind Goliathia and wrapped his arms around her waist. She rolled the throttle under her hand and the bike gave a satisfying vroom. A swift gust ushered the mizzle away. To the west, the sea was alive with tiny sparkles of light.

'To the beach, then,' Goliathia said.

'To the beach,' Jason agreed.

The Apocalypse Chess Club

by Philip S Rollason

1. e5

One black pawn. Two impossible spaces.

'e freaking 5,' she said to no one. Then she circled to check. 'Hello?' Her call was swallowed by the perimeter of trees. She'd not spoken for days and the sound of her voice, new and unexpected, teased a smile from the corner of her lips. 'The Italian,' she called. 'Original.' The words died at the tree line. There was no reply.

There was nothing.

Maybe they were hiding, she thought. Most probably gone. She took a second spin, looking all around, her eyes coming to rest on the mini digger. Then she looked to the rectangular mound.

'No, Papi,' she said. 'Just no.'

2. Tables

She'd visit every Sunday. Every Sunday and Christmas. Roast dinner, tinfoil topped, sliding around on the passenger seat, she'd drive duty bound through the twisted roads all the way to the top of the moor. Beyond, it seemed. Through rain and gales and snow and occasional outbreaks of sunshine. Always, without fail, on those rare golden days he'd say, 'S'good Cornish light, maid. Comes with a pinch of saffron, see.' Then he'd crumple half his face in a wink. 'Just like your hair.' Each time she gave the same arid answer.

'Papi, Mum's Swedish,' and she'd flick a lock in his direction as if to score a point. Or whenever there was the faintest dusting of snow, out came the sledge, ready and waiting when she pulled into the courtyard.

'Built her for you that year the great blizzard were forecast.' He'd nod his welcome. 'Never gave so much as a flake though, did he? Bleddy weatherman got his tealeaves in a twist. More like a *weather or not man*, I reckon.' He'd smack his lips, the way he always did when he'd made a point known. 'Plenty o' snow since. Never did take her out.' Another smack.

'Well, education called...'

It was a sumless game. Stock question, stock answer, right off the shelf. 'S'good Cornish rain,' 'S'good Cornish gale,' 'S'good 'n rare Cornish snow.' She often wondered if he knew that each visit had been played out time and time again. Like tired TV re-runs that had lost their first-aired charm. He was getting old, she'd conceded. So old now that company had overtaken conversation. Or perhaps, she thought, it was his way of knowing outcomes.

Weather and welcomes dealt with, they'd go to the kitchen. She'd lay the table for one, *tada!* the meat of the day and ease him into the chair. Then he'd jive his hips, produce his teeth from his pocket, one blow for luck and in they went. She didn't see the use, he never seemed to chew, practically inhaling everything on the plate as if at any second it would be stolen away. All the while, as he breathed it in, he'd bemoan her life choices.

'That Darwin forgot more about evolution than the rest o' you know put together. Bet he's spinning in his grave at you lot. Bio-Evolution,' he'd pout, gravy down his white, prickled chin. 'You wanna get a proper job.'

'Evolutionary Biology,' she'd correct.

'Well, he's in God's good house now.'

'Ironic,' was all she ever answered. Then she'd take a theatrical bow and say, 'Scene.'

She was waiting, of course, for the inevitable turn in the episode. A real fan favourite. The part she had come for if she had come for anything at all. He'd tip the last of the gravy straight into his mouth, a puckered drain, sucking until the most of it had run. Then, 'Bagsie white,' she'd say.

'Fat chance, Dave,' he'd say, right on script.

She'd clean up then, and they'd go out over the brow of the hill to the bottom of the field and the stump of old oak.

'When God struck her down, I knew what to make of her.'

He'd carved what was left of the tree into a table.

The fallen trunk he'd used to build two notched wedges as chairs.

'This is chess,' he said, the first time he took her down. 'You're gonna lose, but you're gonna learn. An' maybe, the best you can hope for, you'll learn to lose.'

It was beautiful. The squares he'd cut, stained and re-set. The numbers and letters, stamped and painted in around them. The pieces he'd turned and carved, all lined up in a particular way. She was instantly hooked. She had to know how it all worked.

3. Foxes

She studied Papi's grave more than the board. Puzzling half the afternoon until the early evening chill settled a mist in the valley.

'By the book, Dave. Openings are always by the book.' She never knew why he'd called her Dave. She supposed it was one of his strange mockeries. Like that toothless smile when he told her she was going to hell. He was a hard man to be around at times. She thought it was just to push people away, to be alone. 'You like it up here, don't you, away from everyone?' she'd asked one summer afternoon, as she cleaned the table and washed his plate.

'Yep,' he'd said. 'But then there's meat o' the day to consider. An' chess,' he scrunched up his face, the trademark wink. 'An' you, Dave.'

'Beef, boardgames and me. That's quite the roll call.'

'I'll not be round forever, mind. Best get a game while 'e can. Fact, I was thinking just this morning, if God'll grant it, an' he's a kind lord be known, I'll see if I can't come back an' haunt you.'

'You'll haunt me? You already haunt me,' she said, shooting a wink right back.

'Well someone's gotta beat 'e at chess an'um, when I'm gone?'

She shook her head.

'Tell 'e what, you can even choose the colour.'

'White,' she'd snapped.

'Hold on, I ain't dead yet,' he'd said.

She looked to the board, then back to his grave, Papi's words from that day playing in her head. Then she picked up a knight and, by the book, set it down.

'Knight f3,' she called to the trees. Imagining the other player was watching. She'd have been watching if she was the embodied ghost of Papi, playing midnight chess moves against last survivor strangers. 'Hellooo. I moved the horsey,' she all-but sang, looking for a rise. 'Your mooove.' Still nothing. No matter, she thought, today was a day for smiling. Today, she was no longer alone.

She pottered around that evening, making dinner, checking the level in the generator, failing to read in any meaningful way. Thoughts of some unknowable person, down there in the dark, planning untold number of moves ahead, frayed her concentration so that she eventually gave in to their fancy, deciding, in her distraction, to name the mystery player, the Opponent. At least, she thought, until they'd formally met.

The fantasy swelled, inventing the Opponent's gender as she washed her one plate, one fork, one cup. Papi had said, in one of his nonsensical taunts, that more men played chess, that that was why she'd lost. By his reasoning then, the Opponent was likely male. But then she knew from experience that women were better survivors. She counted herself as proof. Partly through this, and partly through the absurdity that no amount of X chromosomes could repopulate humanity, the Opponent was conjured female. Enchanted now, she divined personality from the move of just one pawn. Axe-murdering pushed as far back as could be held, she began to nurture a gentle warmth around the Opponent's simple intention to play chess. How mischievous, she thought, how gutsy to sit at a stranger's chess board by night. And how good natured to silently wait for a move in reply. She predicted, Knight c6, as the Opponent's next move. It's what Papi would have played. It's what she would have played. Of course, she was getting ahead of herself. The game was still young. Anything was possible.

And so it went, move after move, opening exchanges of imagined conversations, while she stood alone drying and then setting out the cup, the plate, and the fork, ready for the morning.

As the evening wore on though, doubt set a rot at the edges of her optimism. The nightly feeling that it was just her in the whole wide world pressed in on the house, persuading her with its proving silence. The pawn had moved. That was for certain. But the rest, was it not just the manifest whispers of her need, and of the secret loneliness she kept from herself? By the time sleep had begun its numbing spell to draw her to bed, she was convinced that the simple answer was more often the right answer. That a bird or a squirrel had most probably knocked the pawn whilst scratching around for food. That it was merely chance for it to have come to stand by the rules. And by the book.

The next day she woke late with a pin sharp headache and a sea in her stomach that whipped up like a storm was in the off. She did a mental check for other symptoms. It can lie dormant for months, she thought, then in a few short days... She decided that she was probably clear, and if she wasn't, well, the last person alive was the last person alive. Who would there be to mull the history over? The Opponent?

Past the kitchen table, skipping breakfast for fear of seeing it twice, she stepped an uneasy gait down into the valley, disaster playing in her head. She pictured the mess, the aftermath of a busy squirrel sending the pieces all about the table and onto the floor. Then, a thieving magpie, caught by the dull glint of the misty morning sun on the head of a pawn, wiping the Opponent from existence with the stroke of a wing. Or even the classic mischiefs of a cunning fox, playing up for indiscernible gains. Out to fool her. Nature had been given so many human things, she reminded herself, that weren't human at all.

Down through the mist floor and to the under smell of earth and stillness, she was guided in by the dark glowing beacons of Papi's grave and chess table.

'Rug o' mist bird,' she said as she passed the mound, and over to the board. She'd taken to Papi's way of talking. A calming familiar.

Even before she reached the table, she could see the pattern had changed. Knight c6, just as she'd predicted. Hardly breaking stride, seized in motion by her butterflied stomach, she made her move as she passed, then on into the trees.

'Your move,' she shouted, swinging around to march away, stopping in the half turn. She looked back, sweeping a gaze across the forest, the trees nothing but a blurred binary language backing into the mist. 'And...' She took a deep breath. Then out it came as if it were one long word, 'I-would-very-much-like-to-meet-you-if-you'd-want-to-sit-and-play-with-me-that-would-be-okay.'

Still nothing.

Foxes, she thought. Against all the odds, it was definitely probably bleddy foxes. What it was definitely not, she decided, was the ghost of Papi.

She walked past the grave without looking. 'Bishop c4. By the book, Papi. Just like you taught me.'

4. Moving

The winter had been stubborn that year, holding them well into March. She'd decided it was time. Her last Sunday visit brought no roast dinner, only bulk buy pasta, tinned tomatoes and a boot full of toilet roll.

'Hi, Papi,' she said as he opened the door giving the usual nod of welcome. He noticed the box of cans in her arms and seemed to shrink at the sight of them.

'Don't worry, there's booze in the back,' she said.

He stood stock still.

'We'll hunker down here for a few weeks, 'til all of this blows over. And anyway, who better to take care of me than my very own Papi, right?' Her smile came beneath a frown, but he hadn't seen. He'd not stopped staring at the cans, eyelids half mast, body sagging with each breath. She practised another smile, in case he looked up, but she could feel the lie stiffening her lips. 'I'll get the rest,' she said.

He looked up just as she left.

'What's meat o' the day?'

She made a bed up on the sofa and, light as needle in groove, they settled into a routine. Each morning she'd rise when he did, always too early. She'd make oats with water and a little salt, attend to chores. They'd listen to the radio, read books, cautiously watch the telly. After lunch, it was down to the board, rain or shine, to play. Papi could be contrary, as could she, but, whenever they sat down in that valley, they each softened. Just enough. It was almost idyllic, those short few months, as good as they'd had it. Just look to the side of the government warnings, adjust the volume each hour for the news and everything was going to be just fine.

Then the needle skipped.

She'd thought the radio would keep on broadcasting forever, the first and the last of globalisation. But there it was. Twisting the knob, moving the line up and down through the frequencies, gave nothing but a vacant steely hiss. The public service announcements were no more. The TV had been playing the same prerecorded warnings for weeks. The 'Black Burn', they'd been calling it. Then that stopped too. That day it was like the world had turned off. Like it was just her and him, up there on the moor, guessing what was safe, awaiting further instructions. She was thankful the taps still gave water, that the toilet flushed and the generator ran, but she knew that eventually they would all stop and she'd have to go out. She dreaded the day. Out, they'd been told, was not to be trusted.

The mornings grew tense then. They each busied alone, reading, chopping wood or pulling out weeds or some other menial avoidance. Their exchanges had become short, functional. Those little afternoon miracles sustained them though, like a solenoid switch that flicked to bring them back together. He'd lean on her down the hill and she'd take a bottle to help the afternoon go. Of course, openings were always by the book and, if she missed a move, he'd press the advantage, setting strange lines with unknowable intention that always paid, come the endgame. And he was never more alive to her than when he issued the inevitable 'Checkmate'. Like his life's work really was to teach her how to lose. Even the games when they both knew she was beaten, many moves from mate, when she tipped her king, Papi would say, 'Stand him back up. Play on now. I think 'e can get out o' this one.'

She never did.

'Checkmate.' Back to life.

The table was much more than chess then and, between moves, they'd talk of old times. Before she'd gone away.

'When I was little,' she said, 'I always thought your head looked like the top of a pawn.'

'I had hair back then.'

'You didn't,' she said.

He brushed his liver-spotted scalp.

'I thought that's why you always played as white, to get an unfair advantage, you fit right in as the ninth pawn.'

'Ha. For sacrifice an' for glory,' he said.

They both laughed. He moved a pawn to a square she covered in the sixth row. She took a sip of wine. Stared at the pawn.

'I loved coming to stay back then. I mean, I still do.'

'Oh, you stayed often, remember?'

'Mum-'

'Absent,' he said with a smack of his lips. 'Some bleddy pair they were. Missed the most of you.'

'I was no angel, they say.'

'Rubbish. Ansum you were, but weeks it was sometimes. Drop you to school, pick you up. An' through all your wet beds an' night wanderings.'

She raised an eyebrow, took another sip, then took the pawn.

'Oh yes. I'd find 'e stood straight up facing a wall talking all sorts of sideways. Cracked me up, you did. No bother though, good as gold an' back to bed.'

'Wow,' she said.

He began to count them off. 'Tie your laces, me. Lamping, that's a skill. Times tables, that was me.' He looked to the tree line. 'All them animal books.'

'Carried me in your womb for nine months,' she joked.

'If I had one,' he half joked back. 'Drive a car, that was me too.'

'Tractor,' she said.

'Same difference,' he said. 'An' the digger.'

She stifled a smile. 'Your dearly departed apple trees. Complete success of course.'

'Dug a hole didn't 'e? Filled it in again? Those apples

never ripened right anyhow.'

'They certainly haven't since,' she said, and she took another sip.

'Only thing I see she taught you was how to drink. Did a bleddy good job too by the state o' that recycling.'

'Can I get an amen?' she said.

'Why d'you bother to put them out anyhow? No one's comin' for 'em.'

She shrugged. 'Drunk optimism?'

'Well don't get too far ahead of yourself.' He moved a bishop half way across the board. 'Check. There 'e go, your move.' He hooked a thumb back up the hill towards the house. 'Learned to ride your bike down the field, that's another one. Must o' been about ... twelve?'

'Eleven,' she said.

'Too old,' he smacked. Then, his toothless grin. 'Hit this 'ere tree more than a few times, like a bike magnet it was.' He tapped the table. 'When I saw her laying over, me first thought was, Dave's been out 'ere sleep riding an' crashed her down.'

She giggled like a little girl, and he let out his big belly laugh.

But contrary was contrary.

She believed it was her that had gotten into him that day, with the row. When she let herself think about it, later on, it could only have been her that brought it to the farm. No one else had been up there for years.

'World's gone bleddy mad, no morals, no guidance. No faith.' He'd begun to preach.

'I dunno, there's common decency, the social contract it's–'

'I mean, look what happened when all this kicked off. Every man for himself, wan'it?'

'And woman,' she said. Her blood was rising.

'Exactly, Dave. An' what does that make us, eh? Two generations from a Godless race, that's what I reckon.' Another smack, sermon delivered.

'What do you mean, what does that make us?' She couldn't stop herself. 'Your great grandfather, a couple of million times removed, no splits, no branches, one line, straight back down your family tree, was a sea cucumber.' He made a kind of crackling growling sound in his throat. 'So, oh father and lord above, from which all knowledge doth fount, what does *that* make us?'

'Well, not a bleddy vegetable,' he snapped, turning away in a wheezing fit. She leaned across the board and he pushed her back with a hand, the other cupped tight to his mouth.

'Sorry Papi,' was all she could say. They'd gotten into it about belief before and 'Sorry Papi' was how it always ended. He coughed for some time. When he eventually turned back, their eyes locked.

'S'nothin,' he said, hands hardly hidden beneath the table. He looked to his lap and wiped the blood spots on his trousers. She thought he'd never looked so old as he did then.

5. Empty

Breakfast was for snoozers. She wasn't sure how it worked, but that was her new motto. The Opponent had kept coming, night after night, and so, each morning, she skipped straight from bed to table, to study her next move. Hunger, she'd decided, was an agent of concentration.

They were deep into the mid game, exchanging pieces for positions. The centre was hers, but the Opponent was a rook to the good. The queen for queen that black had offered up then, made perfect sense. A castle ahead, they planned to make it tell. To grind it out. She played out line after line all that morning, finally giving in to her empty stomach when lunchtime came around. Pasta again, cold from the fridge, and she grabbed last night's bottle and a glass on her way to the door. Then, today could be the day, she thought. No point in being rude. She returned to the kitchen and took a second glass from the cupboard.

When she reached the table, she gave herself a deep pour, put the empty glass black side and checked the lines again. If she took the exchange, then black would have the centre, her position unplayable. But if she didn't, the Opponent would move to block the offering, and the centre would be lost anyway. It was Papi-like in its simplicity.

'Seriously,' she said to his grave. 'Coaching from beyond. Not cool.' Then she moved to mitigate a sure collapse.

She sat for ten minutes more. Sipping her wine, playing as black, deciding that all was not necessarily lost. That she too had some Papi-like moves to play. And that she'd earned them the hard way. Right there at the stump. When her glass was empty, she stood.

'Well, Papi,' she said. '*You* don't drink red. Blood o' the devil n' all.' She pushed the quarter-full bottle black side. 'Let's hope,' she said to the trees, 'that you do.'

*

For snoozers, she thought, skimming across the kitchen floor the next morning. She hoped the wine would become a thing. Take their relationship to the next level. One more step towards meeting the Opponent. Hazed in the fantasy, she opened the door and stepped her shin hard into the side of the sledge.

'What the f–' she said, grabbing her leg to check for a cut, while the wine bottle rolled and chimed on the floor. This definitely felt like one of Papi's mischiefs, the sledge, last night's empty on top, laid by the door as a trap. It had his fingerprints all over it. She rubbed the reddening hump on her shin. Resolving the how of it all in the soothing, turning grimace into grin, she decided that the Opponent must have brought the sledge back up and set the bottle on its back. A returning, thank you, for the gifted wine. How kind. And it was her fault anyway, daydreaming, not looking where she was going. She stood the empty with the others, next to the full plastic tub, grabbed the reins, and led the sledge over the brow and into the valley, sliding it back by his graveside. That's where Papi would want it, she thought. Then she looked to the table and there, black side, was the unused glass.

'Straight out of the bottle,' she called to the trees. 'Classy.'

6. e4

The blue smell of diesel fumes would forever remind her of the first time Papi had sat her atop the mini digger. How strange it had felt to move the bucket and arm. Like a mechanical extension of herself that she just had to figure out. It had been a few years since girl and machine had become one. Now when she wanted to lift, the scoop would pitch instead, or she'd push the body of the digger up when she'd only wanted to tip. So, back and forth, she scraped the black heap Papi had made that morning back into the hole. When she'd filled it to ground level, she marched back to the house. She'd thought to burst in, tell him off for playing foreman when he was sick. But as she entered the front room, she found him lying limp and pale in the bed on the sofa. It was like a frost had settled over him.

'Oh God...'

'Don't you bring him into this,' he said, his voice popping and croaking. 'An' what have 'e done with me grave? A man's prerogative, that. Dig his own endings.' He lurched into a coughing fit. The wheezing had gotten worse the last few days.

'Let me get you back upstairs,' she said.

'No,' he managed between coughs.

She waited until it passed.

'I'll stay 'ere from now on,' he croaked. Then he rattled another cough to clear his throat, and swallowed. 'You won't have to lump me down them stairs. When time comes.'

'You're not–'

'No need,' he said. 'I know.'

'And that?' She nodded to the sledge he'd put at the foot of the sofa. 'To take you down...'

'That's the plan.'

She turned to the side and closed her eyes. 'No, Papi,' she said.

'A dead weight is twice the weight,' he said.

'Look, I think–'

'I know, I know,' he said, his breath rasping in his throat.

She hurried to the kitchen and brought him some water, then held his head so that he could drink.

'There'll be someone at the hospital,' she said. 'Plymouth's probably our best...' She trailed off, the hope too hollow to hold together. Too selfish.

'Nonsense,' he said. 'Never set a foot in Devon, never will. West o' Tamar, that's God's country.' His voice sounded from some place far off inside him, cracked and low, like all the Papi had wilted from it.

She was on her knees, holding his hands. They felt like sticks in tissue paper.

'We're okay,' she said. 'We're okay.'

'Don't fuss now, I'm 'appy enough. Just tip that there Cornish soil on me head.' He tried to smack his dried lips but all that came was a soundless suck. Then another fit stiffened him, and he lurched and spat.

The next day was a Sunday. He'd crawled out early and re-dug the hole while she slept on the floor by the sofa. She'd have given him hell but she could see he'd spent everything, so she spared him her fears, waited until he'd finished, then helped him back to the sofa.

By midday, his coughs were all red. Then they turned black. She pulled the chair from the kitchen and sat it next to the sofa, cooling his brow and wetting his lips, telling him stories about a young girl called Dave and her kind, wise Papi.

He'd burned all that night and in the morning, when

she was sure his chest had stopped its shallow risings, she kissed his bald head and closed his eyes.

She buried him that evening, and it was just like he'd said. The bed downstairs, the sledge, the digger, it was all planned out like one of his chess schemes. She hardly had to think, Papi had done it all. So she grieved as she set him on the sledge, and she heaved to dislodge the dismay as the diesel fumes covered her in their sweetness.

When the digger had done its part, she sat in silence by the stump table and stared at the grave until her tears dried. It was so quiet then. No birds, no breeze, no hidden hum of distant machines. The world really had been turned off.

'Bagsie white,' she said, and she lifted a pawn to her lips. She held it there for a moment, then eased it down. 'e4.' Then she climbed the hill and lay in the bed on the sofa.

7. Endgame

It was the first falling of snow in the last knockings of winter. She lay in Papi's bed, looking at the white topped branches out of the window, thinking about the story of a lonely girl that played chess with a ghost, and how it would end. Check mate, she supposed, and back to life.

A robin flit into view, landing on a branch. A Christmas card framed through the window. It fixed her with its black-bead eyes, shifting along the branch to get a better look, sending snow falling in icing sugar dustings as it hopped and danced. Chest aglow, puffed up against the cold, it sang its soundless refrain, tipped its head, and was gone. She fixed on the black of the branch uncovered by the robin. Then she sat bolt up.

A witness.

She rushed downstairs, slid her bare feet into her boots and opened the front door. The cold pushed in through her pyjamas, stopping her in a cloud of breath on the threshold. All around there was a fine frosted layer of snow, highlighting trees and disguising the field and there, she could hardly believe it, two perfectly cast sets of prints. One leading to, and one from the house. They were undeniably real. The Opponent was undeniably real. She'd hoped to find prints down in the valley. One set coming from the trees to the board, and then one more leaving. She thought she might track the Opponent through the forest to their hiding place but this, this was unbelievable. They'd come up to the house again. Perhaps they were plucking up the courage to reveal themselves. If they meant her harm, they could've done anything while she slept. Or worse, taken all the wine. One thing was for sure, a Papi come down from heaven doesn't leave footprints, even if he is visiting by the grace of God. Especially, she thought, if he's visiting by the grace of God. She pulled her coat on and, careful not to step on the twin trails, creaked stride for stride over the brow and down into the morning mist. She'd have to stay up all of the next night and wait for them to come back. Was there coffee at the back of the cupboard somewhere? Maybe the Opponent was waiting at the table right now, it was such a beautiful morning to be revealed. She thought to go back and make tea, but then they might not like tea without milk. She hurried on.

Papi's twin beacons unneeded, she followed the trail

to the table.

'Hello,' she called. 'Hello?'

Nothing.

The footprints led just there, to the game. They circled around the board so that the grass and mud showed through, but that's where they ended. She checked for a move, the pieces like ghosts under a sheet of snow. Even with the covering, she could see that the pattern had changed. Castled. It was a Papi move, for sure.

'No, Papi,' she said without looking. 'Just no.'

She looked back over the tracks and began to puzzle it out. Three sets now, off into the white. The Opponent had kept coming, kept playing. Just like she had. And last night they'd left a trail, just like ... A sudden constriction, a shrivelling, dropped down through her. The feeling was bottomless.

She tramped up the hill, leaving drops of ice and melted pools through the front room and up the stairs and there, sat in a dark circle on the bedroom carpet, were Papi's slippers. She took them in hand. They were cold and wet and she gripped them tight so that their frigid truth fell in drops to the floor.

There was no Opponent. There was no Papi. There was nothing. Just her and fear and the return of those piteous adolescent night wanderings.

She threw the slippers against the wall and beat back down the hill in a flurry of breath, the unthought, the unsaid, rising up from the fathoms. The snow hadn't touched Papi's grave and, as she stamped and slid into the valley, it raised up like a black backed island in a great white sea. She reached the mound, desperate cold breaths stinging in her chest, needling the pressure, scratching at it to burst. She knew it would. It tasted like copper surging up her throat, rushing across her tongue.

'How could you leave me?' she cried.

Papi was right. 'Absent,' he'd said. And now it was just her.

She fell to her knees. She wanted to shake the frozen earth, somehow rearrange. Then she lay in the snow and grieved anew.

The prints made train tracks, running up and over the hill. Out of sight. Even with new beginnings, she thought, everything still ends. She'd been there so many times, they'd played so many games, yet the valley appeared now as a foreign place. The trees had crept closer while she lay there. The branches reaching their black fingers out and over, as if to make spring's first buds of her. The table was so tall. The spaces Papi had carved away so that they could fit their legs under the board, appeared now as caves he'd gouged out of a cliff with his bare hands. And with his love. The mini digger, made full-sized, its arm a massive upturned 'V' against the sky, looked so powerful and cold, so unwieldy. And the sledge... She caught sight of something on the underside, a limp piece of paper taped beneath the slats. Pulling herself across, she yanked it free. It was an envelope. The ink on the outside had ballooned and kaleidoscoped with the wet from the snow, but the handwriting was unmistakably his. It read, '*Congratulations!*' She turned on her back in the snow and tore it open. The front of the card showed a pencil drawn sledge being held in the air by two red balloons, the words,

'*Well Done*' written within them. She opened it up.

'*To my little David Attenborough. Congratulations on your A Levels, we're all so very proud of you. Don't forget to visit between your Galapagos expeditions and BBC documentaries. When you're back for Christmas we'll take this beauty down the hill. If there's no snow I'm sure we can find some more apple trees for you to skat down. All my love Papi. X*

p.s. Papi's advice for university: Be yourself, Dave. Everyone else is already taken. And anyhow, there really is no other person you're better at being.'

She pulled the card and her knees to her chest.

All morning, she lay cold and wet by his side. When the snow had melted the prints away, she shivered up on the digger and watched the naked forest drip and steam and sway, forming shapes, playing gentle memories that came to pass the day. Then, as the afternoon light began to fade, she moved at last to the table. A saffron sun lit its last across the board, casting shadows reaching through the lines. She twisted a lock of her hair.

'Sorry, Papi,' she said, lifting a pawn to her lips, revealing her queen. She smudged a tear with the back of her hand, kissed the domed white head, then gently set the piece down. 'There 'e go,' she said. 'Your move.'

Slagoon's Breath

by T J Dockree

The old fisherman hunkered down and looked young Bobby in the eye. 'It's a scary story, boy. You sure you want to hear it?'

Bobby nodded, his longing for a good story fed rather than diminished by the terror he felt at this one-eyed giant crouched before him. Bobby watched a small fly wander over the old man's leather eye patch, which barely concealed the vivid scars beneath. His brothers had dared him to steal it. Bobby couldn't think of any forfeit worse than what might happen if he reached up and pulled the patch away. What horror lay beneath?

Two teenage faces spied on him through a gap under the Slagoon sign. Old Fred glared at them. They ducked out of sight but their attempts to be quiet failed, in snorted gasps of laughter.

Fred grunted. 'I hope the nightmares you're going

to have tonight will be worth what your babysitters are offering you. How old are you? Six?'

'Seven!' Bobby puffed his chest out in pride.

The old man laughed and brushed the dirt off a bench in front of the pub porch. 'Sit down.' He patted the bench and Bobby climbed up. 'Well, let's begin, shall we?

'It was a stormy night, and all the shutters were banging on the windows. Gates kept flying open because people forgot to shut them properly. Annoying, is that.'

Fred sucked at his pipe and exhaled. Bobby coughed and waved the bitter, choking fumes away from his face.

'We didn't want to go out, but we couldn't ignore the flare for help. We could hear 'em screaming, even from the shore, as their souls were thrown from the ship into the deep below.' Fred looked sombre and shook his head. 'If we'd a known why, we'd a stayed away. But we thought a ship was going down and people needed rescuing, so we launched the lifeboat and headed out.

'When we got closer, we saw why the waves were so big. It wasn't because of the storm but because there was something under the water churning it all up - like when you're playing monsters and battles in the bath, and you get water all over the floor.' Fred pulled the pipe from his mouth and leant closer to Bobby. 'Then we saw the tentacles!' He shuddered involuntarily and pulled up his sleeve. A set of large white circular welts mottled his bronzed old skin.

'It got us. It curled one of its tentacles under our lifeboat and squeezed us, like we were a sponge. Tighter and tighter, like a boa constrictor, it was! Until the boat popped and cracked and fell apart. It kept squeezing and squeezing and me and Billy were stuck in its grip. I shouted and hollered but poor Billy was unconscious.' Fred mumbled and calmed himself by sucking at his pipe. 'Then, he tossed us up in the air. I thought we were free! But no! That blighter was gonna eat us!

'Billy fell first and disappeared into his mouth. I tell you, I was so scared, knowing I was next. I prayed so hard, and I didn't believe in God then!' He tapped the pipe out on the ground. The warm ashes glowed then dissolved from grey to black into the damp earth. 'Then I fell into that monster's maw.'

'He ate you?' Bobby squeaked.

Fred nodded solemnly, opened a tobacco pouch, and waited.

'But how did you escape?' Bobby asked.

A voice from the other side of the wall interrupted the tale. 'Phil! Steve! What are you two doing down there? Where's your brother? He better not be in there or, God help me, I'll beat the pair of you to the other side of Cornwall.'

Fred stood up and slipped something into Bobby's pocket. 'Time to be off, son.'

'But I want to hear what happened!'

'And I want to tell yer, lad, but I'm no match for your mum over there and she's just fulfilling the curse of Nanny Trenown.'

The gate banged open. Bobby's mum entered, dragging a boy at each side by the ear.

'Bobby B! What have I told you about coming here? Home! Right now!'

'But Mum! I need to know how the story ends!'

'And you!' Mum let go of one of the boys to jab her finger at Fred. 'I've told you not to go filling my children's heads with your stories. What have you been telling him?'

Fred filled up his pipe. 'It's just a story. He knows it ends well 'cos I'm here and I'm safe, aren't I?'

Mrs B pursed her skinny, ruby lips and grabbed Bobby by the arm. 'That may be so, but I don't want him having nightmares like all the other kids in the village.' She marched away, her boys dragging behind like a flotilla in the wake of a battleship.

The fisherman settled back to enjoy his pipe, humming himself a little song about kraken and mermaids and sea serpents.

Bobby found the wooden kraken in his pocket when he got undressed. Once he'd scrambled into bed, he stroked the faint, round notches that marked the suckers. He placed it on the nightstand and lay down, watching to see if the creature would yield clues to its tale. But the Cornish oak simply watched him back. Bobby's eyes closed without enlightenment.

That night he dreamt of old Fred and the kraken. Fred was out fishing in his boat, smoking his pipe and talking to the night air. The sea below began to bubble and churn. Massive tentacles erupted, throwing Fred and his boat into the air. Bobby watched as Fred fell towards the gaping mouth of the kraken below. A scream pierced the air, waking him up.

Everyone was talking about the coastguard hunt for Fred and his boat the next day. The search went on for weeks. His boat washed up on the beach a month later, undamaged. But they never found Fred. Only the kids dared to suggest: 'Maybe he got eaten, again.'

The Slagoon stood silent for fifteen years.

'Hey, Steve! Baby bro's here from the big smoke. Come say hi!'

Steve threw his tea towel on the bar and picked Bobby up in a big bear hug.

Phil pushed between them, waving his phone. 'Group selfie!'

'Hey, do you remember coming up here as kids? And we dared you to steal old Fred's eye patch?'

Bobby chuckled. 'I remember you cowards hiding behind the wall! Did you ever hear his stories?'

'All the kids in the village did. We used to creep up here at night to hear them. Especially on a full moon, like tonight...' Phil lowered his voice in a ghostly tremor, '... because that's when he told his Kraken story. Then we'd dare each other to go for a swim in the sea.'

Bobby laughed. 'Did you ever find out what happened at the end of that story?'

'Nobody knows! Somebody's mum always dragged us away before he finished.'

'When we bought the pub, we tried to find some photos of him but the only thing we came across was his amazing whisky.' Steve grabbed a bottle of Slagoon's Breath and held it up to the light. They watched it slosh around in the bottle like a restless sea.

'Let's give a toast to the old man!'

'To old Fred!' The brothers chinked glasses and

savoured hints of gorse and elderberry.

'Same again! Straight up!' Phil demanded, banging his empty glass on the bar.

Steve frowned. 'Slagoon's Breath is for savouring, not getting drunk on. One more glass and you'll be passed out.'

'Sounds like a challenge, Phil. You up for it?' Bobby placed his empty glass next to Phil's.

'You're on!'

'Okay. Let me put some cushions down first.' Steve carefully placed a cushion six feet away behind Bobby and another cushion five and a half feet away behind Phil. He poured the golden liquid into their glasses. 'Okay, gentlemen. I wish you a good sleep and happy dreams.'

Bobby and Phil looked at each other and knocked their drinks back in one. Phil's eyes rolled up as he fell backwards. Bobby looked at Phil lying on the floor and leaned forward. Steve caught him and rescued the glass from his hand.

'Deirdra! Can you help me with these two, a minute?'

Bobby woke to the sound of screaming seagulls. The world outside was grey except for a glimmer of sun peeping above the horizon. The wooden kraken on the bedside table caught his eye. He picked it up and rubbed the contoured tentacles. He had to get up. He had to know.

The steep, cobbled lane led down from the pub between skinny, tall houses with tiny brightly painted doors and colour-matched plant pots on grey slate steps. He'd sat on most of those steps as a child, with different friends. He'd knock and say hi later.

When he arrived at the cove, he remembered Phil's

comment about going swimming after hearing Fred's kraken story. He shivered and looked out at the still sea. Then he spotted the name on an upturned boat: Slagoon.

The boat was heavier than it looked. He dragged it across the small stretch of sand and pushed it into the water. When the engine turned over and leapt to life, Bobby let out a whoop of joy. He motored out, past the harbour and onto the calm expanse beyond, wondering why he'd been so afraid of the sea when he was growing up.

He checked the contents of the boat. There were two long boxes, one on each side. He opened the one to his left and found a harpoon. It was thick and sturdy and looked heavier than a little boat should be able to carry. He looked inside the other box and found a tripod, presumably for the harpoon.

The boat rocked. Bobby grabbed the sides to stop his stomach lurching. It's just a wave, he told himself. Man up! He peered over the side to look at the water below.

A large object was swimming beneath him. He gasped as long red tentacles erupted from the water, suckers quivering. Bobby grabbed the tripod and fumbled with it. On the starboard side, a huge head appeared. Bobby reached for the harpoon, then stopped. Would this thing get angry if he got a weapon out?

He looked up at the giant squid head, its eyes peeping, child-like, into the boat. It didn't seem afraid or angry, just inquisitive.

Bobby reached out to touch it. It backed away, then came back closer, lifting a tentacle towards him. As Bobby stroked the tentacle tip, it purred.

'You're not so scary. What was all the fuss about?'

He heard a loud 'scree' and the boat dropped into a deep sea-walled trough. Another head emerged from the sea, four or five times larger than the friendly squid. As it rose higher, its momentum started to suck the boat up with it. Then the rising wall of water collapsed on itself, drenching Bobby.

The creature stopped. And belched.

A small dot was ejected from its maw, getting bigger and bigger and screaming louder and louder as it fell towards Bobby. It hit the water. Slap! The kraken gently sank low and swam away.

The back of a man's head bobbed up ten yards away. Bobby watched and waited. He did not want to paddle over to find a dead guy. Then the head coughed, arms erupted and thrashed about.

Bobby grabbed a paddle and eased the boat forward. He reached over the side and grabbed an arm. The man screamed and flailed harder. Bobby let him go. 'Hey, I'm trying to help you. Stop thrashing about or you'll drown us both.'

The arms sculled round to face Bobby. Bobby gazed at the old man before him, grey hair stuck to his forehead above a leather eye patch, now ribbon.

'Are you a ghost?' Bobby finally blurted.

'I'll be a ghost if you don't get me in that boat, laddie.'

Bobby grabbed the old man's collar and heaved him up into the boat. Once seated, Fred shakily patted his pockets and found his pipe.

'We all thought you were dead. How did you survive?' Bobby asked.

Fred looked at the harpoon next to Bobby. 'Is this my

boat?' Without waiting for an answer, Fred fumbled under his seat and brought out a tin box that had been stuck there with gaffer tape. His few remaining teeth danced in delight as he opened the tin and pulled out a baccy pouch. 'You'll have to wait a wee while. lad. I've not had a smoke for 15 years, and I've been craving this moment for just that long.' He filled the pipe bowl, lit it, and sucked. A smile of ecstasy was followed by a coughing fit. 'But perhaps,' he coughed again, 'it's over-rated. Nasty habit. Glad I gave it up now.' He knocked the tobacco into the sea, which hissed as it sucked it in.

He looked at Bobby. 'So, which one are you then?' He sucked at the empty pipe and pulled a face.

'I'm Bobby, sir. I was seven when last we spoke.'

'So, you're the one made it happen.' Fred squinted at his rescuer.

'Made what happen, sir?'

'You ended the curse, young man. The curse to tell a tale I couldn't finish until it ended. Which it has. Just now.'

'A curse?'

'Old Nanny Trenown didn't like my stories 'cos they scared her kids, so she cursed me.' Fred sniffed. 'You took your time. I've been in that thing 15 years!'

'Oh wow. I'm so sorry! I didn't know. We just heard you went fishing then ... disappeared.'

'Yeah, I went fishing, met the beast who lifted me out of my boat, tossed me in the air and gulped me down.'

'Just like your story.'

'Yep, just like my story.'

'Wait. You had tentacle marks on your arm!'

'Oh these?' Fred pulled his sleeve up. 'They're from the first time it ate me.'

'You mean, that was a true story?'

'I might have embellished it a bit.'

'So, were you actually eaten the first time?'

'Oh yeah. But it only ate me. It didn't hurt anyone else.'

'So how did you escape the first time?'

The boat rocked.

'Not sure I'm going to be allowed to tell you that yet.

Guess the curse bit is still on.' The boat settled and the old fisherman pulled the cord to start the engine. 'I'd like to get ashore, if it's all the same to you, lad.'

'Oh, I'd be very happy not to see you get eaten again. Especially if I'm in the boat with you. Just in case it thinks I'm you.'

They journeyed to the beach in silence. Bobby dragged the boat back to where he'd found it while Fred picked up a handful of sand and staggered to a seat. 'Got to get my land legs back!'

Bobby pulled the wooden kraken from his pocket and offered it to the old man.

Fred waved it away. 'Don't give that thing to me, boy! I might need your help getting out of that brute again someday.'

Bobby looked at the carving. 'Is this how you got out the first time? Did Billy have this and rescue you?'

A set of barrel waves pounded onto the beach and Fred jumped up from his seat. He walked briskly up the hill.

Bobby followed him. 'Oh, come on! Don't I get any clues?'

'Nah, don't think so! I've got a very special case of whisky set by. See you up at the Slagoon!'

Of Red Riding Hood, Grandmas & Wolves

by Abigail Elizabeth Ottley

With a skill born of practice, I pick my way through the piles of dog shit that punctuate the concrete yard. Remarkably, they are all the work of the single dog in residence, an arthritic, rheumy-eyed poodle. Hats off to it. Despite its geriatric condition and years of sterling service, day after day, it comes up with the goods. This is a dog that probably doesn't remember the last time it was walked; and an animal, moreover, that fights boredom by pooping in a rainbow of colours from mustard yellow through liverish brown to multiple shades of green. It's true what they say: shit happens.

I know some people will object to my tone but, hell, I call it how I see it. I'm a medical and psychiatric nurse turned registered 'carer' in retirement so I like to think I more than qualify for 'angel of mercy' status. You have to remember, though, I don't choose my calls. I go where I'm sent. All I'm saying is there aren't too many places where the shit count hits double figures. And I'm not complaining either. I know I'd be on a loser. It could be dog-shit central wall-to-wall, and no one would ever pick up.

This yard belongs to a regular of mine, Mrs Jenny Pascoe. A tad eccentric, Jenny is the long-standing widow of Kenwyn Pascoe, at one time a small farmer in these parts. A good deal has changed since Pascoe's day. There's been a lot of so-called progress. As Jenny observes ruefully: 'There be not much proper farming hereabouts.'

It's true. The smaller farms have all but disappeared; though a few, like the Pascoe place, have morphed into smallholdings. Many have been abandoned; unloved and neglected, their moss-covered ruins scar this rugged landscape like old bones. Others have been revived and re-purposed by 'developers' with a canny eye to the future. Farmhouses, barns, even old lavs, have been tarted up and sold on. Over time, they have become the backbone of a thriving holiday trade. It's a shame but you can't blame those who have sold out to the waves of 'in-comers'. This far west, folk have limited options. It's *carpe diem*, as they say.

In her prime, Jenny Pascoe must have been a force to be reckoned with; even now, at eighty-six, she still has most of her marbles but both her eyesight and hearing are failing. In addition, she seems not to be eating and, more recently, she's gone 'off her legs'. Poor nutrition and increasing immobility: these are significant red flags for the future. Six months ago, she was fair to middling, and retaining some independence; now I think if I came twice a day it might not be enough.

Fortunately for Jenny, given her recent decline, she shares her ramshackle farmhouse home with the two remaining anchors of her life. They are Dandy the poodle, who looks, if that is possible, even older, and frailer than his mistress, and Peran, her largely silent, moon-faced son.

Peran, in his forties, is both his mother's official carer and a part-time agricultural hand. He is also well known for frequenting his local and being fond of a pint. Although he manages to feed Jenny breakfast, Peran neither cooks nor cleans. His habitual response to the dog shit problem is to leave his wellies at the door.

'Nobody comes here so us never bothers,' he once told me with tranquil indifference. I was wobbling on one leg, having stepped in something nasty. 'You'm mind you don't fall over now, bird.' He whistled brightly as he passed.

It seems that Peran is home today because the front door is slightly ajar. Its rotting wood and peeling paintwork would look arty reproduced for social media. In real life, all you see is the pressing need for repair. There is no sign of Peran's work boots, however, and no sign either of the poodle. My gaze takes in the threadbare hall runner and the unstained wood of the stairs.

'Hello? Mrs Pascoe?' I wonder if the old lady might be sleeping.

The house wears its silence like a comfortable sweater, wrapping itself against the chill and I think, not for the first time, that coming here is like stepping into history. It's as if the old place is haunted by the ghosts of its younger, more vibrant self. My next thought, however, is more practical. Is Mrs Pascoe safe? Perhaps Peran, departing in a hurry, left the house open to the winds. He isn't exactly security conscious, though for that it's difficult to blame him. They're in the middle of nowhere here. An intruder would have to come by car.

'Lunch, Mrs Pascoe. I'm a bit pushed today but we'll see about a wash and a change of bedding before I get you fed and watered. What's in the trough today? Is it Shepherd's Pie Ping Ping?'

I'm not being rude about the trough. It's a thing we do. Livestock and farming. Light-hearted reminders of Mrs P's working past. Mrs P enjoys a joke.

Out of courtesy, I always knock but this time, before I can do so, the parlour door creaks open to reveal Peran, still in his work boots, looming up on the threshold as solid as Trencrom Hill. His eyes, more usually flat and unresponsive, are wild with emotion. It might be defiance, or possibly anger. Perhaps even fear.

'Ma's had a bit of a fall. I've called an ambulance.'

Peran's white, lunar countenance looms over me. I am not sure he is telling me the truth. Also, his bulk is now so close to me I can't miss the smell of him. Old socks and nicotine, a top note of last night's booze. I am not a small man but, for a Cornishman, Peran is a big one. Taller and more muscular than I, he is packing a lot more weight. I wonder if he is blocking my path in a deliberate attempt to intimidate me or whether he is just being stupid. He's never been the sharpest knife in the drawer, so it's difficult to tell.

Over Peran's shoulder I can see Mrs P, sprawled on the floor in her nightdress, obviously in need of assistance. I take a chance and duck nimbly under the brawny, outstretched arm.

'What's happened here? Did she fall? When?'

Mrs P is deathly pale but breathing. It would be helpful to understand exactly what has occurred.

'I don't ... rightly know,' Peran stammers. 'She ... she were like it when I came in.'

Peran pushes out his lip like a defiant, sullen schoolboy. His eyes follow mine to the mud on his boots, his face flushes red.

'I been out getting logs,' he volunteers, without my asking the question. 'I reckon she must've tried to get out of bed.'

Something about his manner doesn't quite sit right but my priority must be the patient. I quickly establish she is not bleeding and that, although still dazed, she is conscious. It is also clear that the old lady is in considerable pain.

Peran says he hasn't moved his mother or attempted to move her. He insists he has no idea how she came to fall. He admits he was out of the room for a time but says, 'it was only for a minute'. His mother was awake when he left her. She had not at any time that day complained of feeling dizzy or ill.

I let the pressure off a bit, telling Peran he's done very well. I ask for some pillows and a blanket which he seems happy to supply. When Mrs P is propped up and tucked in, he turns his attention back to me.

'What now?' he asks.

'Your mother's in shock. Do you have a hot water bottle? Not too hot, mind. Maybe wrap it in a nice soft towel.'

Peran stays rooted to the spot, his flat eyes unfocused.

'Peran, your mother may be going into shock. I need your help.'

Only then does he lumber away, vanishing into the hall.

The paramedics, well-scrubbed and shiny, eager-eyed and smart as paint, present like overgrown children on their first day in school. Despite this, however, they prove calm and competent. I am confident they've got this.

Still, when Mrs Pascoe hears the word 'hospital', she is roused to surprising resistance.

'My Dandy will fret,' she says. 'I really can't go.'

'Peran will look after Dandy,' I tell her.

Mrs Pascoe appears unimpressed.

Meanwhile, our immediate problem is getting the patient to the ambulance. Her left hip is likely broken and both the door frame and the hallway are sufficiently narrow that this promises to be difficult. To make matters worse, the patient is steadfast in her refusal of pain relief. Both paramedics are behaving with considerable restraint.

'Don't fuss,' she says to the more juvenile-looking of her two fresh-faced rescuers. She cocks her head like an elderly owl. 'What age are you, lad? I'd say you are barely out of school.'

The young man flushes to the roots of his hair and his partner snorts with merriment.

'I'm older than you think,' he says. He flashes her a smile. 'Old enough to deal with a looker like you and that's no mistake.'

Well done, lad, I think to myself. Never let 'em

best you. Once the patients start calling the shots, your authority is under threat.

'Will it be Truro?' says Mrs P, her voice a fluting treble. Big eyes, sad as Dandy's, search the young man's face.

He nods and he pats her arm. 'No worries. I'll look after you.'

Mrs P simpers and blushes like a girl.

Meanwhile the other man is shuffling paperwork. He has already done his best to clear a path to the door.

'Any relatives?'

'There's her son, Peran. I think he's still in the kitchen.'

I glance at my watch. It is horribly late. There will have been complaints.

We hear Mrs Pascoe is in hospital with a suspected fractured hip. 'Complications' are mentioned but not fully explained. On the following Monday, though, I'm in hospital myself, admitted for long-awaited surgery, so it's a full month later, on my first day back, that Mrs Pascoe turns up on my list. A scribbled note in the margin reads *Recently discharged, Treliske.*

The thing about this business that people don't 'get' is the pressure we care-providers are under. Our schedules are packed; there's no travel time allowed; and visits, even at the best of times, are under-allocated. The result is we're running late almost as soon as we start. And there is absolutely nothing we can do except buckle down and work our socks off. We know we can't win but we try to stop our lateness from running out of control. How can you shower, dress and breakfast someone in the twenty minutes allowed by their care plan? It's simply not possible. Yet you have to wash them and you can't leave them hungry. That's without the poor buggers – all too many – who are lying in a wet bed, or worse. It's no wonder, is it, that every week we have carers off with stress? Physician, heal thyself.

About Mrs Pascoe, though, I am genuinely pleased. She's a sweet little lady who has worked all her life and has few pleasures left to her. I'm down for a tea-time visit, so I decide to take a few flowers. We're not supposed to do stuff like this but, honestly, where's the harm?

So, come five o'clock, I pull into the yard with a dozen yellow tulips on my car seat. They are glorious, resplendent, like an armful of sunshine, wrapped up in cellophane and tied with a shiny orange bow. I am inordinately pleased with myself, looking forward to making my entrance. What a great guy I have turned out to be.

As I approach the house, though, I am thrown out of kilter. Eventually, it registers: the absence of dog shit. I cannot see a single steaming pile. What is more, the lawn has been mowed and the overgrown hedges trimmed back. The old place has assumed an air of something like respectability. True, Peran's work boots, lagged in mud as usual, stand guard at the door but the exterior of the farmhouse has been utterly transformed. The once flailing drainpipe is now secured to the wall and the window frames have been painted. There are pristine nets at all the windows, and the windows themselves have been cleaned.

Inside the house, my amazement continues. Just about everything is cleaner and lighter. It smells better too. The kitchen is tidy: no dog scraps on the floor, no mountains of unwashed laundry; and not a single dirty plate festers in the sink. Instead, there is a fragrance of lily-of-the-valley

CORNWALL: SECRET & HIDDEN

which I trace to a diffuser on the hallstand. Has Peran been kidnapped and replaced with a cyborg? Does all this presage the end of the world?

It seems not because inside the parlour nothing much has changed. Mrs Pascoe, clad only in her brushed nylon nightie and a once-white shawl, is supported by a pair of grubby pillows in her grubby, unmade bed. She seems to me more than usually pale; the atmosphere is musty; the commode is full to overflowing; there's a dubious stain on the rug. These things apart, Mrs P looks okay. Only her pallor is worrying. I make a mental note to ask about her pain.

I grin. 'Must be nice to be home.'

I am genuinely pleased to see her. I am waiting to tell her how she needs to get up and muck out the barn. But Mrs Pascoe's failing eyes narrow to sharp and uncompromising slits. There's an urgency behind them that arrests and holds my gaze. There is something, too, about her small head with its delicate bird-like skull, her thinning hair and baby pink scalp that brings home to me with exceptional force her extreme vulnerability. I begin to feel anxious. I'm not sure why.

Mrs Pascoe opens her eyes wide and jerks a thumb in the direction of the door. This might be construed, I suppose, as a gesture of warning but I'm tired and it's my first day back. I can't force her to talk to me if she is not feeling up to it. It's not uncommon for elders to suffer some slight depressive illness in the wake of a stay in hospital. They find it hard to re-adjust to being so much alone.

'Tulips,' I say lamely.

Awkwardly too. I am as bashful as a would-be suitor

who miscalculates his welcome by entering unannounced. As I and my tulips are brushed aside, I am amused to find myself flustered. Only when I say I will look for a vase does she manage a limp little smile. It seems there is no place here for sunshine today.

So, I give her a bed-bath, change her soiled bedding, fetch a clean nightdress. Very gently, I brush out her hair and weave it into two shining plaits. She checks they are right by raising one liver-spotted hand in a gesture I find poignantly girlish. I prepare and heat a simple meal and serve it on a cheap painted tray.

Between us, there are few words and no cheerful banter. When I ask about pain relief, she denies being in pain. I'm about to take my leave when I wonder aloud what has happened to Dandy. Mrs Pascoe says nothing, but I see her start, or maybe even flinch. As I leave, though, I notice two things: firstly, Dandy the poodle's old leash no longer on a hook in the hallway; and, secondly, something so completely without precedent I wonder how I missed it at all. Bright, audacious, bold as a flag, it is hanging near the door I came in by. Brand spanking new, extremely stylish, and doubtless no less expensive, it is a softly gleaming, cherry-red, full-length leather coat.

I decide to put these matters on hold until the following morning. The coat is a mystery but one I can put to one side. Too weary for even a microwave meal, I make myself a sandwich. Shortly after eating it, I am tucked up in bed.

Having slept through my alarm, I begin the next day late and very bad-tempered. When the phone rings, I'm shaving. The boss is calling from home.

'Mrs Pascoe's off your list,' he says.

'What's up?' I flick the soap from my razor. 'Don't tell me that great lump of a son has decided to complain.'

It sometimes happens that a relative, usually a husband or son, will object to a male nurse in the home, most often where the situation involves intimate care.

'Dead,' says the boss. This early in the day, he has no time for the niceties. 'Eight o'clock yesterday. Seems she took a tumble on the stairs.'

'What?'

This single, inadequate word is all I can manage. I am, after all, only half awake. Then, in turn, I am shocked and saddened; and, finally, alarmed. In my memory, I see with a troubling new clarity Mrs Pascoe in her brushed nylon nightie. She has a look in her eyes that I can't pin down. Is it possible it was fear? I wonder if I have made a mistake. Have I failed the old lady? Yellow tulips are for friendship. My sadness at her death is sharpened by a nasty stab of guilt.

'Surely there will have to be an inquest?' I say, suddenly remembering the telephone. There is a brief pause before I add, 'How did she get upstairs?'

Six weeks later, the Pascoe place comes up for sale. Peran Pascoe, we hear on the grapevine, is set to be wed. A classy bit of stuff, by all accounts, a real good looker. A picture turns up in the local rag. Peran is suited and booted. True to all reports, his new wife is very attractive indeed. It sounds like a fairy tale, doesn't it, a story from a picture book? How neatly the pieces of Peran's life have fallen into place. I can't help wondering, though, what Little Red Riding Hood might have seen in an oaf like Peran and where, indeed, a man like Peran would even meet a woman like that.

Given there never was an inquest, one question will always haunt me. How did Mrs Pascoe find her way upstairs?

Unblinded

by Ella Walsworth-Bell

'Katya, don't worry. If he pulls at it, or knocks it, just pop it back on again.' The midwife is younger than me. Her long blonde hair brushes her shoulders, each strand catching the light. 'You know it doesn't hurt him. It fits perfectly, and it's all soft on his face. I promise.'

'Okay.' I step closer to my baby. My little David. His body is warm and soft and he smells of my milk. His skin is silk under my fingertips and his head nestles into my palm. Keeping my hand still, I feel him drift into sleep. My thumb rests against the black plastic of his headset.

'Should I take it off, sometimes?' I ask. 'When he's sleeping, I mean. It's not as though he can see then, can he?'

'Even newborns respond to darkness. The headset will pick up on his lack of movement and go into night mode. Then you can get some rest.' She looks up at me, and grins.

'Goodness knows what we did without these.'

'Mmm.' I bite my lip.

'Such a dear little thing, isn't he?' Pink lovehearts float from her cheeks and her pupils are glowing stars. She pauses. 'Are you OK, though? On your own?'

Loneliness throbs, but I keep my expression neutral. 'I'm fine. I've got David now, haven't I?' Gently, I lift my hand away from my boy's face. 'I'll stay next to him. I'm not that tired, but I might take in a Dreamie or something.'

Her voice softens. 'Keep your settings on private. Little ones can't take in all the information. They tire easily. He'll only be given rough shapes to begin with. Each day his visual input will be increased, dependent on his retinal responses.'

As young as she is, she knows her stuff. And yes, David will keep on the headset. It's the only way, for now. I can't risk attracting any attention.

The girl waves, pixelates for a second, then re-appears. 'Sorry, forgot to say. Don't forget your face-to-face appointment tomorrow, will you?'

'I won't.' I flick her a Smile emoji, to keep her happy. And so she doesn't suspect a thing.

As if I'll really plug into a Dreamie. Why would I waste precious hours on more of the Corporation's manufactured junk? I swing the filter back to 'As natural'. The fake daylight. I just have to see him for what he is. My baby: fresh from the womb. Pale and beautiful in his white sleepsuit. I stroke his forehead and pause when my fingers hit the rigid headset. Every instinct in my body wants to rip it away, but I daren't. Not yet.

When I was a kid, we didn't need all this blasted technology. If we wanted a day out, my mum and I headed down to our secret beach. Cornwall was great for that, even back in the mid 2030s, before the UV radiation grew more dangerous. It sounds crazy now, but we jumped in the car and drove for an hour just to get to our favourite spot.

Rinsey Cove.

I keep my eyes shut, blocking out the garish colours and jarring images that pop up in the view through my headset, uninvited. My podmate, Paolo, taught me how to do this. 'Close your eyes,' he'd whisper in my ear. 'Listen to your heart.'

I think of the Cove, and memories bubble up. Sunlight shining on a pure blue sea. Pink thrift flowers swaying on the clifftops.

Mum and I scrambled down a rocky path and threw off our shoes, raced headlong across the sand to the sea.

'Ooh, it's freezing,' I mock-gasped as a wave tugged my ankles.

Her hand held mine tight, as if I'd drift away. 'Let's sit up by the rockpools in the sunshine.'

Our secret beach was only uncovered at low tide. We lay flat on the rocks risking the sun's rays warming our faces. When the sea rose, we left. A lump forms in my throat, thinking of my mum and the culling. Keep your memories, we were told, your parents are giving their lives for you. With fewer people, the Earth's resources will last longer. Save the environment: sign up for the cull.

I swallow, remembering.

Afterwards, everyone stayed in their pods, to minimise their impact on the planet. And then came the headsets, to make up for not going outside. The technology is astounding. I can enter 'Seaside Views' and all around me will be golden beaches and rippling waves. But without sand between the toes, or salt scenting the breeze.

Your heartrate has increased, my virtual assistant tells me. Her smooth voice sings into both ears, as if I'm having the thought myself. *What about trying an exercise programme? There's 2,252 others taking part in Astral Power Yoga right now. Would you like to join them?*

'No, thank you, Rosie.' The piano music stops. She's right, though. Paolo's been gone a whole month, and I need to keep strong. I stride the edges of the room. It's imperative to maintain my fitness levels, so I'm useful to them in some way.

It's invigorating to swing my arms on my own. I huff the piped air in and out. My chest expands and releases. If I can feel my own body, I know I'm still inside it. Tucked away somewhere.

A cheerful face pops up on my feed. *How's it going in the world of baby?* A ginger tom kitten romps and rolls into the corner of the room, all whiskered surprise when it bumps into the walls. My work colleague's sent me a V-GIF. I bung her a Laughing emoji, adding that I'm pretty busy. With a flash of inspiration, I find a giant cartoon of a pink baby pulling a face. A perfect out-of-office reply: *Gotta deal with a nappy or three. May be gone some time.*

That should keep everyone off my back.

I scroll down to MyMessage. It's low-tech, and that's why we use it. You get a measly 200 characters in a boxy green font next to your username. Hardly anyone's on it these days, because it's so old. On the plus side, it's secure and unmonitored. Paolo's there – yes! – and we launch into guarded conversation.

- *The present has arrived.*
- *Fantastic news. Is it what we expected?*
- *The blue one.* I glance at the crib, and dissolve with happiness.
- *All intact? And you?*
- *Good.*
- *When will the delivery be? We're close enough.*
- *Tomorrow at eleven.*

I breathe in, and out. Slowly and carefully, so that my heart doesn't judder, alerting Rosie.

Breaking free from the chat, I delete the App completely. It's best there's no record of it. I just hope the weather will be fine. It should be; we've been told there are no clouds now.

Chimes sound softly in my ear the next morning. The permit arrives by secure mail, with the exit code for the door. A journey. Last time I made one was when Paolo had his check-up. And then, well ... he got away, didn't he? Took his chance to join a free faction. I stayed, like a reluctant roach scuttling into stale air. I've had time to regret my fear, and time to wallow in my loneliness. Now, I'm determined. For our baby's sake.

It's unusual to get an appointment at the hospital in person, but the consultant is worried that baby David has the same condition as Paolo. Retinal dysphasia, otherwise known as total blindness. If so, then a headset will be pointless for him, as it was for his father.

The Corporation is now stricter on those born with

disabilities, and my stomach churns. I go on automatic: change David, feed him, dress in my protective suit and walk the few steps to the EV.

The vehicle's metal door handle is cold to the touch. If my baby can't see, life will be harder for him. No surgeon can repair his visual faculties. But he would be like his father, with a face free of the headset. Free: unblinded. I'd be able to stroke his soft skin, feel his eyelashes whisper against my fingertips. And perhaps he'd have more insight into our world. Paolo always thought more clearly than me.

'I'm one of the lucky ones,' he'd say. 'Can't see, so I'm not distracted by all that rubbish they shove in.'

I sigh, remembering the mellow curve of his voice. He'd fold me in his arms and tell me to close my eyes. 'Touch me, Katya. Hold me. This is reality.'

I swallow and pull the heavy door open. Click David's crib into the back seat. He twists his head this way and that, bashing his headset. Letting out a wail, he lifts his hands to his face. His fingernails have grown and he claws at the skin, impatient. I soothe him, and turn on Seamusic to calm him.

The journey in itself is uneventful. The vehicle vibrates with movement. Cruise control kicks in and I find myself tapping on the floor as I always do, forgetting the automated steering and gearbox.

At the hospital entrance, the car's engine stops thrumming. I override the safety protocols and lower the windshield. There's a metal barrier stopping us.

Katya, why have you paused your journey? Rosie asks me.

I stammer an answer. 'G-g-gates aren't open. Don't know why.' My heart's pounding. If they check Paolo's history, they'll be suspicious. Drones will be sent. And these days, they're always armed.

A tinny voice belts out from a loudspeaker, asking me for my hospital number. I panic, and delve through a ton of emails before I get to the original. Typing the digits painstakingly into an old-fashioned keypad, my hands are shaking. David cries, and my stomach clutches in fear.

Finally – slowly – the barrier rises. *Katya, please follow the GPS route to clinic room B*, Rosie instructs.

When I get there, the consultant walks into the room and his footsteps tap on the floor. Unevenly, as if his audio is glitching. His avatar's kitted out in a smart suit and glasses. I wonder if he'd worn them, long ago.

'Good morning. Katya, isn't it?' He bends over the crib and suddenly I smell his breath. Off-mint and coffee tabs, all mixed together. Ugh. David's father smelt of warmth and life and fresh aftershave.

I step back.

'And how's baby?' he asks. 'Any response to the headset?'

'Well, he's not keen. But I understand that's normal.'

'Oh, completely. Optical nerve takes ten days or so to start properly processing the visual information. It's all new for him.' A laugh seeps from his lips. 'Soon all these sets'll be defunct, anyway.'

'I heard.' My voice is light, upbeat.

'Implantation's the way forward. And there's no limit to how young we can start that. No bulky headsets, or power outtages.'

'Wonderful.'

'Now, let's have a look at these little peepers.'

My visual feed blurs. I shake my head, annoyed. Then I realise he's removed David's headset. He's protecting me from seeing his naked face.

'Privacy settings are on,' he confirms. The man's bulky physique hovers over my son like a raincloud. In his hand he holds – I hope – an opthalmoscope. I glance at the table, but any other instruments are blurred out. My heart pounds, thinking of needles, and the culling.

David whimpers, and I fumble for his hand. 'Shhh. Let the doctor see.'

'Mmm hmm. And the other one.'

I need to know. 'How are they?'

A bright light bursts from the man's hand like a shaft of fresh sunlight. I blink in fear, then logic aids my memory. A torch. To check the pupils.

'And off.' The man comes back into focus. His hands are empty, as if they've never held any tools. He nods. 'Not to worry. Quick reactions to light, tracks objects well. Despite his father's ... impairment, this one's absolutely fine.'

I'm lightheaded with relief. My baby is healthy, and mine to keep. 'You're sure?'

'Certain. So, managing on your own, are you?'

'Er ... yes.'

'Mmm. Heard what happened. Still, you'll be paired again in no time. Pods are built for families, aren't they.' He puts a cold palm on my arm, and I freeze. Shaking him off, I pick up David's crib. A business card slices into my in-tray and I delete Chas Okonwe, Corp-registered Eye Specialist, in seconds. No, thank you.

*

On the way back from the clinic I watch the GPS marker, desperately trying to remember the atlas of my childhood. Aha – that tiny road on the left. We're here.

'Rosie, I need to stop.'

Is everything alright, Katya? Shall I report a problem?

'No, thank you. I'm going to feed David for ten minutes. And change his nappy.'

The EV system receives the message, and the engine stops. I hit the red override button, so I can open the door.

How long would you like to log the delay?

'Sixty minutes.' The maximum. The dashboard begins a countdown of red digits. Fifty-nine. Fifty-eight. I try not to think about what happens when the allocated time runs out.

'We're here, little one. Let's find my special beach.' I lift him and he stirs, his headset biting into my arm. 'Not long now, I promise.'

Out beyond the car, beyond the cliffs, all is blue. Blue sparkling sea and blue clear sky. My headset registers too bright and my brain throbs.

'This is it,' I murmur, half to myself. I listen for the whirr of drones, and when there are none, I slam the door closed. If they were there, I wouldn't get long. They'd query my intentions and then shoot to kill. The Corporation has no truck with dissidents.

I shiver.

The path is exactly where I remember it, though. Brambles kick against my legs, and the coconut scent of gorse flowers hangs in the air. A stonechat chirrups, and it's not my audio sending me Wildlife wake-up calls. This is Mother Nature herself.

I scramble down stone steps to the beach, ringed by cliffs. The headset glitches – ALERT: LOW SIGNAL – and I breathe out. Paolo's right. He told me the granite cliffs would be high enough to block the input channels. No-one can track me. No-one will find me.

Bold yellow empty sand stretches before us. The sea is a glaring primary blue: I believe these images, despite a lack of detail in the graphics. The fleet of rebel sailing ships will arrive soon. I'm starting to feel nurtured. I'm starting to feel free.

I slip off my shoes. Wander down to the sea, step by slow step, as my mother used to do with me. The sand is warm beneath my toes. And gritty. I'd forgotten the grit. Perhaps my feet are softer now.

'Here we are, then.' I sit facing the sea and hold David across my lap. He shifts his head left and right, searching for me. His set must be reading an error message, too.

'Right. This is it.' I smooth his cheek with my thumb and he stills. 'Ah, let's just...' With shaking hands, I ease the headset away, freeing his face. He blinks. 'There you go. All gone.'

He screws up his forehead, gears up to cry.

'Don't. Look, I'll do it too.' I breathe in deep, taste salt on my tongue. 'See.' Raising my headset, I unloop the earpieces.

Shoot. The world is a blur. An endless dizzy blur. Sickened, I shake my head. My eyes are weak; I've worn the set for too many years. I scrunch my face tight, then widen my eyes, as if trying to escape a dream. Stars form and re-form, like a fizz effect.

Daylight is painfully bright. All the colours are weak

and anaemic, without enhancements. The flowers on the clifftop are a pale line of smudged pink. And nothing is clear. The beach is a long smudge of grey-beige. The ocean is as if shrouded in thick fog. Nausea hits me. Christ, I won't see the boats coming. I won't see the drones, even!

David whines, and I focus on his hazy shape.

There's a twitch of movement. Ah, that blob is his head, and those two dark patches are his eyes. I concentrate again, as if solving a logic puzzle.

The sun warms my face, and I wonder how much time I have left on the car. I need to fix this; I need to see. Panicking, scooping up sand, I rub his tiny fingers. They flex, withdraw, then extend towards the sensation again. I settle down, and wait for my vision to return. All I need to do is wait. Surely.

My heart pounds and my breath races in and out. I'm only getting shadows and blurs. The shades of colour are insipid and weak.

Perhaps I need to forget the bright blues and jarring yellows? Nature's palette is soft pastel hues, rather than artificial intensities. Real soil is brown; grains of sand are a mellow fawn colour. David has a naturalistic skin tone, varying in detail across his arm. I see him, finally. I stare, lost in his beauty. Each messy twisted curl of his dark hair. Each delicate eyelash. Each blotchy freckle. Each miniature fingernail.

And yes, his face is there. Without his headset. He's mesmerised by me, and I sink into the pools of his soft brown eyes. Behind him, the beach gradually returns into focus, a glittering backdrop of subtle colour and intricate patterns.

A shout comes from offshore. I squint at the wide ocean and see a small boat. The fleet has come. To take us away from sealed pods and fake feeds. Away from the Corporation and its culls. Into the real world: to live in harmony with nature. Paolo calls out, across the water. 'Katya, it's me. I love you. Both of you.'

I hold up a wriggling David. 'Look,' I say to him. 'There's your Daddy. We're free.'

These Little Moments in Time

by Lamorna Ireland

A gentle mist drew in and blanketed over the dormant creek. The cottages stirred into an early morning slumber and moor hens peppered the water's surface.

This was just how Jack Trebilcock liked it. Peaceful. Isolated. Hazy.

It was a far cry from the fast-paced chaos of his day to day on the corporate hamster wheel and every year he asked himself why he didn't visit this place more often.

It was that time of year again, and he felt that familiar mix of excitement and remembrance, a splash of dread thrown in for good measure. He always hated the emptiness that followed.

Jack negotiated the cobbled terrain leading down to the retreating water, the sludgy silt on a slow reveal beneath the surface. The tide was going down, making his short walk to their bench a lot easier than previous years. It looked as understated as always, the discoloured timber boards merging in with its concrete side supports, a cluster of emerging crocuses acting as a splash of colour against the grey palette.

A quick glance at his watch told him there was one minute to go. He took his place on one side of the bench, a panoramic view of the estuary before him. A pair of swans glided along the edge of the embankment, momentarily distracting Jack as a familiar voice soothed his soul.

'Hello, dear boy.'

Jack smiled warmly at the old man occupying the other side of the bench, the steel blue eyes they shared twinkling in the morning sun.

'Hi, Dad.'

'Well now. This spot gets prettier on every visit, don't you think?'

Jack nodded his agreement, his gaze on his father rather than the view.

'How's your m-'

'Mum's fine,' Jack said, chuckling.

'That predictable, am I?'

'It's your first question every time.' Jack smiled. 'Mum's doing OK, Dad. She's keeping herself busy with the newest member of the family.'

A short, hearty laugh escaped the old man's lungs as he locked his fingers together across his portly belly. 'Christ. Another baby. What's that? Number four your sister is on now? She always did have a maternal streak, bless her heart.'

Jack nodded his agreement a second time. He chanced

a look back on the water, a small creeping fear of his father disappearing should he take his eyes off him for even a moment. It felt alien to him that there was this whole new extension to their family that his father had never met. He wondered how that made his dear old dad feel. He considered asking him, but he never liked to tinge this precious hour with any feelings of remorse.

'And what about you, m'boy? Any chance of seeing a baby on your lap on our next meet?'

'Dad,' Jack said, his voice failing to mask that sadness. 'You know it doesn't work like that.'

'I know, I know. Humour your old man, will you? How close am I to having a fifth grandchild? Unless your sister beats you on that one too.'

Jack's gaze was back on the water. He didn't want to tell him how his short-lived marriage had broken apart spectacularly, just a couple of days ago. He didn't want to go into scrutinising detail about his work habits, a coping mechanism for his failed marriage. He just didn't want to disappoint him.

'You never know, Dad.' Jack smiled.

An elderly lady in her long trench coat released three collies from the front door of one of the waterfront cottages, their excited barks echoing across the creek. Jack and his father watched them in companionable silence, the furry companions weaving in and out of each other and around the lady's legs, excited for their morning trek. Jack had a strange moment of yearning to be one of those dogs. Not a care in the world, not a work deadline in sight. Just the overwhelming excitement for those morning walkies.

'You're working too hard again, boy.'

'Wha- how did you...?'

'I can see it in your eyes. Jesus, Jack – between the two of us, you're not supposed to be the one with that dead expression in your eyes.'

It was a slight involuntary movement: Jack rubbed his face, his elbows poised on his knees. 'Can you not ... say things like that please, Dad.'

'Why? We've both come to terms with the inevitable. At least, I have. You're almost there.'

Jack shook his head, incredulous, his face muscles aching from all the smiling. Peter Trebilcock, his dear, dear father – he'd always been good at making him smile, even when he didn't fancy it.

'So, what would you like to do?' Peter asked, shifting his gaze back out to the water with contentment.

Jack looked around, askant in his manner, and retrieved a steel hip flask from an inside pocket of his jacket. Another hearty laugh erupted from his dad and he rubbed his hands with glee like a little boy in a sweet shop.

'Now you're talking, m'boy!'

Jack felt his father's hard gaze on his hand as he took the first long draw from the flask, some of that wretched office rigidness melting away from him. He waited for Jack to pass the flask over to the other side of the bench and, with bated breath, reached out to grab it. They were never sure if these things would work. Peter chortled as his fingers successfully wrapped around the cold steel and lifted it in toast to his son across the way.

'Cheers, me 'andsome.'

The woody, warming liquid had trickled down Jack's throat with ease, a hint of vanilla noted in the flavour. He wondered silently whether his father was enjoying the same experience right now.

Peter smacked his lips together and handed the flask back. 'That's a good whiskey.'

'You should know. It's from your collection,' Jack commented, checking the contents of the flask. The whiskey seemed untouched, despite his father's guzzling efforts.

'The 1989 vintage?'

Jack laughed. 'The very same.'

Minutes trickled by in glorious companionship and soon the father and son duo had fallen into one of their games of Black Jacks.

'What else do you have stashed in that coat of yours?' Peter asked, as Jack dealt the cards for the second time. 'Every year you get more organised.'

'Do I?'

'You OK there, boy?'

'It just ... gets harder. We have ten minutes left.' Jack's voice was thick, his throat a solid, painful lump. 'It just gets harder ... every year.'

'I know. My sweet boy. We find ourselves with a unique gift here. But you've got to live your life.'

'Yeah – alright, Dad,' Jack scoffed, retiring his cards to the bench.

'No, don't 'alright Dad,' me! I can see in you exactly what happened to me. Overworked. Full speed ahead through the week, waiting for it to be the weekend. Waiting for it to be your next holiday. Waiting for it to be summer. And now I worry that you're hanging on for this every year. It's not healthy, Jack. You've got to live for the moment.

Like these moments.' He gestured to the quiet creek in front of them. 'Do you come down here at all other than to see me?'

'Ok, I get your point, Dad.'

'Well, do you?'

His father was right, of course. There was something special about this secret spot of theirs. But why did it only occur once a year?

'I love you, my dear, dear boy. I love this little catch up of ours.'

Jack was about to say 'me too' when his words were cut short.

'But...' Peter smiled, reaching across and grasping his son's warm hands, remembering a time when they were smaller than his. 'Perhaps it's time to stop living for this one moment and live for lots of tiny moments in time that life has to offer. Bring that gorgeous wife down here.'

A groan escaped Jack's lungs, his knees juddering and giving him away.

'Alright, bring your mother then. We have two minutes left. We're going to have to cover the taboo topic of your divorce next time.'

Despite himself, Jack felt a ripple of laughter before giving in to it. 'I love you, Dad.'

'And I you, Son. Please, do your old man a favour. Live that precious life of yours. Have more moments like these and unplug yourself from that bloody job of yours more often. Come on – you live near one of the most beautiful spots in the entire world!'

'I will. I promise.'

'That's my boy. Now, take it all in and breathe.'

Jack did as he was told, angling himself in time to witness a bevy of swans, their graceful movements cutting through the water's surface, tiny ripples following suit. Two rowing boats click clacked together as a murmuration of starlings dominated the grey sky.

'It really is beautiful here. Right, Dad?'

When a response never came, Jack didn't need to see the vacant seat beside him. Instead, he listened to his father's words and he breathed in deeply, his lungs filling with that glorious fresh air around him.

'You're right, Dad,' Jack said, knowing those words would reach his father wherever he was. 'One more hour. Our little secret.'

The Shell Necklace

by Anne Rainbow

5 am. My journal lies open, and this morning's words float in a pool of light cast from the desk lamp.

> *Full moon yesterday. Spring tides tomorrow. It's high now. So high, I hear the waves pounding on the shore. Breaking shells. Crushing them.*

I stand to admire the moonlight slithering across the inky surface of the sea. Beside me, Linka raises his glossy black head.

'Not much longer, Linka.'

He knows, from my tone, it's a no and rests his head on his paws. I settle in my seat and pick up my fountain pen. The ink is red. I write three more words and blot them dry.

Moments later, I pull on my waterproof jacket and step into my size eleven Wellington boots. As I let myself out of the side door, the scent of seaweed draws me through the darkness towards the coastal path.

Linka pushes past me and his silhouette trots ahead. I'm in no hurry. I love this hour of the day. No one else around. Only the sound of the waves and the wind swirling above me.

As I turn to follow the narrow path alongside a field of corn, with the steep cliff falling to my right, I pluck an ear. It's almost harvest time. I feel it in my blood.

Where this field meets the next, Linka, too old to clamber over the stile, sits, panting, waiting for me to open the gate. Then he's off again.

When we reach Onjohn Cove, I take the path down to the beach and Linka investigates the shoreline while I sit on my usual rock.

My timing is good. I tap my watch face five times. 'Eight-teen twen-ty-one.'

I'm standing with my two brothers at the entrance to the cist, a chamber cut into the rock. Our latest victim's hair hangs in golden ringlets over her bare shoulders and her eyes plead for mercy. As the moon catches the surface of the lunulae adorning her neck, my whole being warms at the sight of that precious metal, a mix of gold and tin. Two wafer-thin crescents, Cornish, through and through.

Each time the tide rushes forward, we hold her down. And she gasps. And gasps. And then stops.

'Twen-ty twen-ty-one,' I whisper, tapping my watch face five times again. The image of our sacrifice vanishes, and – perfect timing – today's golden disc peeps above the horizon, casting light across the bay. My ritual over, I soak in the magic of this moment, savouring the memories stamped into my veins. Soon, I'll enjoy a sacrifice for real, rather than reliving one from the past.

Cocooned in her sleeping bag, Hazel eases herself into a sitting position and slides the gingham curtain along its plastic-coated elastic rail. Resting her head against the paper-thin wall of the caravan, she watches the sun rise.

Beads of condensation frame her view. Trees that had been shadows only moments ago surrender to the light. Bent almost double by the prevailing wind, their feathery branches reveal tiny leaves, more visible now that day has broken.

Hazel sighs. The day would now proceed, a replica of yesterday. A cup of coffee, perched on the steps of the caravan, looking out to sea. Waking Jessica. Helping her to wash and dress. Breakfast.

Hazel tiptoes to the bunkroom door and gazes at her sleeping child. So easy to please. So easily entertained. Browsing the gift shop, finding more treasures to remind herself of her holiday.

A walk into St Merryn could while away the morning. By lunchtime, the tide would be out. Hazel could pack a picnic. They could go down to the beach. Build sandcastles. Collect shells.

Yes, today would be another day. Just another day. Another lonely day.

Jessica holds the shell high above her head, like a trophy.

'Mummy! Look at this one. It's perfect.'

Two golden curls escape the confines of Jessica's straw hat and coil against her freckled face. Hazel pushes her own blonde locks back out of her eyes, fighting a losing battle against the sea breeze.

'Let me see. Oh yes, darling. Beautiful. You're such a clever girl. How many do we have now?' she says, offering her shoulder bag to Jessica.

Jessica peers inside and counts out loud, 'One, two,' and then silently, because that's the grown-up way. 'Twelve!' she announces, placing her new find with the rest.

Hazel looks skyward and closes her eyes. David would have been so proud. After years of trying for a baby, the birth had been difficult, and the doctor had explained that Jessica would always have problems with learning. The damage to the right-hand side of her brain would also affect her physical development on her left-hand side. Jess would need constant physio care. They'd thought they would cope, but then came David's diagnosis.

'How many more do we need, Mummy?' asks Jessica, pulling at Hazel's arm and dragging her back to the present.

'Oh, perhaps one more?' she says, wiping a tear away with one hand and tucking Jessica's errant curls back into place with the other.

Jessica skips off to continue her search and soon finds another mess of seaweed deposited by the tide. She crouches, resting her hands on her knees. Now and then, she picks something up, examines it and discards it.

Hazel runs her gaze beyond Jessica, eastwards along the beach to where the feeble stream bleeds into the sea. The spot where children build dams is devoid of action.

The ice-cream van that parks by the footpath from the pub to the beach has long gone, signalling that the best of this day is over. The beach at the western end is also bare, sporting only two rainbow-striped windbreaks, separating the territories marked out by holidaymakers.

Between Hazel and the cliff, though, a crowd of semi-clad suntanned lads are playing football, with piles of discarded clothes as makeshift goalposts.

A lone seagull screeches as it swoops down from the cliffs and, while Hazel follows its flight, a cloud crosses in front of the sun. She shivers and digs her hands deep into the pockets of her fleece jacket, pulling it closer around her. Helen is about to set off to catch up with Jessica, when a Labrador races past. It scourges a trail in the wet sand, catching a ball in its mouth, and trots towards Hazel, wagging its tail.

A voice floats from some distance behind Hazel: 'Linka! Linka! Here, boy!'

Linka ignores the call and drops the ball at Hazel's feet.

'Oh, so you want to play, do you?' Hazel throws the ball towards the water's edge and Linka races off.

'Hey, thanks,' says Linka's owner, touching Hazel on the arm.

Hazel swings around to face him and the treasure trove in her shoulder bag clinks.

He backs off, with both hands in the air. 'Oops! Something broken?'

Hazel investigates the collection of shells. 'No,' she says, laughing.

Linka races back to them, ball in mouth, delighted to

find he now has two grown-ups to play with.

'Here, boy! Here Linka. Sit. Sit!' To Hazel, he adds: 'He's just trying to be friendly. I'm Tim, by the way. I live over there.'

He points to a house high on the cliff, above the sand dunes. 'The one with the blue shutters. I bought it a month ago. Still unpacking boxes.'

'Lucky you. I've always wanted to stay in one of those.' She shows Tim a tiny key attached to a cord, strung around her neck. 'We're in a caravan, and it's quite a trek back up the hill to the campsite.'

'Yes, lucky me,' he says. 'Sensible to carry your key like that.'

'I never risk leaving valuables on the beach. And if I go into the sea, I can't lose it.'

Tim throws the ball for Linka. 'From my lounge, I have a wonderful view of the beach. I've noticed you several times recently, with your little girl.'

'Today, we're collecting shells,' Hazel explains. 'Well, Jessica is the collector, and I'm in charge of the bag.'

'Jessica? Lovely name ... How old is she?'

'Seven. And I'm Hazel.'

'Hazel,' he repeats, letting the 'el' linger on his tongue.

Linka arrives once again and drops the ball at Hazel's feet. Tim throws it towards the cliffs. Linka races off while the seagull swoops, its screeches competing with the crashing sounds of the waves and the wind howling around them.

'So, Hazel, you're here on holiday?'

'Yes, I'm a teacher. We come every year for the long summer holiday. It's my favourite place. You?'

'My first time. We always used to … I, I mean, I…' His voice trails off as he traces a curve in the sand with his big toe. 'Sorry, I'm not making much sense,' he says, sinking to his knees and busying himself studying a solitary strip of seaweed.

Hazel turns her attention to the seagull who has now found a mate to fly in circles high above the cliff top.

Tim stands and offers Hazel a shell. 'To add to your collection.'

'Thanks. That's a beaut. Bigger than all the others.'

'You're welcome. What's your plan for the rest of today? What's left of it.'

'We – Jess and I – we're going to make these shells into a necklace for her,' says Hazel, dropping the new shell into her bag.

'Nice idea. An improvement on the key-on-a-string necklace.'

'Yes. Her dad and I…' Hazel's turn to trail off. She clears her throat. 'You on your own? In that big house?'

Tim takes his eyes off Linka who is trotting towards them and focuses on Hazel instead. 'Yes. Well, on my own with Linka. As I said, I bought the place last month. Needed somewhere to think. And plan what to do next.'

'You like it here?'

'Very much. And Linka does too, don't you, boy?'

Linka drops the ball at Tim's feet and waits at his side.

'Unusual name: Linka,' says Hazel.

'It's Polish. Means mannish. My wife … we had Linka as a puppy, but now…'

'We've never had pets. And I'm glad. Not sure I would have coped.'

'Oh, Linka is company for me, aren't you, boy?'

Linka wags his tail, as patient as ever.

Hazel sighs. A few clouds skid across the sky as if racing to escape the rays of the dying sun; and, in the far distance, more clouds, heavy with the promise of rain. 'It'll be dusk soon. Time I called Jessica.'

As Hazel takes a step forward, Tim touches her arm, stopping her. 'Can Linka and I walk back with you, across the beach?'

Hazel gives Linka an affectionate rub on the head. 'Of course. Jessica! Come on, darling. Teatime.'

Jessica runs lop-sided like a puppy, over eager to arrive at her destination. 'Coming!'

'Let me be your guide,' says Tim, linking arms with Hazel and steering her through the maze of puddles left by the outgoing tide. 'This beach, as you no doubt know, is Harlyn Bay but, ahead of us, is Bloodhound Cove and Greenclose Cove, and then, where you'll take the track up to the campsite, that's Onjohn Cove.'

'Oh! I've always called it Boat Cove. And beyond that: Cellars.'

'The Cellars is the name of the house on the cliff top. The Hellyer family used to press pilchards there. Catch them. Salt them. Pack them into barrels. Ship them to Italy.'

'For a newcomer, you're very knowledgeable about this place. The geography. The history. I teach History.'

'What period?'

'Right now? With the sixth formers, Tudor history. Next on the agenda is Henry the Eighth and all those wives.'

'Sixteenth century, then. Same time as the witch

Mother Ivey cursed the Hellyer family for caring more about money than the health of the locals.'

'Cursed them? In what way?'

'Quite simple. Death to any man who tilled the soil.'

'Fascinating,' says Hazel. 'You don't believe in witchcraft, though, surely?'

'But of course! And time travel.'

'I believe time can seem to stand still. And that it can go slow and go fast. Like this holiday. Speeding past.'

'What if you could tap the face of your watch and be transported back in time? How cool would that be?'

Hazel laughs. 'I could interview Henry the Eighth! That would impress my students.'

With the tide far out, Tim and Hazel skirt the rocks rather than having to clamber over them. All the while, Jessica paddles along the shore and Linka races in and out of the sea.

At the mouth of Onjohn Cove, Tim takes Hazel's hand. 'I'd love to spend more time with you. Perhaps you and Jessica could join Linka and me on a walk sometime? We could take the cliff path around to Trevone. There's a lovely beach there.'

'I'd like that, and I'm sure Jess would too,' she says. 'Tomorrow? We go home the day after.'

'Tomorrow, yes,' says Tim, releasing her. 'And this evening? After Jessica has gone to sleep, maybe we could meet?'

Hazel glances across at Jessica who is heading their way, skipping alongside Linka. Every evening had been spent, alone, reading, these past six weeks. But Jessica slept soundly, thanks to her medication. Surely, she'd come to no harm tucked up in bed in the caravan.

'Yes,' Hazel says.

Tim's smile travels from his lips to his eyes and she holds his stare for a few moments.

'Which is your van?' he says, when they reach the stile by the path up to the campsite.

'First on the left by the gate. But I'll meet you here.'

'What time?'

'Nine?'

'Nine it is,' says Tim. 'I'll look forward to that.'

Hazel watches as Tim strides along the cliff path, Linka at his side. Linka's tail, wagging. Tim's long legs, tanned and purposeful with every step he takes over the uneven ground. Above her, the two gulls dance together, one chasing the other.

Jessica tugs at Hazel's hand. 'Who was that man? I liked his dog. I wish we had a dog. What's his name?'

'The dog? Or the man?'

'The man, Mummy. Was he looking for shells too?'

'No, darling. He was looking for something else. And his name is Tim.'

'Short for Timothy?'

'I guess.'

'I like this beach, Mummy. Are we coming again tomorrow?'

'Yes, darling. Tomorrow should be sunny again, and you'll be wearing your new shell necklace.'

Tonight, she adds to herself, while you're in the Land of Nod, I'm going on a date.

Hazel empties the collection of shells into the sink and washes them. She scoops them into a towel and spreads it out on the table.

'Now, Jessica. While I make your tea, you pat them dry and arrange them in size, from biggest to smallest.'

Jessica picks up the biggest shell. 'I didn't find this one, Mummy.'

'No, darling. Tim found it. It's a present for you, from him.'

One by one, the shells are pierced and strung onto the cord, with Tim's shell in the central position. Hazel ties knots between each pair of shells to keep them apart.

Jessica eats her tea and watches all the while, jumping up when it's time for the necklace to be tied around her neck.

'It's beautiful, Mummy.'

'As beautiful as you, my darling. Now, time for bed.'

'Another story, Mummy, please.'

'You know the rules. One story each night. Now, take your medicine and then it's lights out.'

Hazel closes Jessica's door and leans against the partition wall. How much effort should she make to meet a man in the dark? What should she wear?

She draws the gingham curtains and strips off. Washing at the sink, naked, the prospect of starting a new relationship excites her. Whoever comes into her life has to understand that she comes with baggage. She doesn't like the word, but it's a fact.

Tim is attractive. Lovely house overlooking the beach. She revisits their exchange. When she'd looked into his eyes, she'd recognised his sad expression; she'd seen it in the mirror every day for too long. And when he'd touched her, held her arm as she walked across the beach, held her hand ... it had felt good. How long had it been since anyone – apart from Jess – had touched her?

Her own fault! Since the day David had died, she'd built a wall around herself to prevent her friends getting close but, staring at this stranger, she had at last felt the spell of misery lifting.

She smiles, a genuine smile, for the first time in ages.

I watch them as they trudge up the steep path to the campsite. Mother and child, hand in hand. Inseparable? I think not.

The key to Jessica hangs around Hazel's neck. Not gold. Not even a Cornish mix of gold and tin.

As I pass alongside the field of corn, I smile. Tonight's harvest will be sweet.

Back at my desk, I check my notes from this morning.

Engage. Ensnare.

I tick both entries.
Only one more entry left:

Enslave.

A Stumble in the Dark

by Greg Richards

Six pints at The Magpies and a carton of chips on the way home was usually the most Ian hoped for on a Friday night. That was as much as he wanted, in all honesty. He'd never been one to dream big, he knew big dreams required big effort. Instead, he felt lucky to have the life he had.

That's not to say he was completely satisfied with his lot. Like most people, he would often daydream of those little extras that he might just acquire one day. A car that wasn't starting to make worrying sounds if you got above 50, a house with an extra bedroom to use as a proper office, a girlfriend; those things that would make life a bit easier, a little more enjoyable. But Ian was a realist and knew that no-one ever got everything they wanted. So he made no real effort to increase his fortunes, happy to see what came his way.

He enjoyed his evenings at The Magpies. There was

a good crowd there who were always up for a proper conversation. Never, or at least rarely, anything serious but always something he could muster an opinion on. This evening's conversation had ranged from who would be the next James Bond, to whether pasta or potatoes were better and the big issue of koalas versus sloths.

As he strolled home he went over some of the issues again, seeing if they had been fully explored, in case they came up the next night. The conversation was rarely the same twice but Ian liked to try and have some spontaneous ideas ready on the off chance. Thinking it all through meant he wasn't really paying particular attention to where he was going. He didn't feel the need to. He'd walked these roads thousands of times since his childhood, in the light and the dark, in every season and weather. There was a bin on a footpath slightly off the main road, placed handily around the spot he usually finished his chips, so he was automatically strolling in that general direction, his feet walking the same ground they had on hundreds of Fridays previously. Never before had they stumbled on anything. Until tonight.

The drink consumed and his lack of attention combined to bring Ian down to the ground, in a very slow, low impact stumble. It was the sort of fall that goes on slightly too long, the faller knowing contact with the ground is inevitable but gravity cruelly giving them a bit of time to think about it, to unsuccessfully run through some alternative options such as flailing their arms around or walking along bent over for a while. It was the sort of drawn-out fall that happens a lot at wedding receptions. Ian might have been embarrassed about it had anyone been around to see him. Instead he was mainly confused as he had never come across anything discarded along this path before.

His mind instantly started chastising whoever, probably a tourist, had littered the path. He would have to tell the others at the pub tomorrow, he was sure they would be as annoyed as him once he gave them all the details of this latest fly-tipping incident. He looked back to see what it actually was that had brought him to the ground and was very surprised to see what looked like a treasure chest.

Ian tried to recall exactly how many drinks he had drunk that evening. He wasn't sure if it were his eyes or his brain that was playing tricks on him. Six feet away there seemed to be a solid wooden chest with pearl necklaces and some other kinds of jewellery dangling over the edge. The lid was slightly open after his kick and the inside seemed to be full of golden coins, with the occasional precious stone in amongst them.

Instinctively, Ian looked around to see if there was anyone else there. Whether he was looking for someone to reassure him or to see if someone were tricking him he wasn't sure. There was no-one there to do either.

He slowly stood up and made his way to the chest. He expected it to change. He expected that as he got closer his eyes would bring the object into focus and he would realise it was just an old cardboard box or a piece of driftwood, something that happened to look like a chest from this particular angle in the half light of the moon. But the closer he got the more solid it looked. It was a child's drawing of a treasure chest come to life and, for some reason, left on a footpath in the middle of his village. He opened the lid fully, which gave a very satisfying creak, to find it was indeed full to the brim with what could only be described as treasure.

Ian looked around again. He was having a hard time processing this, and the fact that everything else around him looked exactly the same as normal made it all the harder to comprehend. There was the bin he had been heading towards, his empty chip carton lying some way from it where he'd fallen. There was the bench where people only sat to tie their laces or remove a stone from their shoe. The 'main' road was still behind him, lined with dozens of houses, all dark and quiet at this time of night. The footpath to the beach lay ahead. It was just light enough to see down as far as the bend, where it skirted the local holiday park.

As he surveyed the area, he realised the grass verge either side of the path had been kicked up in places. He looked closer, not knowing what he expected to find. He felt slightly ridiculous, like a child playing Sherlock Holmes. But it seemed to him as if there were two different sets of footprints, facing different ways. At a guess they must have been from heavy boots, judging by how much they had disturbed the ground. Had two people fought over the chest? As his eyes followed the footprints down the path, he now saw that there were a few coins and gems scattered, as if they had fallen out. He scooped them up and put them in his pocket, before looking back to where the chest now sat. It wasn't somewhere natural to leave... well anything really, but especially something so valuable. Perhaps it had been dropped and left during a fight. But if that were the case, where were the fighters now?

Realising that he might not be alone for long, Ian's mind gave him two possibilities. First, pick up the chip carton, put it in the bin, and walk home as if nothing had happened. This seemed like the easy option, although at the back of his mind he felt like maybe he would get in trouble for not reporting this. But what was he reporting? And who to? He had no idea. It was safe to assume therefore, that he was keeping this information to himself. Which brought him to option two, keep the treasure. This seemed much more high risk. There were bound to be problems connected with it. That said, he couldn't ignore the fact this option meant he would have a chest full of treasure.

Had Ian been presented this as hypothetical in the pub, he would have spent an equal amount of time weighing up the two options, thinking about the pros and cons of each choice. In reality he made his mind up incredibly quickly: he would keep it. He bent down, shut the lid, grabbed the handles on either side and lifted. It became very clear, very quickly, that the treasure was far too heavy for Ian to carry all the way home. He put it straight back down again.

Looking at it, the chest didn't appear much bigger than the beer multipacks Ian occasionally bought at the supermarket. He stared at it and tried to work out if it were the chest itself that was so heavy or the contents. Either way it was obvious he was going to have to come up with an alternative method of transportation. He had plenty of boxes and bags at home that he could put the treasure in, to spread the load over a couple of runs. But he couldn't leave the chest where it was while he ran back and forth through the village all night, especially if its rightful owner was nearby. He needed a plan, fast.

He could hide it under a bush for now; that was a saying, wasn't it? Or was that where you hid talent? And come to think of it, wasn't it a bushel rather than a bush? What the hell was a bushel anyway?

He was getting distracted. Adrenaline was rushing through his body, making his heart beat and his mind race. Take a few deep breaths, that was the answer. Ian could never remember if you were supposed to breathe in through your nose and then out through your mouth or the other way around, so he did three of each to be on the safe side. It seemed to work.

Sitting on the chest with his eyes closed he ran through the situation. He had a chest full of treasure that was so heavy he needed to split it into smaller loads. Until he could do that, he needed to hide it. But because of the weight he couldn't move it far, so it would have to be somewhere very close. The beach popped into his head. Of course! Where better to hide treasure? He was on the path to the beach; it was the obvious choice. Probably whoever had lost it had brought it up from there in the first place. His mental image of the beach was replaced with one of a pirate, which Ian instantly dismissed. He needed to stay calm and rational.

At that moment, he thought he heard footsteps in the distance. He turned his attention back towards the road. Was that someone singing or someone shouting? Either way, it was time to move. He mustered all his strength and picked up the chest again. It was still as heavy but knowing he only had a short walk down to the beach gave him hope. Fear gave him the impetus he needed to actually move forward. Then, once he started, the weight actually helped carry him forward. He was at the beach in no time.

As he approached the sands the corner of his eye caught shadows moving at the far end of the car park. This gave his willpower a boost, enough to walk as far as he could into the shallow dunes where he could hide the chest properly. He managed a fair distance before collapsing down, completely exhausted. Only then did he consciously acknowledge that his plan had involved burying the treasure, which of course meant digging a hole.

The extra walk into the dunes now seemed a completely unnecessary waste of energy. He chastised himself as he sat and got his breath back, all the while listening out for any sign of life. The crashing waves usually calmed him but tonight he cursed them for drowning out any other sound. He tried telling himself he had imagined the footsteps, the shadows were probably trees in the wind, while at the same time trying to mentally prepare himself for the fact he was going to have to dig this hole with his hands before he could leave the chest here.

By the time he was finally finished, covered in sweat and every limb aching, it had been nearly three hours since he'd left The Magpies. His head was pounding and he could feel the beginnings of a hangover already. Now that the chest was safely under a foot of sand he was happy to forget about it for the night. A big glass of water, and his bed, suddenly seemed much more valuable.

When he awoke the next afternoon, his head was thumping, his brain making it clear that it was unhappy. Likewise his red raw throat reminded him that he had forgotten to drink that glass of water when he'd got in. Getting up, his back joined in with the complaints and made it clear that collapsing on the sofa, instead of making the extra effort to get to his bed, wasn't the best option in the long run. Ian knocked back a couple of painkillers to sort them all out, then made a cup of tea so he could do some real thinking.

He'd made a lot of quick decisions last night and he wasn't sure if they'd all been for the best. Chief amongst them was deciding to keep the treasure in the first place. What the hell was he going to do with it? It's not like you can pay for your shopping with a doubloon, or get a round in with some pieces of eight. Everything's contactless now anyway. Nor did he imagine you could deposit them in the bank without lots of questions, and lots of paperwork, for which he wouldn't have answers.

Many of the questions would probably be around 'where had it come from?' Ian would have liked those answers himself. He could only imagine that it was not from an entirely legal source. This meant either he would become the chief suspect in some unknown case or, perhaps more worryingly, the actual perpetrators of this presumed crime would be looking for him. Neither were a situation he wanted to be in.

A course of action therefore presented itself: leave the treasure where it was. As far as he could figure there was nothing linking him to it. Possibly some DNA somewhere, maybe a fingerprint on the handle, but Ian had never been in trouble with the police before so they wouldn't have anything on record. Leaving the treasure where it was would mean no-one would be looking for him. If someone else found the treasure, good luck to them. He wouldn't know, and wouldn't want to know. Of course, it would also mean he was no better off than the previous night, but then he was no worse off either. It was a tough decision but he decided to leave it where it was, so he could carry on his life as normal.

It wasn't one particular thing that had led him to change his mind. In the weeks that followed, the treasure rarely left Ian's thoughts. While he was sure he had done the right thing at first, with every day that went by he was less and less convinced. As he walked down to the beach in the middle of the calm autumn night, he couldn't explain to himself why he had decided to pick up his shovel and dig up the treasure. There had been no big epiphany moment, it was more a culmination of half a dozen small moments.

There was his 'date' of course, which had definitely been going well, until she asked, 'What's the most exciting thing that's ever happened to you?' and he obviously couldn't tell her. Not only could he not tell her, he also couldn't think of anything apart from how much he wanted to tell her. So he had sat 'umming' for a full minute before saying, 'Pass'. Both of them were fairly quiet for the short remainder of the evening, and she hadn't responded to any of his messages since.

There had been nothing in the news, no gossip in the local online forum, not so much as a passing remark about treasure in any shop, pub or bus stop. Ian knew, because he had been hypervigilant to every conversation recently, sure that someone would know something. Every time he saw a face that he didn't recognise he instantly assumed they were going to point at him and shout, 'You!' Then he would know he'd been found out. But nothing happened and the fear he had felt on the night gradually subsided.

He tried to talk about it without talking about it, by posing the hypothetical question: 'What would you do if you were given a box of treasure?' at the pub. He was careful not to say 'found' in case it raised suspicions. Not that it mattered. Everyone thought it too implausible, and it raised too many questions that Ian didn't want to, or couldn't, answer.

Then the bills started mounting up. All at once there was the unforeseen car repair, the broken window, the need for a new coat. Every time he thought to himself, 'If I just had a bit of that treasure money...'

Of course, he did have a bit of the treasure money. Days later he had found the few pieces he had picked up off the path and pocketed absent-mindedly at the time. Not enough to make him rich, but enough to convince him the whole thing wasn't a drunken dream. They were frustratingly real. Some quick internet research had given him reason enough to think the coins he'd picked up were definitely worth a fair amount. He'd even got the details of some specialists who could appraise them properly but he had stopped short of contacting them. He felt like he'd be finding out how much he'd lost instead of how much he'd kept. While they remained unvalued, they could still theoretically be worthless. That was what he kept trying to tell himself whenever he started daydreaming about the holidays he could go on, or buying a boat, or buying a big house, or the pub, or both. So he tried to believe the coins were worthless. But, if they weren't, then how much was sat waiting under the sand?

Which had all led to this: Ian spending the small hours

digging holes at his local beach. He was sure tonight he'd found the right spot, even more sure than he was last night. It must have been further down than he remembered. Or maybe it was a bit more to the right, he could easily widen the hole that way if needed. It was a clear night, he had a few more hours to dig. When he found it later at least he wouldn't have to fill the hole back in this time, that was always the hardest part. But, tonight, Ian felt lucky.

'Look Up'
by Kate Barden

❝*A* *nd above all, watch with glittering eyes the whole world around you because the greatest secrets are always hidden in the most unlikely places. Those who don't believe in magic will never find it.*❞

Roald Dahl

The tall man chased her up the stairs, his brown arms outstretched, reaching for her heels. She screamed, delighted, and ran into her bedroom. She dived onto the bed, snatched a pillow and swung it round. He grabbed it and the two of them were a laughing, pillowy, feathery snow globe of two people, one tall and tanned and hairy and muscular, the other delicate, fair, round cheeked, shouting and jumping and coughing and laughing and laughing and laughing...

There is always magic Ammo...in every room...

*

The door slammed and every frame in the cottage juddered.

'Sorry! The wind took it ... there must be another door open down here.'

A wet duffle coat was tossed onto the back of a wooden chair.

Grip it!

It tried its best to grip it, but the chair was too slidey and the coat crumpled onto the kitchen floor in an undignified heap.

Ugh...

Muddy boots were prised off, separating themselves from damp socks, which were peeled away from clammy feet with pale wrinkling skin on their toes. Vapour began to rise from the relaxed footwear as it lay warming on the tiled floor.

Aaaaahhhhh...

'I'm putting the kettle on! Want anything?'

Bare feet padded around the kitchen, chilly hands filled the kettle, took a mug from the cupboard, dropped a teabag in and then pulled hard on the fridge door. Amelie splashed some milk on top of the teabag and down the side of the mug, onto the work top and down the door of the cupboard below, onto the floor. The milk bottle plastic screw top jumped down from the side, rolled under the kitchen table and hid behind a thick oak leg.

Now you see me...

Tea made, Amelie carried her mug to the lounge, being cautious not to trip on the tiny lip on the threshold between there and the kitchen. This tricky little step-up had caught her out yesterday, and as she had stumbled, she had thrown chocolate milkshake onto the shoulders of the stiff-backed winged armchair which, with retro stylishness, protected itself by proudly wearing a hand-embroidered antimacassar, circa 1968.

Mmmm...do you like it...?

Her mum, who had at the time been restlessly flicking the pages of Drishti Yoga magazine, was recipient of the chocolate shampoo and politely asked Amelie to

Choosing the battered, deep, red leather two-seater sofa over the armchair, Amelie plonked herself down, adjusted the cushions to prop herself up and put her bare feet on the tiled coffee table. Sometimes there was a wave of ... what ... sadness? ... things felt a bit off; a bit wonky, out of line.

And the objects around us watch us and play tricks on us and when we're asleep they get together and have a party...

Amelie had been on holiday in this cottage for three days. It was May half term and today it had rained, so she had run back from the beach before the rain changed from pouring down to pouring across. She knew it would do this, as she had been to Cornwall on holiday every year of her life. Not to this particular town...

or village?

...her mum, Katie, tried to find somewhere new every

year and this seemed, so far, like an excellent place for exploring, pretty much right on the beach.

'I thought we'd go paddle boarding.'

Katie's muffled voice travelled from the bedroom, across the landing, down the stairs and into the lounge. It reached Amelie just as she was about to nod off ...*thought we'd go paddle-boarding...* and just before she let her mug drop on to the grey shaggy rug.

> *Oh, do stroke me...just a little...*
> *Look, this rug...it's probably a*
> *friendly furry creature, waiting*
> *for you to stroke him...*

'...thought we'd go paddle-boarding...'

Amelie righted herself and her mug. 'When?'

'Now?' Katie was already stuffing towels into a carrier bag; a carrier bag which was far too small for two large bath towels. The bag stretched its sides as far apart as it could.

> *Nnnnnncccccccceee.*

Its handles would never touch and so were rendered useless and it would have to be carried like a toddler cradled in arms.

'Grab some toast or something while I find goggles. Do we need goggles for paddle boarding? I've got your cozzie and a towel and my cozzie and a towel. Not sure if we need goggles. I'll google it. Google goggles. Hilarious. Oh you've got tea. Did you make me one? Doesn't matter. I'll get a takeaway, or a milkshake. Oh yes, let's get milkshake from that veggie cafe on our way.'

Katie moved and spoke with such speed and efficiency, one could imagine that she inhabited a different plane of time; a plane where extra time was created if one moved quickly enough and crammed more tasks and jobs into five minutes than was possible on mortal earth as we know it.

'It's raining...' Amelie's voice tailed off ... things were definitely a bit out of sorts. The intrusions weren't always this frequent and she was wishing for an afternoon curled up on the slippery leather sofa with her mum and the turquoise fluffy blanket she would bring down from the bedroom, and they would eat cheese and crackers and watch something on the telly. But Katie liked to be busy. Productive. Distracted. From her own waves? Her own intrusive whisperings?

'We're going in the sea! It doesn't matter about the rain. Shift your bum, Ams. Come on. Cafe, then we'll find the paddle board teacher on the beach and have a go. Maybe go round the castle?! Yes! Let's do that! That'll be cool'.

Amelie almost wished that her mum wouldn't say things like 'cool' or even worse 'rad', which she'd heard her say to her uncle Ben on the phone the other day. But generally her mum was 'cool' and Amelie didn't really mind at all that they spent such a lot of time together. They had been just the two of them for almost eleven years, although for about nine of those years there was also Magpie the lucky black and white cat, who unluckily was hit by a car but luckily only had to have one leg off.

A magpie is one of the few creatures that can recognise itself in a mirror...

*

Amelie pulled the cord of her yellow hoodie hood tighter, encasing her tanned face in crimped edges, turning it into a golden pie. Katie triumphantly rested the over-stretched carrier bag on her hip like an infant.

Ooo...comfy...

Amelie remembered being carried like this by the tall man who smelled of suntan oil and golden syrup; the man whose skin was warm and prickly on her cheek and who could throw her into the sky, making her tummy feel gloopy and her breath catch on the air before it had time to be breathed back in.

She caught the sound of her mum's voice on the wind. '£30 ... that's great...'

The tall man held her waist and pulled her back from the edge of the stream. Her feet were high off the ground and her hands gripped the wooden branch tightly. 'Hold tight. Ready?' The air rushed past her face as she flew over the stream, arms fully stretched up, she could only just hold on. 'Look up! Look up!' Her welly boot fell from her foot and splashed into the water and the man grabbed her waist again and pulled her back to cool earth. 'Well done, Ammo! You're so brave!' He held her as she dropped from the tree swing, one foot still safely encased in a damp boot, the other naked and cold on the wet leaves. 'Get your welly before it escapes down-stream ... race!' And they ran down the slope, him way out in front, turning to face her and running backwards, pretending to fall over, and then running towards her, scooping her up, tucking her under his arm like a rugby ball...

'And that's enough time to get there and back?'

*

The den was easily the best one they had ever built. Plenty of room for the two of them to lie inside on the blanket, look up at the sky through the sticks and leaves, and eat prawn cocktail crisps and hard boiled eggs dipped in salt and pepper, which had been carefully wrapped in tiny pieces of tin foil, and drink weak orange squash straight from the bottle. Amelie listened to his story, improvised on demand, at her request; always thrilling fables of adventurous children discovering hidden treasure on secluded islands and magic in the woods. The den was shelter when it began to rain, the rain putting out the fire they had built together, another skill he had taught her along with how to hold a knife and how to make a bow and arrow and how to swim and how to say the alphabet backwards and how to...

'Right, we're ready. Aren't we, Ams?'

Their instructor was unhooking the paddle-board and passing it easily out of the van as if it weighed nothing, the muscles on her arms and back as defined as if they had been drawn on with a brown permanent felt-tip pen.

'Hold this and we'll walk down to the sea. Then I'll show you how to get on, stand up, use your paddle and we'll be off, out there.'

The sky, dull grey, mirrored the sea, but the weather was pleasant enough for families to be out, hunting for blennies in rock pools, or playing rounders, enjoying each other, the open freedom and safety of the wide beach.

The waves swallowed her feet, icy around her ankles; the wet sand filled the gaps between her toes. She was carrying her board under her right arm, her fingers only just reaching around the edge, even though it was tucked high up under her armpit.

Hold me tight, girlie...
this could be a bumpy ride!

As they walked out deeper, her legs pushing gently against the waves and her left hand dragging in the water, Amelie hoped she looked surf-style sophisticated, as if this was something she did every day.

Look up...

'Knees. Feet. Up'. Tracey, the instructor, gave the commands, and they headed for the horizon. Tracey was elegant and relaxed, chatting, moving easily through the waves, each stroke powerfully propelling her closer to the castle. Katie, mostly wobbling, breathing hard with each stroke, shrieking when a wave lifted her and shouting words of encouragement to Amelie, capsized four times in ten minutes, spending more time in the sea than on top of it and Amelie, mostly upright, her years as a child gymnast giving her the muscle memory required for good balance and a strong core.

The castle was built on a granite crag which rose out of the sea. Within twenty minutes of leaving the beach, they were circling its island. Tracey's voice washed forwards and backwards, knowledgeable, and if one could hear her properly, it was probably very interesting. '...seals, dolphins, sunfish ... Norman Conquest ... Benedictine monks...'

But Amelie's attention had been grabbed by something else, something other than the history lesson being delivered in the round Cornish accent.

'Look up! Look up!' He said it often, when he wanted her to see the magpies on the bird table, when he threw her in the air, when they were walking side by side and her shoulders were slumpey and she was looking to the ground and he was gently correcting her, making her face front and up, stand tall, fill the space she was in. She heard him, now, 'Look up!'

The figure was slight and pale. Not just pale skin, but pale everything. Clothes, hair, and even the air surrounding the figure was pale, like she was standing in a different atmosphere. An atmosphere where the air was white and visible – not just visible like when you breathe on a cold morning, but visible all the time. A swirling, cloudy white greyness 'like smoke,' Amelie thought. Then suddenly, 'Fire! There's a fire!' The room was filled with smoke and the figure, a girl of about 5, raised her right hand and touched the window.

Amelie wobbled, and fell, hitting the cold water hard and sinking...

All around her was grey and peaceful...

Look up...

The sun was doing its absolute best...

As long as you do your best, Ammo…

…to coax her towards itself…

Look up, darling. It's always brighter when you look up…

…hitting the cold water hard and sinking for a second or two before bobbing up, her buoyancy aid proudly behaving exactly as it had been instructed. A weak noise was escaping from her salty mouth; saline was leaking from her nostrils.

'Mum! Mum!'

Katie spun round and fell in.

Tracey, 'You alright chaps?' paddled deftly back to reach them.

'There's a fire.' Amelie was treading water. 'Up there.'

The castle loomed, grey against grey against grey. Granite against clouds against sky. And they were surrounded by grey water in a grey world.

'The window … the girl … the room is on fire. Get Dad!'

The lights were white. White-white as opposed to creamy-white or yellow-white. They made the bed linen vibrate with their brightness and it hurt her to look at the white walls and the pillow was white hot under her head, so she turned slightly to find a cool patch. She couldn't pull the thin blanket up to snuggle down as it was gripping the far end of the bed with all its might. Even with her eyes closed she could see the white of the room. She could hear voices and strange noises and footsteps. A hot hand held hers. She squinted. 'Ams … Ams. It's OK my girl. Mummy's here.' The pain in her chest made it very difficult to sit up, so she stopped trying. The coughing was hurting her. And what was that smell? She stopped trying to place the smell. She stopped trying to open her eyes. '5th of the 5th 2005 ... 05.05.05.'

'So she's 5...'

'5 and a half, yes...'

'Amelie. Amelie,
can you look up?
I've got you.
Look up for me.'

'Ams ... there's no one there, my girl. What are you on about?'

'The girl. In the window. The room was ... she was looking at me through the smoke...' Amelie was crying. The rain was coming down. The sea was swelling gently.

'Amelie. I need you to calm down, sweetheart. Look at me. Look at me.' Tracey's reassuring soft Cornish accent drew Amelie's eyes towards it as if pulled on a length of string. 'Good girl. Now, put your hands on your board. And you, Katie. That's right. Hands on. We're going to slowly paddle back. You're both fine.'

The soft pink towel wrapped itself around Amelie and held her softly, nuzzling up to her face, a comforting puppy that smelled of soap and coffee.

Hhhhhhhhhuuuuuuuuuhhhhh.

She dug her toes into the stony sand. She looked at her mum who was sipping hot chocolate from a flask which had appeared from Tracey's van, a medicinal magic trick. Huge tears were running down her face, so many and so fast that it was impossible to separate them from the rain. Grief, at last, unhidden. The grey sky cracked open and a slice of light pierced the back of the van, warming Amelie's feet. A pair of magpies landed on the grass near the car park ticket machine. They strutted around a bit. Amelie watched them, as they picked up odd pasty crumbs, bits of ice cream cone, a few crisps.

Look up. On the bird table.
The National bird of Korea,
having a picnic.

Katie's cool hand rested softly on her shoulder, tenderly bringing Amelie back from the den in the garden, gently guiding her back from being five years old and Amelie knew that the sadness of the past could not be hidden. The tall man would always be there, telling her to look up. To look up and marvel at the birds. To look up and face forward. To look up and see the magic.

Don't forget, Ammo.
Look up.

I won't, Dad.

I love you.

Whispers

by Emma Lamerton

I was driving through dirty candy-floss. The sun was giving it a grey tinge as it struggled over the horizon. I know the road well. I drive it every day, but the fog was deceitful that morning. As the headlights picked out the ghost of a tree, a church, a hedge, I was only half sure of where I was. I pulled out a little from the edge of the road. The yellow metal sign was still there, and I managed to avoid it. It was announcing upcoming road closures as the new bypass was being built. *Always a road closure somewhere, another road springing up, a road being widened. And who for?* The streets had been entirely empty on the journey so far. They're only known to be busy in tourist season when sat-navs send wide, shiny vehicles down narrow lanes where oncoming traffic causes panic.

A high-pitched whirring pulled me from my thoughts. As I tried to identify the source, there was a thud against the windscreen. A bird must have hit the car. I pulled over, briefly noticing that my pentacle air freshener was spinning anti-clockwise. I put the hazards on and went to see what I'd hit and if it was hurt.

A few metres behind the car was a small pile of rags. It was rocking slightly, as though being buffeted by the wind. As I crouched down, I soon realised it was a creature, small yet human-like, and it appeared to be dazed. Checking its breathing, I tried to recall first-aid, wondering if the accident needed to be reported. Leaning closer, I wiped my sweaty palms on my coat. I had never seen anything like it in real life: a muddy, child-like face, oversized eyes, wearing a tangle of sackcloth and leaves. I debated whether to talk to it like a person or like an animal when it mumbled.

'...stop, Bucca. I tried ... *an fordh...*' It tried to sit up, but winced and flopped back down.

'Hi,' I ventured, 'I'm sorry, I think my car hit you - are you hurt?'

The little creature tried to sit up again and managed it this time. 'Yes,' it replied.

'Can I...?'

I stopped as the creature again collapsed and seemed to lose consciousness. Carefully, I picked it up; it was heavier than I expected and warm, like a kitten. I took it back to the car. On the passenger seat, I laid it down while I rummaged in the boot. I emptied a box of books and DVDs bound for the charity shop and grabbed the emergency blanket. Carefully placing the blanket in the box, I lowered the creature in and wrapped the blanket over it. It was breathing, but unconscious, and I hoped it would be ok. I placed the box in the passenger footwell where the heater was blowing and carried on towards work.

It was a hectic morning, and everyone wanted my attention. New reports, changes to reports, and my manager wanting a report summarising all the outstanding reports. Eleven o'clock and still on the first, now cold, cup of coffee. I hadn't forgotten about the creature either and was eager to get out at lunch to see how it was doing. Headed to the kitchen, I ran into Frank.

'Hey, Wen!' He smiled. 'How's it going?' Despite being grey, Frank's subtle floral patterned shirt brightened the drab corridor.

'Oh, not too bad. Busy morning.' I nodded to my cold coffee but then realised he wouldn't know it was cold, so I ended up raising my half-empty cup with an awkward smile.

'Tell me about it. Don't suppose you want to join me for lunch? Was thinking of trying the new pizza place...'

'I would, but...' I wondered how to explain the small, possibly injured, probably mythical creature currently in my car.

'Another time maybe?'

'Yes, yes, that would be great.' I got into the kitchen, then leant against the closed door. How typical. I'd liked Frank for ages and had been hoping for a way to have more than a passing conversation, and now ... *the timing.* I put the kettle on and googled *Cornish Pixies* on my phone while I waited. No one seemed to know what they ate, nor did they have any tips on medical care.

In the back of my car, I was relieved that the pixie was ok, and feeling much better.

'I'm just a bit bruised. Thank you, Miss, for looking after me.'

'No problem. Let me see if I can find you something for the bruising...' I rummaged in my rucksack. It contained various stones, herbs, oils and, of course, salt. Nowadays, I knew which ones helped with what and knew how to place a gemstone or a drop of oil to help the world tick along a little more smoothly. I am a witch. I have been sure of it ever since I'd found the book in Nan's secret library, behind the raspberry bushes. Nan had let me keep it, the small volume of spells and wisdom; she had told me that only a proper witch could have found it. This was the first time my talents felt useful, or appropriate, though.

'Here we are.' I put some drops onto a tissue. 'Geranium and lemongrass for bruising. And here,' I handed over a small chunk of rose quartz, 'that should help too.'

'Oh, thank you, Miss, I feel better already!' The pixie smiled. 'And that's a marvellous blanket too, so soft! You really are very kind.'

'You're welcome,' I replied, feeling that the pixie was overlooking the fact that I was partly responsible for the accident.

'I don't mean to be a trouble,' said the pixie, meeting my eyes, 'but perhaps you could do me a favour, if you felt inclined...'

'Oh? How can I help?' I asked, carefully pouring some bottled water into the lid for the pixie.

'It's the Bucca. They keep encouraging the *bras melynyow* - the big yellows, you know, the road builders?'

'The Bucca? Aren't they ... something to do with

the sea?' I remembered reading about them somewhere. Another mythical creature, a water-spirit, something like mermen.

'Yes, Miss, that's right. They don't want sea traffic, so they want it all over land. They complain about all the pollution. We try to explain that most of the extra traffic is all headed to the beaches anyway, but they don't listen. Now the big yellows are at our barrow!'

'How can I help though?' I remembered the road signs; all this was planned and going ahead, a little late for objections. I handed over the lid of water.

'Thank you, Miss. Well, if you could give us a hand moving, Miss, that would be a big help. I mean, we don't know many folk with a vehicle.'

I smiled, lost for a moment in considering that this was perhaps the strangest Thursday I had lived through, but then noticed Frank approaching. I froze - there wasn't time to hide the pixie or come up with something to stop him.

'Hey, Wen, I went to the bakery...' Frank opened the door and hopped into the front passenger seat. 'Want first choice on the pastries I've brought back for the office?' He held out a big paper bag. 'Oh, I didn't realise you were busy. Hi, I'm Frank!' He waved to the pixie as I took a slab of flapjack.

'Hi, Frank, I'm Dewdrop, but they all call me Deedee. Wenna here rescued me this morning, and now she's going to help us move.'

'That's great. Do you need any more help?' Frank smiled a sugary grin as he took another bite of doughnut.

'Well ... oh, you pair are awfully kind. But, yes. There

are a few of us to move.'

'How many?' I asked.

'About five hundred.'

I stared at Deedee, trying to imagine what five hundred pixies looked like.

'I'd be happy to help,' said Frank. 'Count me in!'

That evening, two cars were parked in a field, parcel shelves serving as loading ramps for hundreds of pixies, as they slowly loaded small parcels into the vehicles. I sat with Frank in the front of his car, half-listening to the radio.

'Hope you've got plenty of lavender oil in your kit.' Frank looked sideways at me with a mischievous smile.

'I have.'

'They say moving house is stressful.' Frank nodded at the pixies, illuminated by the headlights.

'They don't look it though, do they?' They seemed well organised and calm. Not quite the mischievous mayhem-makers they're made out to be. 'How did you know that, though, about the lavender?'

'Didn't think you were the only witch in the office, did you?' Frank took a wooden case from the glove box and opened it. There was a layer of small brown bottles filled with various tinctures. These lifted out to reveal a packet of dried leaves and flowers, and finally, a mix of stones in the bottom, accompanied by a bag of runes. 'Deedee's not the first pixie I've met either. Speaking of which–'

There was a tap at the door, which was already open, and Deedee looked up at us.

'We have a small logistical problem, Miss. Wondering if you might help us out a bit?'

'Sure, what's the problem?'

'Well, we're loading up well, and should be done in about half an hour or so. But we, erm, well, we don't know where to move *to*.'

'Oh.' I had assumed that pixies had barrows all over the place, like villages and towns. So if they had to move, then some family or friends somewhere else could find them a bed or a floor to camp on for a night or two.

'I have a map.' Deedee held out some folded-up paper.

I took it and opened it out on my lap. It was of the local area. I could make out the barrow, some of the clay tips and purple regions that seemed to mark the local villages.

'Mind if I climb up?'

'Not at all.' I helped Deedee up onto my lap, and we all looked at the map.

Frank took the opportunity to put some drops of lavender oil onto our coats.

'We don't want to go too far.' Deedee explained the local area was where they hunted and tended the wildlife. They had brooks and streams to look after, so they needed to live somewhere within the confines of this map. Deedee described some vacant badger setts at the base of one of the clay tips as an option, although there was a flood risk in winter.

As I leant over the map to work out how we might get there, my necklace swung out, almost catching Deedee's arm.

'Oh, sorry!' I went to grab my necklace, but Deedee was reaching out to it.

Deedee's hands met their reflections and pressed against the cool dark surface. 'It's perfect! This stone, it feels like *tre*, like home.'

'Black tourmaline?' Frank asked.

'Yes.' I grinned. 'Are you thinking what I'm thinking?'

'Deedee,' Frank asked, 'have you heard of Roche Rock?'

'Oh yes, we know it well.'

'Did you know the rock itself is a mix of quartz and black tourmaline?'

'Like the necklace?' Deedee looked longingly at the pendant again.

'Just like it.'

'We've been there lots, and it has always been a safe-feeling space. I'll go check with the others.'

Deedee disappeared back into the barrow.

I pointed. 'Do you see that? There! It's like the headlights are being reflected or something?'

We looked out of the windscreen as lights twinkled in the barrow, like a distant midnight city. We didn't notice Deedee's return.

Deedee coughed politely, as though not wanting to startle us humans, who probably seemed a little enchanted.

'Everyone is very excited about moving to Roche Rock. We've sent a couple of scout parties to some nearby nests and setts to spread the word that we are moving, and that the big yellows are coming soon. I think we're about done. Troyst will let me know once we are all loaded up.'

'That's great. I wasn't sure what a new barrow would need, geography wise.' I still wondered how this muddy mound would compare to the rocky boulders surrounding the Rock.

'We can settle wherever really,' Deedee said, as she

took a seat in the door pocket. 'We aren't too fussy.'

'Aren't you sad to be leaving, though? This was your home.'

'We aren't *human* about things.' Deedee shrugged. 'We've lived here for hundreds of years, but we will live in other places. We know things change; all we can do is just try to see that they change for the better. I think the Rock will be better.'

'It feels so wrong, though. We shouldn't be forcing you out like this, not for a road. Can't we do something?' I asked.

'You're just humans,' Deedee said apologetically. 'It's not your fault.'

I frowned. 'But we drive the diggers and we make the decisions. It's humans that approve these projects, that decide we need more roads!'

'Well, you *think* you do.' Deedee looked down as though trying to find the words in the tyre treads. 'The Buccas, pixies, knockers – we whisper the ideas to you. Humans just don't get ideas on their own – but I'm not meant to tell you that.'

'But we don't need the roads extended. I don't want a road here. I don't want a bypass destroying this barrow!'

Deedee looked meekly up at me. 'But you didn't feel that way until you met me, did you?'

The sound of an owl eventually broke the silence.

Frank was still distracted by the glittering barrow. 'What are all those lights? I didn't think you had lights in there to start with, but now it's glowing!'

'Not lights.' Deedee laughed. 'We've just moved our stuff off the floor. That's just a layer of gold.'

'And you're not taking it with you?' Frank asked, amazed.

'It's heavy and pretty useless as a metal. We've packed the iron, copper, a bit of silver. The useful stuff. Our ancestors collected a load of gold, but we've never seen the appeal. Plus, it just attracts trouble.'

Troyst appeared and whispered something to Deedee. 'They're all set - we are ready to go!'

Parcel shelves aboard, the cars made their way to the Rock Inn car park and made ready for the pixies to unload. It was a short walk down the road to the Rock itself. Soon, there were streams of pixies flowing along the edge of the road, carrying all manner of packets and furnishings. Empty-handed pixies drifted back to the car park on the other side. They were chattering excitedly; I overheard fragments: '*I'm sure my great-great-granny lived on the Rock back in the day, I can smell her saffron buns!*' '*I'm glad we've bagsied a spot under the big rock, that's going to be where all the action happens, trust me!*' '*Finally, we will have a space for all your art projects. No more accidentally slurping paint-water left on the kitchen table.*' I smiled.

The cars slowly emptied, and the number of pixies coming back was getting fewer and fewer. Deedee was in the last group that came back.

'Thank you, Miss, and Mister! We will be sure to send any especially wonderful ideas your way.' Deedee bowed with a huge warm smile.

'Hang on a minute.' I felt I'd sussed something out. 'We suggested Roche Rock. We must have had that idea. You didn't know about it being black tourmaline, so you couldn't have whispered it to us!'

Deedee looked puzzled. 'You're both witches, though, aren't you?'

'Well, yeah.' I shrugged.

'Well, what's a witch but an approachable human? One that folks and forces can talk to? We mightn't have known about the Rock, but something somewhere did, and told you, put the idea in your head ready. That's how it works. No one alone knows the plan, but it's all out there, being whispered. We were real lucky to run into you both, though. Thanks again for all your help.'

Deedee bowed and turned. Just like that, no pixies could be seen.

Someone tipped off a local archaeological group about gold buried in a certain barrow. The progression of certain big yellows was halted, with historians and archaeologists intrigued by the find. They could test the gold at the site by day, and it was real gold sure enough, although stamped with some unusual designs. Any they took away to sample or study, however, would disappear. The curiosity stopped the bypass; all the enthusiasm for it waned once the mysterious barrow was discovered.

The Buccas stopped encouraging roads after learning about micro-plastics, or at least some of the Buccas did. They take a while to get up to date sometimes. Nowadays, they prefer to remind folk to take their canvas bags when they go shopping and whisper how water tastes so much better from a reusable bottle.

*

The pixies are rarely seen, but you might have noticed some strange ideas come out of the Clays area. Sometimes, they like to cause mischief but, usually, they just like keeping the humans believing that they are in charge. It seems to make them happy.

Frank and I stopped for a drink that Thursday evening. The rest, as they say, *eus istori.*

The Trees Grew Tall

by Claudia Loveland

When I moved to Cornwall and into the big house on the hill with its views over the countryside and across Falmouth Bay – that was in the spring of 1948 – its situation was prominent and exposed. That hardly suited my own situation, so I decided to plant trees.

I started with the open, grassy field at the front, which was crossed by an old footpath. The only person who used the path was the postman. It was his shortcut to the next property, half a mile away.

I remember my first attempt at digging, chatting to Jack as I worked. Jack was my fiancé. We were not officially engaged, but we had promised to spend the rest of our lives together. He was going to train as an architect and wanted to create new landscapes. He approved of the Cornish soil; there were a lot of large stones in it, which he assured me would help with drainage. By the end of the afternoon, my hole was nearly four feet deep, far too deep for a sapling. Jack laughed and suggested I cut a step into the side in order to climb out.

From that day onwards, I kept digging and planting. It became our special time.

I had all my food delivered, of course, as a lady should; the butcher's boy and the grocer left my orders at the back door.

The woman, the first of many who came in twice a week to clean the house, recommended her husband as a gardener. She implied that it was undignified for a lady from London to work as a navvy. She was annoyingly persistent, but eventually gave up, clearly unable to understand my refusal. I believe she disapproved of my slacks, too.

I soon gathered I was a talking point down in the village. When I cycled to the post office, I could see people looking at me with curiosity. That was of no concern to me though, and, after a while, they lost interest.

I planted shrubs as well as trees, and I dug small ponds. I diverted the stream to fill the ponds, and built a weir, creating a small waterfall that spilled over rocks on one side. Over time, I transformed that field.

Within a few years, the postman had to pick his way carefully along the footpath. In fact, after he twisted his ankle – tripping over some garden debris – he conceded and took the longer route. It had indeed become a garden by then, a landscape of shrubs and wildflowers, ponds, and hummocks left by all the digging I had done.

At last, we had it all to ourselves – Jack and I.

Though the years were passing, and I felt at home on my land, I remained an alien in the locality. I clearly failed to meet people's expectations: I had no need of a social life. My digging, the view from the house over the trees and fields and out to sea, these were sufficient.

My conversations with Jack were my mainstay and my consolation. They had taken the place of the letters we used to write while he was away during the war – before he was parachuted into France on D-Day.

Missing, presumed dead, I had been told in 1944.

Yet I knew he would return.

I would wait.

At the time, people said I should buck my ideas up and snap out of it, but they were in no position to understand. I believe I became a little odd in the head, though only for a while. I remember people losing patience with me.

They thought that inheriting my aunt's country house would help me adjust. The annuity that went with it, as long as I actually lived there, would get me off their hands as well. They thought I would forget Jack, but that would never happen.

After twenty summers, the ash trees and the willows were competing with the sycamores. The rhododendrons flourished like colossal weeds. The garden had unfolded across all the fields around the house, with hydrangeas, azaleas and camellias cascading down the slope. Nevertheless, I could always find a reason for more digging while I was waiting for Jack.

It was in the early summer of 1969 that some of my silverware went missing.

First a butter knife: old, an heirloom. It was hallmarked, and had my great aunt's initial, an ornate A, engraved on the handle. I was annoyed that it was missing. I suppose I had become rather fastidious. I had my things. They were not to be interfered with.

A few days later, my grandmother's christening mug was no longer to be seen in its place on the silver tray on the sideboard. This time, I suspected that someone had stolen it.

But who? Certainly not my cleaner; that would be completely out of character. Besides, why would anyone take only these two pieces, and on separate occasions? If they wanted silver, why not take the entire tray of family treasures? Jack suggested asking the police if they had received reports of other puzzling thefts.

That weekend, I was occupied in digging another sizeable hole. Jack was impressed by my stamina. I was certainly strong. It had become a long hole, a wide, deep trench. Standing in it, I could only just see over the mounds of soil I had thrown up beside it.

As I glanced about me, I noticed someone, a man wearing a khaki overcoat, heading in my direction from the side of the house. The coat looked odd on such a fine day. He was apparently trying to follow what remained of the postman's path. Someone from the village, perhaps?

He seemed to be taking care not to be seen from the house and was looking around – presumably to check whether I was in the garden.

I wanted a good look at him and crouched motionless against the side of the hole. He had a young, tanned face, and his brown hair and good features were not unpleasant.

His pace quickened, and I guessed his aim was to dodge behind the bank of hydrangeas beside me. Then, with a surprised gasp, he tripped.

I narrowly avoided being crushed as he tumbled heavily into the trench alongside me.

His head cracked against a large stone. His shrieks, first of surprise, then of pain, ceased abruptly.

Shaken, I watched a flurry of soil and dust settle around him, dislodged from the top of the hole as he fell.

The silence that followed gnawed at my mind. He lay utterly still. His neck was twisted and his head lay at an unnatural angle. I saw a thin dribble of blood at the corner of his mouth. It was not trickling. There was no movement at all.

I wanted Jack. I needed Jack, but unspeakable, long-suppressed images crowded in on me. My hands trembled. My eyes squeezed shut to block out the sight of the body. I had to get away from it.

I scrabbled at the edges of the pit, trying to claw my way out, scattering earth back into the hole. Blood surged and pulsed in my head. I kept my eyes tightly shut as more and more earth fell in around me in my frenzy to escape.

Reaching the top, I slumped against the pile of earth. As the throbbing in my brain slowed and dulled, the pictures in my mind came into appalling focus.

I became conscious of another sound, a moaning, a sobbing. My own heart, crying. I let out a wail of grief for Jack, and my tears flowed as they had wanted to for over twenty years. They overflowed the dam of denial that I had built.

As I quietened, anger – a terrifying fury, volcanic

– rose inside me. He had said he would never leave me. Hundreds went missing, but he said he would always come back. Arrogant, selfish rotter – getting himself killed. Unfaithful, heartless, cruel liar. I would not pity him. I would bury him. Blot him out.

With the anger came energy, and, still unable to look back into the hole, I picked up the shovel and began to push and toss even more soil on top of him. When I was calmer and allowed myself to look, I could see nothing of the body at all.

I knew what I had done. I realised that two people had become one, and neither was coming back.

I worked until I had thrown back all the earth, and then went into the house.

My letter opener – a silver-handled paper-knife – was missing from the dresser. Shaking again, I went into the dining room and poured myself a drink. There, I discovered that the thief had taken other silver keepsakes as well.

I sat at the table, reasoning with myself. This was not a private matter. I would be called to account. Someone would expect him home. Someone would know where he had been. They would report a missing person.

I reflected on what had happened: it had been a sad accident that I had failed to report.

In the days that followed, I lived in constant anticipation of the knock on the door that would herald an investigation. I replayed the events in my mind: I had given a common thief a decent burial. I had saved a family from knowing about a crime.

It was clear, though, that I had put them in a

position I recognised. They would know only that he had disappeared. When would he walk into their lives again? Had he absconded or been abducted? Was he dead? There would be no answer. They would have to wait, as I had waited for Jack.

My waiting was different now. I was no longer watching for Jack's arrival; I was grieving for him. My waiting was for judgement.

A malignant horror festered in my mind. Might that young man still have been alive when I buried him? Would I be accused of murder?

I felt guilty and ashamed; if not guilty of murder, then guilty of stealing his family's grief. I was guilty of stealing his body. I was the thief. I was guilty of keeping them in ignorance; guilty of murdering their rights and trampling their feelings, leaving them hoping for a resolution that could never materialise.

I would wait.

Weeks became months. I could hardly report the matter after all that time.

After a year, I abhorred myself utterly. Two young men dominated my existence, and one of them I now hated as much as I hated myself. The other, my Jack, my life, had been stolen from me. For so many years we had been joined together, now we had been put asunder.

Jack never spoke to me after that day. I had lost him completely.

I continued to dig alone, but my heart and my blood had chilled. My spirit sank lower as each season passed. I still took cuttings from the trees and shrubs, but now I planted

them nearer the house and allowed the bracken and the brambles on the outskirts to work their way towards me, unhindered.

Each year, the ferns surfaced ever closer, unfurling canopies that shrouded the earth beneath. Gradually, garden returned to field, overgrown and impassable.

The trees grew tall and the hedges high, and I lived behind them, in melancholy and in hiding: a life barely worth living.

It was on the tenth anniversary of that devastating day that I heard a loud knock on my front door. No one had arrived at that door in years. It seemed such an extraordinary coincidence. Even before I opened the door, I knew my waiting was at an end.

The man – I had expected it would be a man, or perhaps a man and a woman – was carrying a rucksack. I had expected a briefcase.

His casual clothes surprised me – I had expected a uniform, or at least a suit – but his tone was very polite.

He said this was difficult for him. I said that I understood completely.

He asked if I remembered a day, many years ago, when someone had fallen into the hole I was digging. Of course, I remembered.

I showed him into the dining room, where I had always known this conversation would take place, and we sat on opposite sides of the table.

'It was me,' he said.

I only caught fragments of what he went on to say after that. '...a stupid dare...headache lasted a fortnight...

lucky I didn't kill myself...'

I said nothing.

'...crawled out...in tears, you were...in a bad way...'

I had no words.

He went on talking: '...waited...police never came...no need to come clean...hid them...ten years to the day...'

I thought about all the darkness in my life over those years. The hate. The false guilt. The dread that I might have killed him. The consuming fear of discovery – coupled with an overwhelming need for everything to become known.

I was not the criminal. I was the victim.

'...need to get it sorted...niggling guilt...'

It niggled him?

My remorse had been no mere niggle. I had lived with self-destructive disgust at myself, appalled by what I had done. Every day that I had spent digging without Jack, I was punishing myself, locking myself away.

Now, there was no crime, but I had already served a ten-year sentence: waiting, with both dread and longing, for that knock on the door.

No crime. Was I mad that day, all those years ago? Was I mad now?

He wanted me to forgive him, to release him.

The effrontery.

I listened in silence, nodding when he needed a response.

He reached into his rucksack, and brought out my grandmother's christening mug, engraved with her name and the family crest. He pushed it across the table towards me. Next came the letter-opener, with its long, slim, sharp-tipped blade. Then the small butter knife and a set of four teaspoons.

'...probably missed them...memories...'

A cold rage churned inside me.

I picked up the christening mug and turned it to catch the light. It gave me no pleasure.

I stroked the ornate handle of the letter-opener, and remembered letters received long ago. My fingers slid along the blade. Cold. I thought of Jack lying who knows where. I thought of a young man lying in a trench, a grave.

I picked it up: my letter-opener. It felt substantial and well-balanced in my hand.

'...not live with myself...'

His need to talk gave me time to consider.

This time I did not avert my eyes until his ragged breaths ceased completely.

Then I telephoned the police.

The Girl He Found in the Dark

by Emily Charlotte Ould

Caden shivers. Beneath the moon's glow, his breath comes out in cold clouds. Pounding down a dark alleyway before crossing the main road, his trainers reach soft ground, socks wet and mud-splattered from earlier's football game. The washing machine is broken again, so they'll stay dirty for a while. With the screams at home still drumming in his ears, he marches forward, takes a left, and dips behind a hedge. The grass is still springy from yesterday's rain.

He pushes past the overgrown shrubbery, never stopping, until he sees what he came for. Sliding his headphones down so they circle his neck, he breathes the Cornish air in, letting it glide over his face.

In front of him, the old bus shelter is covered in overgrown foliage and leaves, its structure bowing with age, but it still stands defiant. Rough stonework is just about visible beneath all the brambles, with tangles of thorns poking their way through the empty windows. It's probably dangerous to sit inside; Caden doesn't care.

Back along, this village ran deep in the heart of clay country and was a common route to get where you needed to be – so Caden's grandparents told him. But then the clay industry dried up and a new road was built. The bus shelter got shrouded by plants and tangling nettles and a hedge grew tall before it. Eventually, buses stopped coming altogether.

These days, he can only get around by asking his mum to drive him somewhere – and, lately, she 'doesn't have time to be his personal chauffeur'. He can't wait to start driving.

When he reaches the shelter, he kicks at the brambles blocking the entrance. All the remaining plants that crowd around the granite walls are brown, wilted and rotten. He kicks at another bramble in the shadowy doorway as he gets closer, but instead of stubborn thorns snagging his laces, his trainers suddenly hit something soft and warm.

'Aargh!' somebody screams.

'What the –' He saves himself from falling face first into a bed of nettles and looks up wildly into unfamiliar eyes. 'Who the hell are you?'

Staring back at him through the shadows is a girl, roughly the same age as him. The amber glow from the streetlight on the road lights up her face. Her hair is honey blonde, falling down in wisps come loose from her ponytail, and she leaps up from the bench. A single white headphone dangles from her ear, caught in a tangle of hair.

'Who the hell are you?' she says.

'Caden,' he replies, ripping off a nettle caught in his jeans. 'And this is my spot.'

'Own it, do you?' she scoffs.

'No.'

'Well then. I was here first.' She scowls and presses her hands flat against the wooden slats of the bench, before plonking herself down and bringing her knees close to her chest. She pulls her phone from her pocket and starts scrolling, clearly not about to go anywhere. The white glare from the screen lights up her face in the shadows.

'I've been coming here forever,' Caden says, 'so you definitely weren't here first. Now, do one.'

'Not very friendly, huh?'

'Don't need to be. Not to weirdos hanging out in abandoned bus shelters.'

'Takes one to know one.' She shrugs, looking back at her phone. Caden stands there, stretching out the seconds, waiting for her to back down. But she just carries on scrolling on her phone, like he's not even there. Then, just when he figures he should leave, she glances up at him through thick black lashes and silently budges over. He ducks beside her deeper into the doorway and warily grabs a seat on the mottled old bench.

'I'm Ivy,' she murmurs into the darkness, without looking up. She clicks her phone screen black. Caden tries to smile at her through the gloom, but he's not sure if she can even see much of his face.

'Hi, Ivy,' he says.

She just nods.

Truce.

'What're you doing out here anyway?' he says.

'Could ask you the same thing. You gonna murder me?'

'Don't be stupid. Anyway, I asked first.'

She rolls her eyes, shaking her other headphone loose so it tumbles down against her neck. He can hear the faint sound of ABBA singing a chorus and tries not to smile.

'Came out here to think,' she admits. 'My thoughts can be so loud sometimes. I just needed to get out instead of staring at the bedroom ceiling all night. Lying there. Waiting to fall asleep. I share a room with two other girls; there's only so much snoring in my ear I can take ...' She looks up sharply. 'Not that I need to tell you anything about my life.'

'I know what you mean,' Caden offers. 'Sisters, right?'

She looks at him. 'I'm fostered. Live in a big house down that road.' She points to the left where Caden knows there's a hidden country lane. 'They won't know I'm gone. Our house is full of kids. I just wanted to come out here to feel cold air on my face instead of their gross breathing.'

'Oh,' Caden says. 'Sorry.'

'It's fine. What about you? Why are you out here?'

'I don't know. It sounds stupid.'

'So tell me.'

'Well ...'

'Go on then.'

'Well, I guess ... I can't sleep most nights. So I come here. My house is a little crazy right now. My mum, she just had a baby and it screams all night. I slip out most of the time and she doesn't even know I'm gone either. I think, sometimes, I guess I just need quiet so I can feel like me again.'

'Doesn't your dad help?'

'He left when I was nine,' he replies, staring at his hands. 'The baby has a different dad. Dave, that's his name. Only been with Mum about a year. He works for agencies when he can, so money's never flowing in. Not his fault, I guess. Round here, it's the only type of work you can get. Either that or care work, and I don't reckon he's cut out for that. Doesn't have much patience when it comes to other people if you know what I mean. Mum told him to move in when he got chucked out of his old place, completely loved up, they were, and then they had a baby, so now it's all four of us in a two bedroom house. I can't wait to move out.'

'Wow. And I thought I had problems,' Ivy says.

'You know what I mean.' He nudges his leg against hers. She doesn't move away.

'What's her name? Your baby sister?'

'Pea. And it's half-sister.'

'She's still your sister.' Ivy glares back at him. She pulls out her phone again, shoves her earphones back in, and frowns at the screen. Next to him, her earphones blaze with the noise of Mamma Mia.

Caden winces. He didn't mean to make her feel bad. In the quiet, the air feels thick between them. He could wade right through it and never get any closer to her. And he wants to get closer to her. Looking down, he watches a money spider crawl across the undergrowth at their feet and scuttle over a patch of dead leaves. He glances at Ivy, wondering if she's scared of spiders. But then she reaches down to the ground, splays her fingers against the leaves and lets the spider crawl along her fingertips before circling her wrist. As she leans back against the wall of the bus shelter, the spider begins to climb all the way up her arm. She knows Caden's watching her, but neither of them say a word.

They sit there while midnight passes them by, the rest of the village asleep. When it gets colder, Ivy starts to shiver and Caden offers her his jacket.

'Go on then,' she says and he drapes it over her shoulders. He's never seen a girl look so good in boy's clothing.

'Sorry,' he says, raising his voice a little so she can hear him over her music, 'about what I said before. I didn't mean it like that.'

'It's okay. I know.' She almost smiles. 'It's just ... I'd give anything for a sister. Someone to be a part of me. No matter how stupid life gets. Or how often people leave you. You're lucky. To have that. Don't run away from it. Stupid boy.'

'Okay,' he says. 'I'll try.'

And then she smiles at him. Right there, a proper full-blown smile. The moonlight and the amber glow from the streetlight hits her face all at once. He breathes a sigh of relief, feeling like he's finally got something right. He thinks she's beautiful, even when she scowls, but she's even more beautiful when she smiles at him like that.

Without saying a word, he softly places a hand over hers and, terrified, he waits for her to move away like before. But she doesn't. She stays. They sit there like that, soaking up the quiet and the warmth of each other, and stare out into the night.

'You wanna get outta here?' she asks when it's too cold to keep sitting there. 'Do something else?'

'Depends.' He shrugs. 'You gonna murder me?'

'Shut up.' She laughs.

She jumps up from the bench and stands in front of him, offering her hand. He takes it and, palm against palm, they set off across the grass. Their trainers swish across the field, getting streaked with wet and mud. Dipping out from the hedgerow and onto the main road, they cross and head towards the public footpath.

'Know anywhere good?' she asks.

'What, better than that place?' He jerks his head back towards the old bus stop. 'You're having a laugh, aren't you?'

'Yeah, right.' She grins.

They slip down a footpath lined with trees. Treading bracken and granite stones, they follow the light from Caden's phone in the dark. An owl hoots in the dense thicket of trees while foxes yowl somewhere beyond the path. Ivy holds Caden's hand tighter as badgers snuffle loudly in the bushes out of sight. He laughs and tugs her along, step by step.

Eventually, the path opens wider and they find themselves walking along the clay trails Caden used to walk with his dad – back when he was around. They keep going over the rough stony ground until their eyes get used to the dark and they begin to walk over the patchy hills and low dips in the landscape with ease.

'C'mon, get up here,' Caden calls to Ivy when they find a ridge that rises high above the rest of the trail. 'Sun's coming up.' She climbs up after him until she's standing by his side.

'Wow,' she says, staring at the view before them. 'You

can see for miles.'

'Yep.' Caden looks out across the horizon at all the clay, all the fields surrounding it and the roads and houses that dot the landscape. Across the bay, a fishing boat slowly cuts across the waves of the Atlantic Ocean, a flock of hungry seagulls hovering above it. A little closer, horses graze in the early morning light across patches of green. And to the right, the vast pools of water, turned the lightest shade of blue from the white clay beneath, lie still as ever. Caden smiles sadly, remembering how his dad told him not to swim in them when he was young.

'Not to mess around in, them pools,' he'd said. *'You're better off out here on solid ground.'*

'Hey.' Ivy nudges him, pulling Caden from his thoughts. She stands close and squeezes her palm against his. 'Thanks – for bringing me here.'

He smiles. 'S'alright.'

To the east, the sun peeps over the horizon, letting its golden rays fall across the sea so it glitters like diamonds in the light. Together, they stand, watching the sky change from a weary grey to a bruising purple and, finally, bright, burning orange and blue. Hand in hand, just standing there, watching.

Being.

Belonging.

'It's beautiful,' Ivy whispers.

Caden turns to look at her and watches the fiery colour of the sun reflected in her irises.

'I know,' he says.

Just as the sun burns its brightest, she turns and leans in closer. Blonde hair tickles his cheek as it's swept by the morning breeze and her hands, still clasped against his, are warmer than the sun. Her touch is magic. And, slowly, Caden finds himself ablaze with light and hope, kissing the girl he found in the dark.

Kissing the Stars

by Ulrike Durán Bravo

'Shh!' I hear a mother tell her noisy children. She points at me. 'You'll wake the devil with all your noise. You don't want three years of bad luck, do you?'

A couple walk past and pinch each other on the shoulder when they see me, just in case. A young man makes monkey noises and gestures. A girl giggles, 'Are you sure you're not growing a tail yet?'

I should be used to it, but even after all this time, it hurts.

When I was young, I thought there was something wrong with me. I was spindly and looked like a climbing frame. Unsupervised children would come near, soon crying out in pain when they found themselves scratched. Parents nearby would give me a dirty look and scold their child for touching me.

Let me introduce myself, with the name that you may

know me by best. I am a Monkey Puzzle Tree. I have many names: Araucaria Araucana, Chilean Pine and Pehuén. Those are my scientific, common and ancient names respectively. Finally, we trees have a secret and sacred name. The one humans cannot speak. You may hear it if you listen carefully to leaves whispering and the branches creaking.

Are you listening?

I am here because of colonialism and your desire for the exotic. Due to your ambivalence towards me, I fear the threat of the axe. I was only a seedling, plucked from my mother prematurely, shipped from a country far, far away. To give me strength, when I feel lonely and misunderstood, I dream blue dreams about a wild life in Patagonia: a place exposed to the elements, where my ancestors were the masters of survival.

Listening, listening to creaks and whispers of other trees, to the voices of people, the DNA in my capillaries and the rumblings of the mycorrhizal web, I learnt that while Darwin sailed around Cape Horn in his famous ship, the Beagle, one of his friends collected some of my ancestor's pine cones (each containing two hundred seeds or more). Legend has it, I heard, that to keep them safe, he tied the cones into lover's knots. They returned to Falmouth, Darwin's head buzzing with ideas. He had learnt that mountains and volcanoes take a long time to form.

We also take a long time to grow, at three centimetres a year we grow up to 80 metres high. Some of us live to ten-thousand years old, and our ancestors evolved in the times of the dinosaurs. Come close and look how we have puzzled together our leaves so insects can't crawl inside;

made our leaves triangular, spiky and pointy to protect ourselves from sharp teeth. We grew bark which resisted the heat of the volcanic eruptions, we grew trunks as thick as boulders and as tall as the tallest dinosaur's neck...

So tall we could almost kiss the stars.

When the ice came, we filled our branches and trunks with resin to protect us from the cold. Their flying cousins, the birds, replaced the dinosaurs. Parakeets eat our seeds and spread them in the Patagonian forests. Plant hunters came and spread them all over the world – which is what happened to me.

I heard much while I was a seedling in a bag – figuring out the sequence of events that led to my journey over the Atlantic Ocean all those years ago. I learnt that Scottish plant-hunter Archibald Menzies was offered some of our pine seeds as dessert while at a banquet in Chile. After trying a few, he stashed a whole handful of them in his pocket. On the voyage home, he germinated several seedlings, returning with five healthy plants which he called the Chilean Pine and gifted to Kew Gardens.

I learnt that these young trees were spotted by James Veitch who then employed William Lobb to hunt plants for him in South America, with specific instruction to gather the pine seeds from the Araucaria Araucana. Although William came across as gruff and unsophisticated, Veitch spotted in him the single-mindedness and stamina needed for the job. He showed him some pictures, hand-drawn, of spindly strange-looking pine trees. Exotic, Christmas tree-shaped, with twisted long-nailed fingers as branches. William imagined a thick forest, filled with these Medusa-head like growths, and felt a flicker of excitement for the challenge.

This is where my own personal story starts, so closely entwined with that of the Cornish plant-hunter William Lobb. While he dreamt of us, we dreamt of him, and I remembered my future and imagined my past.

In 1840 William travelled on the HMS Seagull from Falmouth to Rio de Janeiro. His mission was to collect as many interesting seeds and specimens as possible. Landing in Brazil, it did not take him long to find beautiful flowers in vibrant ultramarine, fuchsia and cadmium yellow; swan orchids, begonias and passion-flowers. He marvelled at how plain and simple the nuts and seeds looked; the magic where these beautiful gem-like flowers sprung from. Spurred on by his success, he travelled south, leaving the tropical humidity behind him and reaching the more temperate plains of Argentina.

I know the local gauchos warned him: 'The sea-journey around Cape Horn is dangerous with its many storms, fog and icebergs.'

He listened to stories of capsized and disappeared ships and dreamt of them. William decided to travel overland instead. He bought a mule, and found some local guides. From Mendoza, where the air was still warm and the wine sweet, he took the Uspallata Pass over the Andes and then south along the foothills towards the Araucanía region.

The mountains were so high and so cold, the mule's footprints left no impression on the snow. However, the journey impressed on William's mind forever.

'Is this really better than the sea-journey?' he asked over and over again, worrying about frostbite.

'There is ice by the cape too,' said his poncho-wearing guide whose lungs were used to the high mountain air, low in oxygen.

On their journey, his guide told him about how the local Mapuche tribe were warriors – resisting against the Spaniards for hundreds of years, priding themselves as the only tribe never officially 'conquered'. The Spanish renamed the Mapuche 'Araucanos'; the area 'Araucanía' and hence the official name of their ritual tree becoming 'Araucaria Araucana'.

'Interesting name,' William said.

'No-one is sure where this name came from,' the guide informed him while incessantly chewing coca leaves, which stained his teeth. He insisted they helped with the altitude.

'Maybe because a native word for rebel is "Aw qa".' His accent was strong, and William wasn't sure he had understood correctly. Was his guide trying to warn him about the locals?

The frozen landscape was punishing. Soon, William struggled with fever and fatigue, wishing he had risked the sea instead. While he was shivering and delirious, he worried about meeting the fierce indigenous people. His guide gave him coca-tea to drink and wrapped extra ponchos around him, telling him not to worry, this will help.

In his fever his dreams were clouded in blue, and his bag of seeds was bulging and moving by itself. He saw a seam tear open and strange piskies in bold coloured dresses gliding out of his bag. They fluttered around him, dancing and singing at him in a language he could not understand. Then they flew away never to return. Other times, he dreamt the seeds were infested with maggots and rotten. Either way, in his nightmares all his hard work was for nothing and his collection had disappeared. He felt sick with loss and anxiety, his seeds were his treasure – never mind emerald and sapphires, gold, silver and copper – it was the living, tantalising beauty and fragility of plants that haunted him.

When he woke up, his bag and seeds were still there. He felt better; he was not burning anymore and the pain in his joints and head were gone. Weakened but clear-headed, he trudged on with the mule stubbornly carrying him. William never left his bags out of sight.

At 5,250 feet, just below the snow-line on the exposed ridges of the Andes, somewhere between the cities of Concepción and Valdivia, he found us: his Araucaria Araucana. Majestic, strange and more mystical than he had imagined. Enormous straight trunks with a gnarled, prehistoric nature to them, draped in old man's beard lichens; canopies so high they were no more than parasol-like silhouettes fingering the blueish haze. High above and evergreen in contrast to the deciduous southern beech, lenga and other trees that held on to the last few golden and rusted leaves, hinting at a glorious summer gone. A frozen mist rose from the icy ground, clouding the forest and its secrets. Exhaustion did not diminish the awe that William felt. These trees looked nothing like the hand-drawn pictures he had seen of the small pines at Kew. He was exultant with joy, and felt small in the world. These giants can be mine, he thought. I can take their seeds and grow some of this ancient wilderness at home. This armoured tree, he thought, is power and strength itself.

'Beware the mountain lion,' his guide said, interrupting his thoughts, 'the Patagonian puma living in these forests are known for their strength and their stealth.' William was sure that the guide was deliberately trying to scare him. He was excited to conquer a tree like this despite all the obstacles and bring it home to his Cornwall.

I know from his stories that they stayed in a village where the people welcomed him while the volcano Osorno watched over them. His guide spoke their language, Mapundungun, and translated while they offered him chicha – a mildly psychoactive drink of fermented pine-nuts. There was compote made from calafate, a sloe-like berry. His host, a man named Nahuel, with sharp flickering eyes, explained that they were sub-tribe of the local Mapuche people; people of the earth. This particular tribe called themselves people of the tree – Pehuénche.

William saw how Nahuel and his people decorated and prayed under our branches, gave up offerings and danced around our trunks. Nahuel explained that the Pehuénche know spirits are within all living things and believe us trees sacred: our roots connect Minche Mapu (world below) to Wall Mapu (living world), and up to Wenu Mapu (world above). Being so tall, we are a connection to the blue, the skies, and the dreams of higher spirits. They know their strength comes from us trees, and tell their *ekews*, their stories around us. These stories are passed onto the seeds that they hold, so we can remember what happened before us.

Nahuel told him, translated by the guide, that at the beginning, the people feared our pines might be poisonous. Until there was such a cold winter the earth was hidden under the snow, rivers froze over, the animals left and the tribe was without food. Many old and young died from hunger.

Young people wandered as far as possible to find food but many found nothing. One of the youngsters was making his way home, empty handed, blue from the cold, embarrassed and hungry. A wise old man came out the forest and walked beside him. 'What's the matter?' he asked, so the young man told him of his hungry tribe.

'Why aren't you eating the pine-nuts?'

'They could be poisonous, and Ngenechen, our spirit lord, forbids we eat them. Anyway, they are too hard to chew.'

The old man said, 'The pine-nuts are a gift of food from the trees and spirits above. Boil them in water or toast them on fire. They are only ripe and ready when they fall. So gather as many as possible and store them for the rest of the year.'

So the young man gathered as many pine-nuts (which are as thick as your little finger) as he could fit into his bags and pockets and took them home to celebrate. It is said the Pehuénche never suffered from hunger again.

After the story, William witnessed the Pehuénche hold a branch of our tree up to the sun and thank both the tree and the sun because they did not let them die of hunger and for the gift of sharing their fruits. Oh how I long for that sort of blessing; for people to see me as an important part of their world, not just an entertaining and sometimes inconvenient foreign addition to their landscape.

William was not interested in eating the seeds or

praying: he was eager to harvest the seeds he had travelled so far to collect. The Pehuénche wait until we shoot our cones down like bullets when they are ripe and ready, landing softly on the cushions of moss and fungi between the shields of bamboo. William disregarded Nahuel's stories and collected over 3,000 seeds by shooting cones from the trees with his rifle. I remember well the blast of the gun; the flight through the iced air; the hard landing on the frozen ground. And then the warmth of William's hands around the cone that protected us, huddled tight like bees in a hive before being transferred to the dark, confined mustiness of his bag.

My destiny changed that day – from then on I was to follow a lonely path, all too often to be spited. I was still soft-shelled and vulnerable; naïve to what it meant to be catapulted away from the comfort of my mother-tree.

He kept us, his seeds, safely, closer to his body than the others, checking obsessively, for his nightmares had increased. That Ngenechen (or the puma, or Nahuel) would find his revenge somehow. Whatever he dreamt, we felt.

Travelling further south deeper into Patagonia and Tierra del Fuego, he understood why some call it the land of fire: not just the constant glow of the volcanoes' peaks but a land lit up by its vegetation. He found further jewels in the Chilean fire-bush and lantern tree, both with bright orangey-red flowers glowing like torches in their shrubbery. His search, hunting and gathering for seeds and nuts, for the most beautiful flower and biggest trees, possessed his mind and body.

He eventually travelled back north, now up the coast,

'Kissing the Stars'

and arranged for the seeds and specimens to be sent back to England. He personally oversaw our departure from the port of Valparaiso, before continuing on his adventures. Every night, until receiving notice that we had arrived safely, he dreamt of spiky, scratchy, unfriendly yet beautiful

Araucarian piskies with devilish warrior eyes plotting escape and revenge.

I was one of those specimens, in a bag labelled Chilean Pine.

We were sold to the lords and ladies in the South West of England, adorning their gardens as ornamental trees. My cousin was planted in the gardens at Pencarrow near Bodmin. At parties, Sir William Molesworth enjoyed giving his guests a tour of his rhododendrons, camellias, Iron Age hill fort and Italian Garden. On one occasion, his friend, Charles Austin, remarked about the strange-looking pine tree: 'It would puzzle a monkey to climb that.'

Unfortunately, my cousin in Pencarrow was blown over by a storm in 1905. Better a storm than a saw, but it shook my roots to lose my kin in exile. I had then yet to know what was to happen in Patagonia. Even now, every day, I tremble with fear about the news I will receive. For myself, and my species. I distract myself by watching Shakespeare plays and other frivolities in the small amphitheatre in this garden. I overhear people gossip, laugh and cry. A multitude of voices and stories float around me over the years. Here I have endured storms and droughts; wars and pandemics; peacetimes and festivals; poverty and neglect as well as prosperity and care.

Through the network of dreams and root communication, I learnt that in Patagonia, the timber industry grew and the loggers moved in unsparingly. After the pain of seeing their precious tree almost eliminated from the landscape, the Pehuénche placed their own bodies on the line, forcing the logging companies to kill them if they wanted the trees. The dictatorship sent the army. The Pehuénche people dreamt with us and asked the powerful Araucaria trees to bring a snowstorm. That night clear skies turned dark and it snowed more than ever before. And so the army was prevented from committing their atrocities.

The struggle continues. The climate is changing so fast that we are having a hard time to adapt to fires and flooding. Now our once extensive native territory in Patagonia is only a quarter the size of London. We are considered one of the most endangered species of trees in the world.

Sometimes I dream of breaking out, roaring in anger, crossing the Atlantic and taking up arms to protect the forests of my ancestors. This, alas, I cannot do. Instead, I can try to save myself and hope that you listen.

Amazingly, the gardener walks past with her clipboard, explaining to her assistant that 'they fare best when there are at least five of them together.' She looks over to me and says, 'This old lady could do with some company.' I notice some youngsters in pots ready to be planted. I am humbled.

So, my roots for now are safe in this old Cornish Garden. I enjoy the gentle sea-breeze against my branches. I am lucky this is my home: overlooking rhododendrons, azaleas and camellias that bleed colour in spring; fields of bluebells, and salty wafts of wild-garlic and lily-of-the-valley swirling through the lower air. There are palms and yuccas, ferns and frons, foxgloves and fuchsias. Peering over a wall: an orchard of gillyflowers children like to climb, picking their juicy apples. In the distance, I can occasionally glimpse Falmouth Bay, where once upon a time, I arrived as a 'specimen' in a Packet Ship, from Valparaiso, Chile.

For now, I will be here, remembering my ancestors and dreaming the future in blue; rooting down and rising up, ready to see out centuries if not millennia. The few Pehuenche that are left still pray to us, parakeets still spread our seeds, at least 70 types of insects live in our branches, the British still give each other the Monkey-Puzzle nips when passing us, loggers still fell us.

Next time you see one of us, be it a youngster with spindly climbing-frame appearance or an elder with grand domes kissing the stars, see if you can feel and listen to our *ekews*, our echoes, our stories, our sacred name whispering in our branches.

The Plastic Fairies

by David Allkins

Alex Sullivan looked at his inheritance, before being distracted by something rustling in the bushes. He dismissed it as his imagination and looked back at the two-storey house with ivy creeping over it. The house was surrounded by a small wood in an area forgotten by the rest of the world. He took a picture with his phone and noticed that he had driven into a signal blackspot. Through the glimpses of the curtains, he could see there was lots to sort through.

Alex had no doubt that his late Aunt Marianne's house would be full of possessions. Her years as an artist meant more clutter, with her work incorporating and reusing discarded junk and tech, building three-dimensional collages. Still, she had been his fun relative. Perhaps the only fun member of his family really.

Her single status had made her an ideal childminder

for the summer holidays, while his parents stayed at work, to support the mortgage payments. His summers were spent wandering the countryside together or they would both sit quietly while she typed and he did homework. Or she would go into her art room to work on something. Alex never really questioned what she did there. His parents were always rude about the concept of art, so he just left it alone. Besides, she stressed that there was a room upstairs that he should never enter, so he avoided exploring around the house in general.

Looking back, Alex did think Marianne would have been a good parent if she'd wanted to be. As a small child, due to his parents attempting to read fairy tales at bedtime, he became scared that fairies would take him away if he was naughty and just the idea of this was enough to worry him. Marianne found out about this after he'd had a crying fit from accidentally breaking a glass. She'd told him, fairies didn't want to take children anymore. They were taking dolls and figures instead. The toys would be given a spirit in a magic spring and brought to life to become fairies. Knowing that he was off the hook had reassured Alex a lot. After that, she would make up bedtime stories about the plastic fairies that survived by taking discarded things from abandoned buildings, rubbish tips and scrapyards. Marianne had mixed up traditional fairy tales with science fiction and anything that had been passing. Alex had loved hearing those stories.

While Marianne had left her remaining funds to various causes, she had left the estate to him. Right now for Alex it was a sanctuary. He'd been working hard to establish himself in the financial district of London. His parents had stressed the importance of the long term and having a well-paying job, through his childhood and education. He'd managed to work himself up to a position that was first in the round of redundancies. Rising costs had led to him returning to Cornwall to move back in with his parents. The situation was getting tense. Maybe he could renovate the place and sell it to return to London, but if he hadn't been a success there, what else could he be?

He eventually found the key to the front door through all of those his aunt had left him, including ones with colours painted on the handles.

Alex entered the house and, looking into the living room and the kitchen, established just how much stuff he had to sort through. The leaflets and posters from the CND and Greenham Common. The paperback science fiction and fantasy novels she'd written in the 1970s and 1980s. There were statues, DVDs and a library's worth of books on fairy tales, magic and folklore marking out their territory on all available furniture surfaces and sections of the floor. Alex could not help thinking of the white minimalism that he'd strived for with his apartment, which had been easier to abandon.

He decided to wait a few days before investigating the garden, which was now a reclaimed wilderness.

Had he just heard something? There was another creak. 'It's that cat flap in the front door,' thought Alex. He glanced back in the hall and was sure that the catflap had moved a minute ago. Alex looked around, expecting a stray cat. Then he began to explore the house again.

Inside her art studio, Alex saw Marianne had continued working on the idea of fairies. There were sketches and Polaroids of designs and works in progress. On the table there was a figure that may have started as an ordinary mass market franchise plastic doll but had been turned into something else. It was an androgynous bald figure with black shades, wearing black plastic plate armour, leading into grey full length gloves on the arms and baggy camouflage trousers ending in heavy boots.

Alex stared at this figure, thinking of the childhood stories she'd told him as he'd lain in bed. It didn't look much like a traditional fairy, but maybe she would have stuck wings on it later. Maybe she'd decided to make stories about them or sell sculptures of them as well, but never had the chance.

He decided to look in the upstairs rooms and noticed the door with the sheet of paper attached to it. It was a plain piece of paper with a message written in thick capital letters.

'To be taken care of in the event of my death. The key with a yellow and black handle opens this.'

Alex took out the mass of keys he'd been given, already getting nervous about what might be behind there. That childhood memory of the forbidden still made him breathe faster. He stared at the door as if trying to see through it. The most he'd ever got from her was that it was related to her CND days. So, material about nuclear war that she thought would scare a child. He held up the key pointing it at the lock.

The door disappeared and there was the figure hovering off the ground. Tall, covered with red burning skin, the flames emerging from its shoulders. The only detail that he could see from the burned flesh of the face was two black pits that used to be eyes. As the figure hovered, he saw a backdrop of grey and white dust spreading out to everything, making it like burned wood turned white in a fire. Alex screamed and started to run, forgetting he was at the top of stairs. He stumbled and fell, trying to hunch himself up as he did so.

When he began to revive, he had the sensation that something was looking at him. Lying on the stairs, he saw two very small figures staring at him from the hall.

They were about 10 inches in height. The hands, facial features and heads were slightly too large for their bodies. One had a widow's peak of long dark brown hair tied behind her head. But her face had bat-like features. The eyes, decorated with makeup around them like the circle of an umbrella, were black pupils with golden circles. Her nose was pushed up and back, flattened into a triangle that the long nostrils looked out of. Out of a smiling mouth marked in black lipstick, two tiny sharp teeth poked out from the upper and lower lips. Below the neck, she was wearing a grey jumper of some sort. She had black trousers, with a belt buckle of a golden bat and no shoes. From her back, Alex could see folded bat wings outlining her shape.

The other figure had a face without makeup, wearing a white smock that covered her arms leading to white gloves. Over this smock, was a form of a vest holding USB sticks to its blackness. What could have been her hair, was a mass of wires and cords, some of which stretched down to her waist, all the ends having different connecting points.

'Hello,' said the one with the wings. 'I'm Luna, this is Zygreta. We are what you call fairies.'

'No, you're not,' Alex said automatically. 'There's no

such thing as fairies.' He thought of Marianne's stories and the figure in the art studio room.

Luna reached out her hands. 'I realise, this is a culture shock...'

Alex began to push himself up from the stairs. 'I hit my head. I'm hallucinating. You're a figment of my unconscious.' He sat back down on the stairs staring at Luna. He didn't notice that the fairy called Zygreta was moving nearer, holding one of her longer cords from her head, in her hands.

'No, I'm not,' said Luna, folding her arms. 'Shouldn't you listen to what I'm saying?'

'No, because you're not real and you shouldn't do what people who aren't real tell you to.'

'We haven't got all day.' This new voice had an electronic effect to it. Alex looked down to see Zygreta on the step as she pushed one of the cords through his trousers and into his leg like a needle going through and his surroundings disappeared.

Alex was now in a dark room on an armchair, facing a large blank television. He looked down to see Luna and Zygreta sitting on the arms of the chair. 'Where am I?' Alex asked.

'A shared mental projection, a chat room for the mind,' Zygreta explained.

'Before she died, your aunt left some explanations.' Luna spread her wings out. Alex saw that they had little rotors in them, like the ones that kept drones in the air. 'We also recorded her memories.'

'You can't record memories.'

Luna pointed to herself. 'Fairies, magic, yes we can.'

The television screen flicked on. Alex stared at the face of his aunt Marianne, sitting up in her bed, looking older, thinner and weaker than the last time he remembered.

'Hello, Alex, hope my funeral went all right. You've met Zygreta and Luna already. Well, if this all works out, you should be watching me. Now you know where all my fairy stories came from. All of this started when I finally found the 'well of the little folk' in Cornwall. The story was that children used to baptise their dolls to stop fairies taking them. I did a lot of digging and research and found that the well was supposed to give life to fairies, by giving them a body. According to Zygreta, you should be seeing some of my memories as I keep talking.'

On the screen, Alex saw from Marianne's point-of-view, as she walked across grass, until she came to a clump of thorns and then her gloved hands pushed them away to reveal a pool of water.

'I'd always worried about nuclear war but it got worse as the 1980s started. You're lucky you grew up without the cold war, Alex. I was learning fairy magic just to try to find a way to preserve something if the bomb dropped.'

Marianne took out a plastic doll in a dress from a bag and dropped it in the water. The doll sank from her sight.

'I realised that human society or culture wouldn't survive after a nuclear war. It needed to be a form that didn't need food or water and could survive even without air.'

The doll's head and arms broke the surface, waving about and appealing for help. Marianne's hands removed the doll onto the grass. It moved as if it had gained a whole new range of joints, a muscle structure like a person. Now the screen showed a grey structure of walls, lit by a moving torch.

'I found a forgotten private nuclear shelter that had been built in the 1960s. I helped the fairies set up there and store information and books and materials so that somehow human culture could still live on.'

Marianne kept speaking, the screen showing memories that illustrated her worlds.

'Of course, in the 1980s the home computer arrived and I got one to let the fairies use their magic to play around with it. As the years passed and cheaper computers or junked ones turned up, the fairies got very good with computer hacking and fake online identities and companies. As money is not a solid reality anymore, they made a new form of fairy gold. Eventually, their orders were delivered to my house and I took them to the shelter.'

Now the memories showed the shelter full of different levels and shelves, packed with media, screens, hard drives and phone keyboards with a force of colourful, altered and transformed doll figures working on them.

Alex wondered for a moment if this was all fake footage somehow, but how much would it have cost to produce all of this just for him? His aunt had done what he thought had just been a story. She had created plastic fairies. He was going to have to accept it.

Ok, what had they always told him, to be a success in the city? Make a decision and you could get emotional about it later. 'Okay, so my aunt created you. Now she's passed away, do you want me to drop your packages off once a week?'

'That would be nice,' replied Luna, 'but we've got

a more immediate problem. It's in the locked room that caused you to fall down the stairs.'

Marianne's face appeared on the screen again. 'If I'm going, I'm proud of what I started. And I saw something in you, Alex, that cares about more than numbers and money. But, back in the 1980s, there was a magic cult that thought a way to break the cold war deadlock was to create a demon. Not summon, create. A magical WMD that the USSR couldn't defend against. An embodiment of the destruction and desolation of the bomb. The problem with this? If it's made to turn the world into a wasteland, it won't wait till somebody gives it permission.

'I was too late to stop them making it. With the help of some fairies, I was able to seal it up like a genie in a bottle before it possessed a human. Once it fuses with a human soul, it reaches its full power and destructive potential. The cultists either died in its creation, or within a year afterwards. It's been in that locked room at the top of the stairs, in a container so that we could work out a way to get rid of it. We did, but my death is getting in the way. So Alex, you're going to have to help the fairies get it to their shelter, to exorcise it permanently. I know you'll do your best. You were a great nephew. Goodbye.'

Alex was back to sitting on the stairs facing Luna and Zygreta. He wanted to just go and lie down and absorb this, but he knew that he couldn't. 'How do you exorcise that thing? Wave a crucifix at it?'

'No,' replied Zygreta. 'That demon is an idea. The idea of nuclear war. You break down an idea, by pointing out that it doesn't work and never could.'

'Well, there is also magic stuff and chanting involved,'

added Luna. 'But that's basically what we're doing. We just need to get the container back to our shelter and take care of it.'

Alex wasn't sure if he understood it, but if they knew what they were doing, fine. 'I've got the keys to her truck, with the house. Will the drum fit on the back?'

'Yes.' Luna spread out her wings and rose up into the air. 'Before we do, there should be another spare doll body waiting for us to bring to life later. Get it in the truck and we can save a journey for it. Have you seen it?'

Alex picked up the doll from the art room, unlocked the truck and placed it on the backseat. Then he joined the fairies at the foot of the stairs.

Zygreta raised up her hands and Luna lifted her into the air. Alex walked up the stairs while they flew, unlocking the door and turning on the lights. The window had been boarded up. On the drum and all over the white walls, there were symbols and writing that Alex didn't recognise. In the room, there was nothing but an object like a plastic oil drum, with a yellow and black sticker on it.

'Don't worry,' Zygreta said. 'It's not actually radioactive itself. You won't get poisoned from it. Magic is just symbolism taken to extremes.'

Alex stepped forward and saw the burned figure again. It looked at him from a landscape of grey and white ash, a king of the wasteland.

Alex felt something touch his shoulder. He jumped sideways and saw Luna hovering with Zygreta. 'It can give you visions, Alex, make you see things, but it can't do more than that in the drum.'

Alex moved to the drum and picked it up, repeating

what Luna had said. The drum was surprisingly light and he was able to get it to the back of the van and shut the doors. He got in the driver's seat and opened the door for Luna and Zygreta to land on the passenger seat. 'We'll give you the directions.'

The journey felt longer than it was. Alex drove as slowly and carefully as he could, as the windscreen outside the road kept turning into grey ash, blowing in the breeze. He kept telling himself that it was just in his head, trying to focus his attention on the road and Luna's directions. He even wound down the driver's window so that the cold wind would help him focus. Eventually he got instructions to pull over.

Then the visions stopped and the normal road was back. 'I've stopped seeing things, has it run out of power?'

'It could have,' said Zygra. 'Or just be saving up for a final big push. It's been battering at its prison cell for years. It's not safe till we exorcise it.'

Luna and Zygreta flew ahead through the woodland, Alex carrying the drum and moving slowly. Eventually, they came to what looked like a hill with the trees forming a space around it. Alex thought that he could hear something metal moving. A door in the hill swung open, like a safe built in the earth. The door led to a ramp lit by bars of light to show the grey concrete. Further on, Alex thought that he could make out little dots of light.

Luna and Zygreta swooped into the tunnel. 'Just keep walking, we'll get the exorcism ritual and equipment ready,' called Zygreta as they headed down.

Alex entered the tunnel, moving slowly. He had the sensation of something moving in the drum, pushing at an area of it.

'*No!*' The scream of rage hit his ears. The plastic of the drum cracked, cutting Alex's fingers. The drum split apart.

The force pushed Alex down onto the concrete. The figure that he had seen in the visions, was now clawing at him. He grasped its arms, trying to push it away. The blood in the cuts on his hands ran into the demon's arms. Alex could see the scarred and twisted flesh, smell the burning meat.

'*Let me join your soul. I'll give you powers.*' He heard the voice even though its mouth was a fused scar. He could also hear Luna screaming at the end of the ramp. 'Don't go near it yet, it could jump into you. Zygreta, give me a data stick now.'

Alex tried to twist or kick the demon away.

'*Can't stay this solid long, but long enough to take your skin. Make fusion with your soul.*'

Alex was concentrating as hard as he could to get the thing away physically and mentally. He saw the bat wings of Luna flying down, holding a data stick, but it ended in a spike. The stick went into the flesh of his arm. Alex felt as if he was falling down a hole. He mentally screamed at himself not to pass out, but he couldn't keep himself awake. As his sight faded away, Alex thought he saw winged fairies over him dragging a net, through the form of the demon as it faded away. Then darkness.

Alex woke up looking into the face of Luna, directly staring at him. She was holding out her arms, her hands covering his mouth. He felt different, new and stiff, as if his limbs and senses were just waking up.

'Alex, remain calm. You will get back in your original

body soon enough. We had to move your soul out of it, to avoid the demon taking it. We are removing it from your body. When that happens soon, we will put your soul in and you'll return to normality. Nod if you understand.'

Alex nodded. Luna took her hands away. Alex stood still, holding on to what Luna had said. It was soon going to be over.

'You know that doll body we put in the backseat? We had to put your soul in it as the quickest thing to hand.'

Alex looked down at his new form. The top of plastic armour plates, the long grey gloves, the combat trousers, the boots. He dug in the pockets of the trousers and pulled out the black shades. Fingers slid around the bald head and face. A sense of calm stillness was over him. No breath, no sensations in the stomach, no feelings of cold or warmth. Part of Alex felt that he should be panicking about this, but a larger and stronger part was asking why?

Luna took his hand, 'They're going to start the exorcism. Come on.'

It was like walking through an open air market in a city, as Luna took Alex through the fairies' bunker. So many moving figures, life, light, colour and noise. This was what he thought London was when he was young, before it became a world of grey buildings and suits to him. They walked through areas where films and TV were playing and there was music and dancing. He remembered what Marianne had said about all the work they were doing with companies and accounts. But now, he could almost sense the magic and the data flow as they moved around him.

They passed a glass surface and Alex stopped to look at his new form, putting on the shades. In the glass there was a confident figure, someone new, without the weight of the expectations of who they were supposed to be. Luna tugged on his arm and he walked on.

Luna and Alex came to a room in the shelter, where his body was tied up with cables hanging from the ceiling like a puppet, inside of a chalk circle. Around it, the fairies were typing on keyboards and tablets, while others were speaking words that sounded like Latin being played backwards.

Alex looked up at his body, his face twisted into a snarl, the limbs straining at the bounds. Alex looked away and saw Zygreta tapping on a phone keypad.

'*Let me join with your soul,*' the demon's voice shouted down at Alex. '*I can give you power. I can make them give you what you want.*'

Alex heard himself saying, 'Well what do I want? Can you tell me?'

'*I can see what you want,*' the demon shouted with Alex's voice, '*and that is...*' It paused. Then it thought of something else while pressing against the cables restraining it. The sound of the chanting rose but not enough to drown out the voice loud enough to echo around the room. '*I'll destroy this flesh, before they destroy me. You'll be trapped in that form forever.*'

Alex thought of what he'd seen walking to this room and of trying to get back to London, for the cycle to start again. 'Well, I'd still be here and you won't be.'

The demon walked out from Alex's body as if it was stepping out from a doorway. It looked around and they all heard a wordless howl of anger and frustration. Then it sighed and fell on the floor within the chalk circle. Its body crystallised and broke into fragments, which kept breaking into smaller parts, until it was lost from sight. 'It's gone,' shouted Zygreta. Alex saw Luna reach out and press his neck to the data stick and everything faded out again.

Alex knelt down to say goodbye to Luna and Zygreta at the tunnel entrance, back in his human form. He'd come round in it a few hours earlier, but then just sat there recovering. 'I'm still happy to drop your orders round while I'm sorting out the house.'

'About that.' Zygreta moved forward. 'We may be able to offer you a monthly wage for that and other odd services. The first payment would be in advance of course.'

'How much?'

Zygreta quoted a figure that was more than Alex had been getting in London.

'Well, the house will take a long time to sort out.'

'There's something else.' Luna was holding the doll body that Alex had worn. 'Now that this body has your soul in it, we can't put a fairy spirit in it anymore. It's shaped itself to fit your soul.'

'I'm sorry,' said Alex.

'Well,' Luna began, 'Your aunt said you were working at moving money around. Of course you also know what's currently happening in the world. And in human form, it'll be hard for you to work with the tech we've got set up. So do you want to come back here sometimes and help us work on different projects? We just stick your soul in this body, then put it back again. And you can join us for a while.'

Alex thought about what he had seen and what the fairies were doing. With what he would be paid and inheriting the house, why should he return to London? Especially now he had the chance to become a valued member of a community and be moving money and figures around in a bright exciting world.

'Luna, I'd be happy to keep working with you in whatever form.'

A Letter from the Other Side

by Claudia Loveland

I swear, today is the last day my mother will control my life.

'There's a letter for you,' she'd said. 'In my desk. Bottom drawer. Promise me you'll open it after my funeral, not before.'

The letter is now on the tea-tray, which I set down on the patio table, rather more heavily than I intended.

I'm sitting in my mother's peaceful Cornish garden, trying to relax. I'm still exhausted by weeks of stress. She went downhill so fast. Then there was the time spent preparing for her funeral, still busy, even though she'd arranged it all herself.

There were so many people at the crematorium, and lots I hadn't met before. She'd been the bookkeeper for several local businesses, but balance sheets and payrolls weren't what people remembered her for.

Several of the older crowd told me she'd been 'inspirational'. Someone must have used that word while they were chatting; it became the buzzword at the wake. Germaine Greer would have been proud of her, I gathered. Some of these people know more about my mother than I do.

There's so much I don't know. Are we all like that? Do we all think that our parents were somehow born at the same time as we were?

'She was liberated and liberating,' the local women's rugby captain told me.

I had some doubts, but you don't talk truth at funerals.

'We were close, briefly, a long time ago, and her influence continues.' That was an older man I didn't recognise, and, frankly, it sounded contrived. 'She certainly knew what she wanted.'

Well, he was right about that – and she usually got it. If she couldn't do it by herself, which was rare, she knew how to organise help.

Jenny Jenkins told me she'd asked my mother to be her best friend when they were six years old. '"Oh, no," your mum replied, "I'll never have just one best friend."'

That story was easy to believe; she didn't really need other people, but she got involved with them. She gave so much; you just never knew how much she was holding back.

But clearly, she was wonderful.

I'm clenching my teeth. I let my shoulders drop and my face muscles loosen as I look around the garden in the sunshine.

It's my garden now.

The ivy has taken over one side of the shed and is creeping across its roof. She wouldn't hack it back – she wanted the flowers in the autumn for her bees – but elsewhere everything is very tidy. Flowers and vegetables grow together, the smaller ones sheltered by the taller ones; leaves, flowers and colours complement each other, organised, like everything else, according to her own scheme.

How could she create such serenity and yet be so infuriating?

I'm using my grandmother's tea set, rescued from the glass-fronted cabinet where it's been on display in the cluttered front room of the cottage for as long as I can remember. I have a pot of tea and a plate of biscuits. This letter-reading has become an event. It reminds me of playing tea parties when I was little.

Most of my memories of the house are from my childhood and turbulent teens. For the last twenty-five years, I only saw my mother two or three times a year, if that. The arrangement suited us both. She was self-motivated and very contained, and I suppose I inherited the same gene, suppressed when I came back to live here, after she finally accepted her diagnosis.

I open the envelope. Pale blue.

It contains one small sheet of matching note paper. Where's she been storing vintage stationery all this time? It has a Basildon Bond watermark for goodness' sake; the kind of thing her generation kept because it was too good to throw away.

Her writing changed when her grip failed a couple of years ago; it's unrecognisable here, but not illegible. Elderly.

It's dated over a year ago, around the time I moved in.

I see the word *garden* and shove the letter back into its envelope. More instructions. Is she never going to stop telling me what to do?

Gardening was beyond me when I first came back to live with her. I wanted it to stay that way, but things have changed.

'This one's called something Latin, dear,' she'd say, her tone bordering on patronising. In fact, as soon as I came back, she was teaching me, expecting me to dig and prune.

Well, I suppose it worked; I'm definitely into herbal remedies now.

And I'm staying in Cornwall.

She had already lost so much strength a year ago, but I didn't understand why she wouldn't employ a gardener. Someone who knew what they were doing. Someone who liked dirty fingernails.

Gardening was her thing. It wasn't mine. I'm a nurse, and it infuriated me that she wanted me to start weeding.

This was why I'd left home in the first place: to escape from being told what to do and how to think.

'You don't want to do that, my love.' 'Be back by ten thirty, mind.' 'You'll enjoy this.'

I needed to leave my simmering resentment behind.

I'd grown up knowing that I didn't need a father, not that I'd ever had the option of one. Mine disappeared before I was born, never to be discussed - oh, the arguments - and never to be replaced.

At eighteen, I decided I didn't need a mother either.

So, I stayed in London after my training, and we became the sort of long-distance friends who visit occasionally. Always nice to meet up. Always fine to say goodbye.

It was only after the diagnosis that I thought a dad might have been useful for looking after a sick mum.

I take another look at the letter.

My dear Phoebe, I can imagine you sitting in the garden as you read this.

How does she know? How is she still controlling me?

Please bear with me.

Bear with her? She's been dead for three weeks. I've spent my life trying to avoid having to bear with her.

She was in charge, right to the end. Even a few weeks ago, she was still fussing about thinning out the young calendulas. I'd moved her bed to the window so she could look out over her landscape. 'You'll do it tomorrow, won't you?' It was between a request and an order. This was what came naturally to her. She assumed she was in charge in any situation. She knew she could cope, but she still had to prove it. To whom? There was never any doubt.

I bend forward in the garden seat and pull up a small seedling, at least an inch high, which has taken root between the paving slabs. Cheeky thing.

'Sorry, little tree, you're going on the compost.'

I'm talking to plants now.

Straightening up, conscious of the muscles in my back, I remember her frustration as Parkinson's overwhelmed her. It was completely beyond her control.

I suppose I'll be having memories like this every day, and for a long time. Maybe a few more disputes with her, too.

The late summer sun is still fairly high, but it will soon disappear behind the carn, the hill where Mum lived all her life. We both grew up in this place, and, evidently, she hasn't left yet. I must give it time.

Once there were three generations in this house. Three generations of women. Lots of my grandmother's things are still here, and some of mine and all of Mum's. Everything since she was a little girl.

I take the tea-tray back into the house as the garden goes into shadow; I'll be back again later to feed the chickens.

The letter can wait.

I avoid tripping over the old flat-iron in use as a doorstop. That must have been my great-grandmother's, or maybe it's older than that. So much stuff.

'Just get rid of it,' she said to me a few months ago. She was weary that day. 'All of it. I can't, but you can. Just wait until I've gone, then get the clearance people in.'

It was difficult to hear her. Her voice became so thin towards the end.

'You'll want to keep Grandma's jewellery, though, and her notebooks – all her cures and ointments are there. That tea service is quite nice, not that I've ever used it, and there's a brooch your father gave me. Could be worth a fair bit. You must have it valued.' Her voice became more resolute. 'I never did. Never needed to sell it. Shame to let someone else walk off with it.'

Brooch? I was scarcely aware I'd even had a father.

She hadn't mentioned him in thirty years or more. And wouldn't mention him again.

'You don't have to keep the bees. I know you don't like them.'

Well, thank you, Mother.

'You can sell the hives on. I'll have to show you who to contact.'

'I'll sort it all out,' I said, thinking about the honey, and the beeswax candles, and the egg sales, and the herbal remedies and all the other small ways Mum made a little extra money over the years. And my father.

I found the brooch when she was asleep. Ugly. Victorian. Heavy. Overloaded with diamonds.

Later in the evening, I settle myself on the old sofa; chickens fed and in the henhouse; cats fed and curled up beside me. I've eaten too, and now have the energy to tackle the letter again. It's still irritating me, but I can't keep putting it off.

I scan the next couple of lines. They sound so formal.

I want to assure you that even the thought of you is always precious to me and that I have always cared about you.

My eyes squeeze shut, and I breathe out slowly. So remote.

To be fair, it is, of course, true. She cared too much, perhaps. She was bossy, protective, but I never for a moment doubted her love. I realise how grateful I am.

Did she feel unloved? And here's the old guilt for having moved so far away, for so long. It's rushing towards me like a breaking wave, and I go back to the letter before I'm swamped.

I sincerely regret our lack of contact.

So do I, now.

It wasn't my choice. I wanted us to be together, but it takes two people to make a relationship work.

No, not her choice, but she left me with no alternative. She never left anyone with an alternative. I had to leave, but I wish things could have been different.

The Parkinson's diagnosis is hard, but I feel sure that you will do your best to make the end as easy and comfortable as possible.

I'm so glad that your career has been successful. Putting it on hold now...

I don't want to turn over the page; I sit, staring at the letter.

She's right. We really were this distant twelve months ago. We talked about her end, her final days, and yet we were so far apart. I scrunch the letter in my hand – and have to apologise for elbowing a sleeping cat.

I try to work out if I'm angrier with my mother or myself.

We both did our best, I decide. We did what we could, to cope with life as it was handed to us.

There are things you don't choose and you just have to manage. There are risks. You have to protect yourself, and you pay a price.

What has it cost me? I think of the things I've lost in this process. Well ⁻ my mother. We hurt each other and drifted apart a long time ago, though we bonded again during her last year.

I lost my roots, the land of my mothers, though now she's brought me home. It was a while before I understood that this was what she was doing. She's given me new skills along the way as well. That's a gain.

Losing London, swapping a modern flat and sterile wards for a century-old cottage with its own sustainable eco-system? That's a gain too. Friends are already queuing up to visit. Our relationship improved, and she has to take much of the credit for that.

There are still many things I'll never begin to comprehend, but I'm finding some peace and I promise myself I'll be thankful. I'll leave the past behind. She gave me my beginning, and I gave her a good ending.

Resolution.

I re-arrange both cats, one on my lap and the other beside me, and, flattening out the letter on the arm of the sofa, I relax back into the cushion.

*Putting it on hold now...*I focus and turn over the page... *was probably a hard decision. I imagine reading this will also be difficult for you, but I would be so pleased if we could build a relationship after all these years of separation.*

I understand that this may come as a shock. Your mother and I sat in her garden and talked recently. She says she will give you my letter when the time is right.

My eyes flick to the last line and I'm jolted out of my tenderness. My outraged teenage self comes to the boil inside me.

I don't know when that will be, or how much she'll explain.

Both cats have bolted. I'm sitting on the edge of the sofa. She's still in control. Has nothing changed?

Do make contact if you would like to – from now onwards I will always be hoping for your call – but if you don't want to, I will respect your decision and maintain my distance.

Whatever you decide, I will continue to care about you and hope that you will find much happiness in the future.

There's a mobile number, then an unsteady signature.
Your father.

The Well Keeps its Secret

by Caroline Palmer

'You see that picture on the wall? I am that girl on the sofa looking out of the window. That's me, all those years ago. I was nineteen and now I'm in my sixties. A long time since I was that girl, living in the castle, with her parents and her brother – for a time anyhow.' Kat stroked the photo gently around her brother's face.

'I expect you'd like a look round the castle before a cup of tea. You're my nearest neighbour and you've never been round? Well, we must put that right this moment!'

Kat was entranced by what she saw out of the window. Seven magpies in the trees opposite! She began to sing the old song. *'One for sorrow, two for joy, three for a girl and four for a boy, five for silver, six for gold and seven for the secret that's never been told.'* As she finished, the magpies flew away.

She looked out of the window, lost in thought. Mother

called her to the kitchen for tea. Reluctantly, she dragged herself to her feet and went up the stone steps to find Father and Jim at the wooden table. They'd not lived in the castle long and Kat admired its romantic, medieval look. When she asked Father how old it was, he looked vague.

'How long is a piece of string? One thing I know it is old enough to need lots of repairs. And how are we going to find the money for those?' He put his thumbs in his belt. 'There must be someone who knows cheap stonemasons, cheap carpenters, cheap decorators. Trouble is, once they know we're Londoners and not from Cornwall, they'll milk us!' His tweedy clothes were well cut and had been expensive once. Contractors often thought he might be an eccentric millionaire.

Mother commented pettishly, 'Surely we can afford to get things done, Geoffrey. Cousin Henry did leave us the money to buy this place ... house or castle!'

She was unimpressed with living here. Cold, draughty, shops miles away. She'd have preferred the London suburbs ... but Henry had left them instructions to buy this house. God knows why! She wanted to shop at Harrods – now they could afford to, again. And to replace the string of pearls they'd had to pawn.

It was a valid comment about the house. Such a strange instruction to insist on the family living here, with no choice. It was an unusual, some would say beautiful, building. Looking out over the Redruth-Camborne area, the building was a granite mixture of castle and house; part of this was propped up by huge boulders. It was used as a hunting lodge in the time of King John. There were battlements at the top, but the rooms looked quite ordinary, apart from having large, granite-slab floors. The position was isolated with the nearest house half a mile away. The castle was frequently enveloped in mist.

During the family discussion, Jim remained completely quiet, buried in this month's Climbing News. He'd been a frustrated climber in London; Chelsea being totally without pitches, and roofs being too much of a challenge. This issue was featuring Cornwall and Jim devoured the news of cliff and inland ascents. He feasted his eyes on a picture of Bosigran near Pendeen and started planning a trip if he could commandeer the family car. His father considered the vehicle to be absolutely his and would be unlikely to take him. He was a selfish man.

Tea continued and during the discussion about necessary repairs, things became heated, and the teapot knocked over. It rolled off the table and shattered on the floor. Both parents were highly irritated; they were not yet used to being able to buy what they needed, even what they wanted. Jim was nearest, picking up the pieces and placing them on the table. The impetus of the teapot's fall had been so strong that one large part had wedged itself into a lump of stone in the floor. Jim was intrigued to discover a handle on the flagstone and pulled on it. A big round piece of stone slowly came up. He looked down in excitement. There was a wide vertical tunnel, its darkness rolling down into the distance. Jim cried to his parents and sister: 'Look! See what I've found!'

Jim's parents came over, initially showing desultory interest. Then Jim's father remarked with surprise: 'This must be a dry well! Obviously, the servants in the past needed a well for cooking and washing. It would never get closed up in those days. But perhaps we should?'

Jim spoke passionately against it. His instant, secret plan was to well dive; he'd always wanted to do this. 'Let's keep it. It's not doing any harm. And,' craftily, 'if your posh relatives come round, you'll have something to show them!'

Jim's parents hummed and hah'd but, in the end, they decided to leave it open. It was imperative they finished the house repairs before winter, so they returned to their discussion. Jim's fingers caressed the handle of the well top. First chance he had, he'd be down there exploring. But soon his thoughts turned to refurbishing their handsome building. They should have red velvet curtains and damask hangings. He hoped suitable furniture would be purchased. It would be dreadful to end up with the family's old blue sofa, with broken springs and scratches on the arms from the last cat they'd owned.

The next week the house was empty except for Jim. When he saw the car rolling away down the track, he made ready to climb. Changing hastily, he opened the lid of the well and gradually lowered the rope and then himself in, bit by bit. For a few feet, daylight from the top allowed him to look around. He swung on the rope and gasped. Before him was a silver plated locket on a chain, hooked onto a snag. Deciding he wanted a proper look and to change before his family returned, he climbed up the rope and shut up the well.

That night Kat had a strange dream. She was in the kitchen, unseen. There were two servants in nineteenth century clothes, a man and a woman wearing a locket over her rough clothes. They appeared to be lovers but were arguing. Eventually the woman opened the well lid and pushed the locket down against the side. Then she slammed the lid shut and left the room. Kat awoke, confused by this strange dream. Did it mean anything or was it because she was fascinated by this building?

Jim was fascinated by the locket. He examined it several times, wondering who'd owned it. He decided to go further down the well next time but had to wait a week before his family went out. Right now, Jim had lost all interest in trying out Cornish climbs. As soon as the car disappeared, he got changed and went to the well. He lifted the lid and paid the rope ladder out carefully, then climbed down. He noticed that daylight didn't reach as far and resolved to find his head torch next time. He went six feet further and looked around very carefully. He was rewarded with an ancient, crumpled, mildewed fan hanging snagged on the wall. Again, overjoyed at finding a treasure, he climbed back up the rope. After tidying himself, he shut the well lid. Gloating over his find, he soon heard the car returning, and hid the fan with the locket.

He politely offered his family cups of coffee when they came up to the kitchen, and his mother slapped four large pasties on the table. The pasties were delicious, hot and succulent, bought in Redruth. Smelling like Heaven and tasting like a dream. For once Jim's mother had no complaints to make. She felt drowsy after the meal and retired to the bedroom for a snooze. Jim's father joined her, so soon the gentle sound of snores could be heard.

Kat and Jim decided to climb up to the battlements to look over the countryside. On the north side could be seen Redruth with Camborne further along: southward were the engine houses of the Great Flat Lode. That side held the oldest architecture in sight, but their castle was the most ancient for miles. They also noticed several magpies in the trees below. Both pondered how it had been in the past. Jim made a reference to the well but, after that, changed the subject. Jim wanted to tell Kat of his finds, and Kat wished to tell Jim of her dream, but they both felt too awkward. Soon, holding tightly onto their secrets until it became too cold, they climbed down the stone stairs to the warmth of the kitchen.

That evening, Jim, in the privacy of his room, took out the locket and the fan. He wondered why they were down the well. He probably would never find out.

That night Kat had another dream about the kitchen with the well lid lifted. There was a scruffy-looking man holding an expensive-looking fan. He started at every noise, and it seemed likely it was stolen. Eventually the man took the fan and threw it gently down the well, to catch on the greenery growing inside, so he could reclaim it later. Kat awoke, once again. Both her dreams seemed unthreatening, but they puzzled her. She turned over and went back to sleep.

Some weeks went by before Jim could go down the well again. Stonemasons and carpenters were renovating the castle, and the decorators would be coming after. Jim bided his time and drove over to Bosigran and found some rewarding pitches. He went several times and met some other climbers.

His chance came, eventually; the car left, he readied himself, wearing his head torch. This time Jim descended eighteen feet; daylight seemed so far away, and he noticed it was very cold. He searched the walls carefully and then, with pleasure, saw a string of beads with a cross on. It was black and fitted in his pocket. Once the well lid was closed, he looked up the string of beads online, like he had the locket and fan. He discovered it was called a rosary, used by Catholics for prayer. Squinting at it, he decided it must be pretty old as it had woodworm. Another piece for his collection.

When Kat went to bed that night, she wondered if she would dream again about the kitchen. She'd had no dreams recently. However, she found herself back again, in familiar surroundings. The atmosphere was tense and anxious. There were several finely dressed people in the kitchen, two men and three women. Down at the main door, people were banging and shouting. One of the women kneeled, crossed herself and brought out a rosary. She started to pray fervently. One of the other women eyed her disdainfully, picked up her rosary and put it down the well. These people were clearly expecting a raid, and they braced themselves for it, apart from the third woman who picked up her embroidery and ignored everything. Kat woke again, completely confused. The next thing she knew, it was morning. She longed to tell Jim what was happening but did not.

It was a long time before Jim could descend the well again and he was frustrated. There were several trips to Bosigran to climb with people he'd met. He swam and surfed in the azure water of the North coast.

The last day of the summer, the family decided to have a day out. They tried to persuade Jim to come, but he made his excuses – quite weak ones. His mother grumbled that she'd hardly seen him recently. Suddenly moved, he gave her a big hug and then the car rolled off to Sennen. Climb-ready, he unrolled the ladder, this time dropping it full length. He climbed as far as the rope allowed, searching for anything interesting. His eyes lit up as he spotted a fine golden ring. He reached across with confidence. Then there was a tearing noise above as the ladder came away from the top.

As he fell, he was aware of the cold air and the intense dark. Then he ceased to register any feeling.

The three came home having enjoyed themselves thoroughly. The mother was beginning to think living in Cornwall might be bearable. Kat put on a cup of tea. Her father noticed that the lid was off the well and replaced it.

'It'll be those pesky workmen the last time they came,' he growled. The mother shrugged.

That night Kat dreamt of an empty kitchen and a well with someone falling to the bottom. She was worried as Jim had not come home from surfing. She tossed and turned.

Next morning all three, alarmed, searched for him.

Kat kept her dreams a secret.

The well kept its secret too.

The magpies? They flew away for ever. Seven for the secret that's never been told.

Morwenna

by Jennie Rawling

The day they came for her, the clouds hung heavy in the sky. She pushed the bedcovers back at 5.30. Then she stood at the end of the lane, steaming mug in hand, to watch the sun rise over the valley one last time. By 8 o'clock she'd packed up the last of her belongings, said goodbye to each room, and was standing in the doorway, waiting.

At 8.10 the car crested the hill, trundling down the road and out of sight, behind the cluster of cottages huddled at the edge of the hamlet. Three minutes later it re-emerged at the end of her lane. She didn't move until it came to a stop two metres from her feet, then she turned back inside, breathed in one last scent of home, and stepped out to meet them, a duffel bag in each hand.

The drive out of the valley is a memory she replays often. They passed vacant windows, doors locked from the outside, abandoned gardens, her world watching her go. Everyone else had already gone. Ma had left for the hospital with Aunty Agnes and Uncle Jim in the night when Agnes' waters had broken, leaving Morwenna to say a final goodbye to their home. She was the very last person to leave this beautiful, difficult, giving but unforgiving valley, full to the brim with memories.

As the car chugged up the steep road, Morwenna craned her neck to catch a glimpse of the slightly wonky roof with its sturdy chimney stack. On the bend in the road she was gifted one final, glorious view of the place she had called home all her life. Her eyes widened and she drank it all in – the narrow lanes, the row of cottages shoulder to shoulder, the cluster of other dwellings spaced out around this, each with a small garden and outhouse. She tried to capture every detail in a mental picture to carry with her, and then they were up out of the valley and it was gone.

They drove on in silence. The car didn't have far to go. The residents were all being resettled within a five-mile radius of the hamlet, most of them in one of those characterless newbuild estates. Seeing the box of brick and glass awaiting her, with its 'low maintenance' garden and identikit neighbours, a part of Morwenna's heart curled up and died.

Three days later, on 3 September 1962, they flooded the valley. Water rushed down the narrow lanes and bubbled out of the chimneys, smothering the laughter and idle gossip entrenched in the walls. By the end of the week, a lifetime of memories had been buried in a watery grave.

Sitting now in her not-so-newbuild, Morwenna resurfaces from the distant memory. It's been raining for days. It's constant, relentless. *Another day of this and we'll need a bloody ark.* A little bit of rain doesn't bother her, but this is different. This transforms the paths across the heathland into rivers of peat, which stain your boots and soak into your socks. This lashes at your face and makes your eyes sting. This plasters your trousers to red raw thighs and seeps into your aching joints, clogging them up with rust.

Morwenna stares out the window, fidgeting. Her gaze shifts to the edge of the reservoir, just visible from where she is sitting. The water level is rising. She pictures it creeping up to the village, standing vulnerable and exposed, and sweeping everything away until it reaches her front door. She imagines stepping outside to greet it and walking on into the inevitable.

She wonders if she could swim all the way to the bottom of the valley from here. She knows her home is still standing. Some divers went down there a few years ago, filming for a documentary. She watched it on the BBC. As the camera glided along her little lane she'd held her breath, until there it was, taking shape in the gloom. It looked like a corpse. She swallows but encounters a lump. For 52 years she has looked out at that sliver of water. Most of the other residents have left the new village, moving further up country. Many have moved on to the next life, including her Ma, Agnes and Jim. Only a few remain.

A violent rattling on the table makes her jump. *Christ.* She pushes herself up off the window seat, wincing as the blood rushes back to her tailbone. The phone's screen is lit up with the word 'Elsie' and a smiling, freckly face.

'Hang on,' Morwenna shouts, cursing at the unresponsive touchscreen.

'You've already picked up, Wen,' a distant voice calls back.

'Yes, I know. I'm just...' Morwenna grasps the phone and plants it against her better ear. 'Don't tell me you need a lift, because my battery's dead.'

'*Again*? Wen, you don't drive it enough, you need to help it recharge. Anyway, I told you, I've got my own taxi now.'

'Oh yes. Well after three years of being madam's personal chauffeur it's easy to forget.' She pauses. 'Anyway. It's nice to hear from you. Nobody else calls me.'

'That's because you don't want them to,' Elsie says. 'Look, I'm just on my afternoon break so I can't be long, but there's a lady at work who does home visits–'

'No–'

'You haven't–'

'Not interested.' They've had this conversation too many times. 'I'm not an invalid.'

There's a sigh on the other end of the phone followed by a careful silence. Morwenna knows her friend just cares, but she's never been one for a fuss. Elsie could live in a different world, going on adventures and partying like most twenty-somethings do, but for some reason she's chosen to be here. Studying for a Master's degree in marine biology, when she isn't in lectures she works in the village Co-op. She lives with her mother, in yet another newbuild estate, on the outskirts of the village. Morwenna can picture her dot-to-dot freckles dancing as she tries to control her frustration. When Elsie finally speaks, her voice is small and tight.

'If I hadn't been there when you left the gas on last

time, you could have killed your—'

'Nonsense, I would've been fine. It was only five minutes,' Morwenna says.

'It was twenty. Wen, I have to go. My supervisor's tapping his watch. Charming guy. Talk soon, ok?'

'Ok. Don't take any rubbish from that pillock now.'

Elsie laughs. 'I won't. Bye!'

'Bye.' Morwenna waits for the line to go dead, then places the phone back on the table. She decides to read and settles back in the window seat. The drain outside is overflowing, and there's a waterfall cascading from the gutter. But the rain itself seems to have finally lost its enthusiasm. Tucked in above the radiator, she's nice and toasty. She props the open book on her knee. The lines are fuzzy, and they begin to swim across the page.

She comes to with a jolt and a snort. The book is on the floor, and through the window all is dark. She rises to her feet and shuffles into the kitchen to pour a glass of water. At the back door she listens for rain but all is quiet. The cooker clock reads 11.59. One minute from the witching hour. Fully surfaced from her long nap, the restlessness has returned, and a sudden urge to be in the water takes hold of her. She normally swims in the bay, but tonight she feels a pull in the opposite direction. Her feet begin to move and she follows them, out through the front door.

It's a two-mile walk to the reservoir, but Morwenna's walked it before and she does so now. Her feet splash through puddles ankle-deep. Water seeps into her socks, but she barely notices. She has no idea how long it takes her – she left her phone on the dining room table, and her

watch hasn't worked since last spring. Pulled by an invisible rope, she just keeps walking, until the water lies there waiting in front of her, and she's pulling off her sodden walking shoes to feel the earth underfoot.

She wades in until the water reaches her collar bone, then dives under, the cold engulfing everything. The water embraces her, lubricating creaky joints. A few steady strokes and she resurfaces further out. Treading water, the black night above, dotted with stars, ghostly feet circling below. The valley holds its breath, waiting for her next move. Her heartbeat slows to a steady gu-GUNG, gu-GUNG. She takes a couple of deep breaths, then on the third she fills her lungs and dives down.

Out of the murky depths a chimney emerges and the old house reaches up to greet her. She traces its familiar lines – the guttering that used to clog up with moss, the upper-floor windows with the rusty sash fastenings, now two empty sockets. Her eyes are not so useful in the water, so she sees with her hands.

Forcing her body down to the point of negative buoyancy, she can feel the memories welcoming her home as she slowly begins to sink. The little front garden lies before her, its vegetable patch boasting sturdy turnips and nocturnal potatoes. It had been a good year in the valley, and they were in for a treat that evening: Aunty Agnes' famous vegetable soup. Most vegetable soups were nothing much to shout about, but Agnes' was different. She put thick, rich cream in it. But she didn't mash the veggies down to make them smooth, oh no. She kept the chunks of swede and turnip and carrot and potato thick and juicy. Add in a crunch of celery, a sprinkle of nutmeg and a hearty handful of fresh herbs, and you had before you a bowl of pure heaven. Morwenna has never forgotten that smell. In those days she would bury her face in her bowl and slurp away until she had to come up for air.

The front door of the little house is open, so she lets herself in. The door was never locked, even at night. Who would have come in except your neighbours, and they were always welcome, at any hour. Once or twice, Ma came downstairs in the morning to find one of Peter's boys, Jack or Roger, dropping off a freshly-baked loaf. So she lit the stove and put the water on to boil, and bid them stay for a cup of tea before they headed back to the bakery for a day's work. That was how things were.

The living room is smaller than Morwenna remembers it, its edges blurred. Her body tells her it's nearly time to leave, but she lingers. She's been away so long. Morwenna runs her hands along the familiar rough stone around the fireplace, but it feels different, smoother. She gently windmills her hands and comes to rest against the living room wall, the stone a reassuring hand against her back. Her chest is starting to tighten, and faint alarm bells begin to ring. She has swum underwater all her life, but she's never stayed down this long. *Just a little longer*, she tells herself. Louder alarms kick in, more insistent ones, and a burning begins to spread across her chest. For a brief moment, she blots out her body's warning system, rests her head back and lets her arms drift.

What if she stays? She's home. Finally home, after all this time. She could just... let go. Then the noise would stop. And the pain would be brief and intense, but then it, too, would drift away. They wouldn't be able to tear her away from this place again.

A switch in her brain flicks and her eyes blink open. Her body is screaming for oxygen. She's not even sure she still has time, but she makes a move for the surface anyway. Strong, steady kicks and her eyes focused on the light above.

The burning in her chest grows fiercer. Up ahead, she sees two moons, one cold and ghostly, the other yellow and precise. As the edges of her vision darken she bursts into the air and gasps. Exhausted, she floats on her back until both her breathing and heartbeat are steady, and looks up at Elsie's concerned face.

'Would you mind not blinding me with that bloody thing, please,' she manages.

'Sorry.' Elsie directs the torch beam at her submerged

feet. She watches Morwenna carefully for a moment, before relaxing a little. 'Good swim?'

'Lovely.'

Still on her back, Morwenna kicks to shore, then brings her knees up and clambers out. Elsie wades back to the muddy bank and climbs out, then looks at her friend, shivering and fully clothed.

'I brought a towel,' she says, turning to rummage in her rucksack then handing it over. 'Oh yeah!' she remembers, head back in the bag. 'I thought you might want this too.' She pulls out a bright blue fleece-lined changing robe, light grey in the moonlight.

Morwenna tuts but doesn't refuse it, and begins to peel off her sodden clothes. Elsie looks away until the robe is grabbed from her hands, then gathers up the wet clothing and plops it into a carrier bag. Turning back to her friend, she frowns at her bare feet.

'Where are your shoes?'

Morwenna looks along the shoreline. 'I don't know.'

Elsie shrugs. 'The car's not far.'

'You *drove*?'

'Yes, Wen, I did drive. It's the middle of the bloody night.'

Morwenna frowns. She turns to look back at the water, its surface still masking so many unanswered questions.

'Come on,' Elsie says, 'you're shivering.'

Morwenna nods to herself, then bids the lake a silent farewell. It will still be there in the morning. She turns and follows her friend up the path, through the long grass.

'Oh, I've been thinking.' Elsie takes the older woman's arm companionably. 'It's time I moved out of Mum's place.

And you need a lodger.' She looks straight ahead, aware of her friend's eyes burning into her cheek. 'I could move some of my stuff across in the morning.'

For a full minute there is just the rhythmic whisper of carrier bag against thigh.

'Sounds good.' Morwenna smiles inside.

'Home?' Elsie says.

'Yes. Home.'

Under the Waterfall – A Memoir

by Rachel Fitch

*T*homas Hardy was a novelist and poet. 'Under the Waterfall', one of his less familiar love poems, was written in 1914. The poem itself was written by Hardy on one of his visits to Cornwall. He would enjoy walks with his wife, Emma, down the Valency Valley to Boscastle. Pentargon Waterfall was the waterfall that had inspired him. Though Hardy's poem is written as if it were Emma speaking, this is a view from Hardy's imaginative recollection of his time spent at the waterfall in his words.

It was by the swirling purl of the waterfall, where I had sat and put my pen to the scrap of paper that had lain idle within my pocket since leaving for the rugged Cornish Coast. This was a place of solitude and for my mind to find new delights. Though it did not know this, the landscape of myth and mystique was to be an alliance in combat with the dread of bleakness and the despair from the loss of words and language. The words upon this ruffled, torn paper, were a bid to capture the magical moment of dreams and fantasies. The moment that I dare still to dream, albeit confusedly as if it was like a rare moment of flickering starlight or a glorious sunset that was far too magical for human eyes. But alas, it did happen. As the days grow longer and my mind grows older, I sometimes question the correct nature of the illusive meeting. Nevertheless, upon reading my poetic words again, only I see, only I know the hidden meaning. The meaning existing only for my fickle memory.

'Whenever I plunge my arm, like this,
In a basin of water...'

It is at times when my fingers caress the ice-cold flow of water, whether it is in the simple basin or a natural flow or hear the roaring cascade of running water, the grey fog of my mind disperses revealing the emotions of the past. It takes me back to that one fugitive day that slipped through the unforgivable hands of time. That one burning day in August when I walked upon the Cornish soil under a speckled blue and dappled green canopy, I stumbled across a surprising scene. The picnic was a delightful picture of deep purple grapes and red luscious strawberries; a bottle of wine winked carelessly in the sunlight, but the most heavenly sight of all was the girl lounging on a grey, speckled blanket.

Once over her initial shock at myself, the intruder,

disturbing her afternoon of pleasure, she beckoned me over to her small patch of indulgence. But it was not the delicacies of the picnic that intrigued me, as I fell into the deep black pools of her eyes. I could do nothing to fight against the darkness of their currents that embraced my cumbersome soul. Moreover, I let myself glide and be guided by her mysteries of storms into a world where stars and ships collide. I was lost but was led by her to lie down on her bed of grey softness.

> *'With a hollow boiling voice it speaks*
> *And has spoken since hills were turfless peaks.'*

The increasing thundering sound of the water plunged me further into her hidden depths. Skeleton ribs from sunken ships rose up from the shadowy masses of monsters and long-forgotten daemons. Silver fish darted around our bodies, curiosity fought with nervousness, mesmerised by our bodily forms. I drank it all in. A green thicket parted and the dark swirls of water gave way to a beautiful shaft of light. Flecks of gold floated aimlessly, basking in the warmth of the light. One by one, seals gracefully swam upwards to greet us. Patterns of spots merged into one as they playfully showed off their bewitching dance.

So lost was I in her dark eyes that the timing of the pouring of the wine was missed. Indeed, the rim of the drinking glass pressing onto my lips brings me back to the reality, to the blue sky, the rich grass and the silent, watchful trees that surrounded us. The waterfall's sound dims as she motions me to drink. The cold amber liquid hits my mouth with refreshing notes of woody sweetness.

She pays no attention to the small drip, mirroring the waterfall, upon my chin but gazes, almost solemnly, into my eyes as she brings the glass towards her rose-red lips.

It was such a strange ritual but this intimate moment had been truly written upon the stars. Drinking from the same cup strengthened our connection that was first cemented by the deep pools of her eyes. No words were spoken. We only sat, drank and enjoyed the succulent fruits that were on offer, all the while basking in the glorious summer sun. We were oblivious to the surroundings that were still stirring around us; the wild rabbits hopping in the hedgerows, bees finding their flowers and the fluttering wings of the butterflies could not draw us out of our own little world. I lay back upon the soft blanket and marvelled at how the universe had brought us together. It was what I believed was meant to be.

The afternoon light dims and I watch how she gently cleans the cup in the water. The falling sun sends flares of light that bounce off the smooth cup's surface. The cup tumbles from her delicate fingers and we watch as it splashes into the water. Despite the season, the water is bitterly cold as we plunge our arms in to retrieve the one physical connection that we have together. It is lost. Hidden in a rocky crag of the waterfall but it does seem fitting that a small part of ourselves remains in this place. A token, which only our lips had touched, would always be that link that would forever draw me to this magical place.

'*Though precisely where none has ever known,*
Jammed darkly, nothing to show how prized,
And by now with its smoothness opalised,

Is a drinking glass.'

I look back into her eyes. They are dull and lifeless. The sun has dipped and the magic that had pulsed all around has disappeared. With a hurry, she gathers up the picnic things; with a small nervous hesitation, she leaves the grey blanket upon the ground. She says nothing but steals a few timid glances my way. Her eyes so void of life. I can swim against the currents. Gone are the black swirling stars cruising on the pulse of waves. The magic is no more and, with some trepidation, I go on my way.

As I have said, I sometimes wonder about that day. I sometimes while away the hours recollecting that afternoon. Lost again in the flurry of magical starry waters. I have not felt such magic since. Though this leaves me with a tinge of sadness, I am glad that I still have the touch of magic within me and our connection is still hidden at that waterfall. I still visit there. I still sit, in summer, under the blue skies that dance with the green canopy. I never see her.

Would we have been wild and free ... would we have spent all the Earth's days together ... most of all, I wonder what would have happened if I had picked up that soft, grey blanket ... the grey fur of the selkie.

Hidden in Time:
A Legend of Saint
Wenappa

by Jo Grande

Nobody counted time; the seasons came and went. The days grew longer or shorter as the years turned and children grew up and followed the customs of their day. But things were changing, and the woman who came knew that she would become part of a new era in this land.

I see her walking on dewy wet grass, her long gown trailing damp about her sandalled feet. Her head is bent and her shoulders are drooping, but the fresh air or tears have brought colour to her cheeks, and a fine cloak fit for a queen is bunched around her shoulders and gathered under her chin.

Wenappa follows a grassy track along a narrow tree-lined ridge which obscures a large mound. Trees grow on the mound. Perhaps it is a tinners' tip or burial mound, or perhaps before the trees grew so tall it was an old fort on this high vantage point, with a view across the land to the river and the harbour on the creek at Bissoe; or perhaps people have performed the rites of their old religion here.

She stops in a little dell at the corner of a birch and alder coppice, where two fresh water springs meet to create a pool. The water trickles out from the pool to form a single stream which wanders gently downhill, until it is lost in the wooded valley below. She bends down beside the clear, welling water and dips cupped hands into it, lifting them to her mouth. Then she brushes away the tears on her face with cool damp strokes and marks a cross on her own forehead with a wet finger.

Her brother, Kea, had arrived that day bringing sad news. He and his friend Fili were travelling West together and caught up with the small family group after enquiring along their route. Kea came to tell Wenappa that her aunt, her mother's widowed, youngest sister, had been murdered by Saxon pagans.

'It was nearing Christmas and the group of Christians were travelling North, down from the Welsh Black Mountains,' Kea said.

'They were heading for a place called Talgarth when the pagans spotted them and tracked them down from the mountain and into the pass; and when our aunt and her friends became aware they were being followed they rode at speed through the pass to the pastures of the lower slopes, and towards the safety of the town. But they were caught and killed as they approached it.'

Wenappa burst into tears at the news.

'But she was so young,' she cried, 'more like an older sister to me than an aunt,' and inconsolable, she went out alone.

The aunt she thought of as a sister was also named Wenappa, and now by the welling pool she remembered happy times that they had spent together. She thought of her grieving parents too, her mother and her father, Lord Cynyr Ceinfarfog, and her old home in Wales. The pastures were green at Caer Gogh, the place where she and her brother Kea had spent their childhood.

In those days they had ridden out in springtime to help bring in the sheep for lambing, and her cousin Dewi sometimes came with them riding his chunky Welsh, dappled-grey pony, whose coat in winter always turned white, thick and warm to keep out icy winds and snow.

Later when the long spring grass was cut the children helped to turn the hay as it dried in the sun. Sometimes they also helped build hayricks or rode home together on top of a loaded haycart; and when the sheep came in for shearing, they would gather scraps of wool and pile the rolled-up fleeces ready for sorting, spinning, and weaving into the flannel which clothed and kept them all warm in wintertime.

She remembered her Aunt Non, Dewi's mother, and the summer when all their family went away on a boat to Brittany. Aunt Non gathered a group of Christian women friends together there and built a monastery to house them all. The women called themselves 'Nons,' or 'Nuns,' and Dewi was then called David.

But Wenappa's best memories were of her aunt

Wenappa. From her she had learned useful things, like making medicines and antiseptics from herbs and how to live off the countryside. Together they wove baskets and cloth and made hand tools to suit a multitude of purposes. She was also able to help in caring for sick people. Now, with her husband Selevan and her young son Cybi, in this wild new land of farmers and tin miners, these healing skills would be useful. She had work to do here, and her son Cybi to care for. She knew in her heart that she could not return to Caer Gogh.

Her brother and his friend, Fili, were on a mission from the court of King Arthur to set up Christian monasteries on either side of the Truro river, and the work was to be completed before winter. Kea was also King Arthur's steward, and known as Sir Kay at court. He was the tallest knight in Avalon, and had previously been a monk at Glastonbury, and it was he who welcomed his sister when she came to court to meet and marry the handsome blonde-haired King Selevan of Domnonia, the old name for Cornwall.

It was a land which had been almost overlooked by the Romans who ruled in Britain for so long. Here in the late fifth century the Celts still lived their independent, industrious lives as farmers, and miners of tin which they traded. But there were many Christian newcomers arriving from Wales, and a new name was coined by them at that time. On their maps the land was called 'West Wales', and King Selevan, like many others, travelled West with his Queen Wenappa, and their son Cybi, who was just old enough to ride safely on his pony.

The newcomers had a mission, to spread the Christian message which they had learned from Irish, Welsh and Roman Christians, some of whom stayed behind when the Roman armies returned home. The Romans had left behind a legacy of castle forts and roads, and a modern way of life with the Latin language for those who were educated. But none of this had reached Cornwall. Gradually here the change to Christianity was strengthened further by the re-invention of pagan Druid festivals, to become new Christian celebrations, with pageantry, music, and even dancing.

With all the changes there was also relief from the fear of demons, dark arts and unnecessary sacrifice, and new places were being built for Christian worship and community gatherings, and for healing the sick, and safe retreat.

The solitary walk gave Wenappa time to reflect, and to recover from the news which had shaken and saddened her so much. She knew there were always hazards for travellers to face in unfrequented and unknown places, but she was strong-spirited like her aunt, and determined to work in this land of her Celtic Christian husband, King Selevan (whose name was Cornish for Solomon).

It had been a long, life-changing journey. Their group travelled on horse-back and sometimes on foot following the stone markers, and the tracks along lay lines through high moorland, then over steep coastal pathways and across marsh and deep bog. They had paused to rest at farmsteads and hamlets, and shared their Christian message as they went. But now Wenappa was tired. She longed for the hazardous journey of each day to end, and here they had found a sheltered, green and peaceful spot, more like her old home in Wales. It was sheltered from the wildest winds, far from raging coastal seas and shrieking gulls. Here they could make a home and a settled place to begin their work. Here there were trees to give good shelter from harsh weather, and trickling streams of fresh water. Blackbirds sang in hedgerows and rabbits frolicked in the long grass.

She had longed for stability on their journeying. Now she had found it. As she stood at the edge of the welling pool, Wenappa vowed to continue the work her aunt had shared with her, here.

'This is a sacred place,' she said to the overhanging trees in their spring green, and to the small birds which fluttered there and sang out on the morning air.

'I dedicate this well to the aunt whose name I bear.'

She held her arms out over the pool and spoke again as a breeze brushed the reeds in a whisper and the little birds took flight.

'The well-spring of Wenappa, God bless this place!'

She lowered her arms and allowed the cloak to swaddle them again, and she stood for a moment in silence. The unshed tears had cleared from her eyes, and she smiled as she spoke her thoughts aloud.

'This is our home. I'll build a church on the hill and a place for wanderers and pilgrims, a monastery where travellers may stay and rest; and those who are sick will be cared for.'

Then she turned and made her way thoughtfully back down the hill to the small hamlet by the stream.

*

Cybi, with his thick mop of curly hair and bright blue eyes came running up the hill and flung himself upon her.

'Come quickly, Mother,' he cried. He was growing up fast and he pulled hard at her hand, dragging her with him down the hill.

'We are going to Bissoe, to the harbour. The horses are saddled and ready! A man has fallen into deep mud as his ship came up to the quay. He is a Roman, and they cannot get him out!'

Together mother and son broke into a run, and Wenappa noticed as they passed the site where her new church was starting to be built that the over-wet cob mix was sagging under construction. The workmen were tin miners and not accustomed to building walls.

But there was no time to stop. She called out to them, 'Come quickly! There has been an accident at the port! Bring your shovels and spades. There is a poor man in trouble. He's trapped in mud on the ebbing tide!'

She grabbed a long length of rope with knots at intervals along its length. The men had been using it to measure distances on the ground. She coiled it up quickly, running on as she looped it over her arm. Cybi and the workmen ran after her, hard on her heels and carrying their spades.

The horses were ready. All was movement and speed. A horse and cart appeared. The men who had been 'builders' minutes before were now riding on board. Selevan was already up on his horse and away at a gallop down the track.

Wenappa pulled the rope coil over her head and across

one shoulder. She mounted her own horse in seconds.

'Follow me. I'll make a way through,' she shouted to her son.

Cybi was close behind on his pony. They rode together galloping after the others and soon overtaking the cart. It was almost a mile to the harbour. They splashed through streams past Trehaddle and through Cusgarne, and covered the ground in minutes.

There was just a little water left puddled in the harbour. The exposed mud filled the air with the earthy smell of rotting vegetation and sea water as the tide reached its lowest ebb.

The ship was tied against the quay and already unloaded. Pottery, glass and bales of cloth were landed and stacked up; and ingots of tin and copper together with cooking utensils and other tin, copper and iron objects were all waiting to be loaded on board. A crowd of workers and disembarked travellers stood helplessly watching the exhausted struggles of a poor man who was desperately trying to claw a path to the edge of the creek. But his efforts were weakening all the time.

Some people were rushing about trying to find a means of rescue as Wenappa and Cybi clattered onto the quay, and Wenappa leapt down from her horse giving the reins to Cybi.

'Take the horses back to the trees and tie them up there,' she cried, pointing back the way they'd come. Then she turned, and looked out over the creek.

Vast areas of deep mud lay exposed by the low tide, spreading out on either side of the inlet in long, wide slicks, with a central furrow of river water forming a slack stream, which slithered slowly through the middle. People had been throwing wood planks and logs onto the mud, with anything else they could find, in the hope of making pathways or handholds for the struggling seaman who had tried to reach for them. But now, sunk up to his waist, his struggling had ceased.

Wenappa ran, carrying the coil of rope with her. She saw her husband leap down from the quay onto an old wooden door which had been dropped beside the quay wall. She quickly tied one end of her rope to a mooring post and then reached down, calling her husband's name.

'Selevan, Selevan! Take the rope!'

He looked up at her and she dropped the coiled rope down onto his shoulder. It was a long, strong coil, and Selevan set out from his platform unwinding it slowly from his body as he took long leaping strides from a plank to a tree-trunk log, and then from tree-trunk to another plank, just as they lay thrown in a haphazard pathway across the mud.

Slowly he closed the gap between himself and the sinking man. He carefully balanced himself on a thick plank and with all his strength he hurled the rope. He watched it unfurl as it flew towards the poor exhausted Roman. It was grabbed in desperate, shaking hands and immediately wrapped, splashing and wet around his slippery body, looped up by him and then tied off in front.

Selevan hoped the knots that the man had tied would hold. He called to the people on the quay.

'All of you pull!' he cried. 'Haul, steady and slow and strong. Haul, haul...' The men on the quay grasped the rope and the rhythm and hauled away, reaching for each new knot along the slippery length of builders' rope, knot by spaced knot in unison like good seamen.

Selevan stood, knee deep in mud as his wooden plank platform slowly sank beneath his weight. But gradually the trapped man's body was lifting, moving out of the mud and coming towards him. He could see the poor fellow was faint and struggling to breathe.

He held out his arms and grabbed him as he came near, and then holding together they were drawn towards the quay.

Many hands reached out to pull them up onto the solid decking of the quay. Cybi had come to his mother and was watching with wonder as the pile of wet, muddy rope increased around her feet.

They laid the exhausted Roman on a pallet bed. They washed him clean with fresh water, and covered him in blankets. Then they gave a cheer for Selevan, calling him 'Levan' as he heaved himself back to safety, because he had risen, like bread-dough from the river mud. (Or maybe it was because Saint Selevan was too much of a mouthful to say?) But it is true that this man lifted spirits.

The Roman had come from the North near the wall of Hadrian. He was a stone mason, skilled in building and making repairs to the wall.

Wenappa looked at her own weary troop of builders now all leaning on the spades, which they had not needed after all. She smiled. All would be well. God had sent her a leader for her local team. The little church would now grow quickly under his supervision, and the monastery with its hospital would be built as well.

*

Gwennap port at Bissoe is gone, but Gwennap (Churchtown) still bears Wenappa's name in its short form, with the 'G', (which the Romans could not pronounce) added: GWENNAP. Her churchland is marked by parish boundaries and the word 'Llanwennap' on maps (which means 'the Churchland or Parish of Wenappa'). The area includes the 'mining collapse' at Gwennap Pit, made famous by John Wesley, who preached there. St Wenappa's church in Gwennap now stands as a Victorian monument to golden times, when the 'Gwennap triangle' with its copper and tin production was the richest place in the world; and many come from overseas to find their mining ancestors in the graveyard.

The Network of Mine

by Alice Thomas

I always wished I could praise the sun with my phantom hands, feeling its warmth. The dense smoke clouds, however, have crept beneath it, bringing howling winds and many shreds of rain across the roaring coast. They brought instead the cold and misery from the burrowed tunnels of the Bodmin mines, which were closed down a long time ago.

Seagulls chuckled above in the blue sky, almost insulting to my senses. They flew around the terracotta ruins, laden with buildings with their tops removed. A coat of gravel was layered over those structures, adding to their centuries-long roughness.

At the centre of that rubble, I noticed a tent wobbled by a harsh burst of wind. You stood out well next to a broken wall, bellowing at that device of yours. You held it right across your fingers, placing it over your ear. Such odd behaviour indeed.

I saw your friend emerging from the tent. With flowing strands of amber hair, she moved over with hands in pockets of her long raincoat. She told you that your friends were planning to go home because of the vicious weather. I don't blame the young maid for thinking that.

You said to your friend that this trip was the perfect opportunity to find treasure there, for this can lead to your best opportunities.

Your friend apologised. She would rather want to be safe and not place herself in jeopardy, telling you that some risks were not worth it.

She walked off with the other two folks, vanishing away into the thick, open fog. Your eyes watched over them, adjusting your feet through a flurry of gusty streaks. You dashed into the wide opening, smelling the dry, bitter air. Your hood flicked out, allowing for a better sight of all that rain whipping into different angles. You muttered you can do this and swore to get the prizes in those uncharted fields.

With a heavy breath, you stumbled across the weary rocks. A warm device shot light from your palm, acting like your personal torch. Bats flew out. You flinched, with your arms covering your temples for protection, but you lowered them as if it was nothing. Those tiny buggers should be the least of your worries.

After a series of irregular slabs of cracked rock, you made it to the main hall. Rusted mine tracks were wrapped over the tall platforms, towering over the pits of wood and metal. Some of those stairs nearby were worn out after many years. The entire state of that mine had gotten worse since most of the miners stopped working there. I still couldn't understand why they have left that place alone.

A wall tapped, knocking into a different rhythm. You twitched your head to follow where it came from. It must have been nothing. I saw your lips pressed together. You dismissed such hits as rocks falling on the surface while approaching for a smoother and brighter landing.

You produced a map out of your stuffed bag and showed it to your eyes. The pencilled marks appeared on the sheet to show which materials to discover there. Gold, copper, silver, tin and the rest of the goodies. I doubt if any of them were loose enough to collect without needing a pickaxe. You didn't bring one yourself, which was rather silly, of course.

On that document, I saw a major pathway from the starting hall, which lead towards a fork. One passage from it pointed to a narrow room, which was marked with a 'R' next to it. Another path pointed through a snake line into a vast chamber, presented with a written name of 'Southern Mine'. The third path led through a long winding road towards a tiny cell, with an X marking the spot of gold nearby.

The 'R' room was known as the last retreat; I'd say it was a good place to start your perilous expedition. A place of rest and safety, along with other useful tools and supplies. In fact, I would have begged you so much to make a bee-line for it.

But you ended up taking the path leading to gold. You wanted to collect treasure without having to waste time in other fruitful areas. Your muttering sounded like you demanded to grab the goods and head out of the caves without hesitation.

When you arrived at the small cell, it was desolated. The tattered boxes were lined up as storage for the goods, serving as seats to eat a pasty on by their crusts. Not a neat set for a clean guest to visit, but it was good as a place for a break if you ask me.

You must have lucked out when you found an acceptable pick-axe by a nearby crate. You pulled it off the ground. While it sported rust around its metal part, it whacked on the rocky wall without breaking. Lucky you! I imagine it will become extremely useful for collecting minerals from the tight cracks within the bunches of stone. The whole environment had seen better days, though.

Your feet must have ached with sore muscles after walking through the mines. The misty wind howling from the long tunnels there didn't help either with the lasting spot of humidity. I had soot in my nostrils when I worked there once; it made my snot speckled dark.

The knocking returned. It rang straight into your ears, repeating every ten seconds. So often that the rhythms had mixed into an irregular string of noises. You felt them like torture, hammering into your own senses. That was easy to experience for any soft person from a later generation.

You knelt on the floor. Your fingers reached into the rucksack. You drew out your map again. A slit ripped across the middle. You tried to patch it back together, but then it got stained by a few big drops from the ceiling. I could see the lines blended into splotches, made from the tears of fatigue. Your doubts about where to go next must have stacked up like piles of paper.

The knocking grew louder, enough to give you a crushing headache. Did you realise why it became intolerable for you to handle? Your mouth opened wider, showing your coffee-bordered teeth. Your hand rubbed around your forehead, rubbing sweat into your temples. The heat puffed into your coat, which produced the opposite sensation to when you were outside in the pissing rain. It was like a cruel bout of fever.

After swallowing a few tablets of aspirin, you marched on through the next tunnel, strolling your feet across the bumpy surface. Your toe stubbed on a fallen rock, which must have stung into some throbbing pain. Your mouth kept all the noise, sucking in your cracked lips. You then limped further along the fissured walls.

The structures became less uniform on each batch of a hundred steps. By the weakened mind, the path warped into patterns of bubbles, with rigid textures and water seeping through its large cracks. That road spiralled on for ages.

The knocking rattled through like waves. Louder, softer, harder. Your sense of direction was disoriented, scrunching your face, hampering your head down like a heavy weight. Your legs zig-zagged over the layers of rock, dirt, and slabs. You almost slipped on the damp parts, and you almost lost your fingers through a broad fissure in a wall.

All of your missteps have drained your energy. Your food supplies in your bag have dwindled down to only biscuits, next to your dried up bottles. You hunched over in sheer fatigue, catching droplets with your tongue. They left a sour bite of salt and copper over your taste buds. I wouldn't collect water from those rusted parts, which came from the torch holders burnt out into creaking thorns.

Your map unfolded again. Its diagrams had sense withered out of them. One part shaped like a chamber; another poked into a hole, leading to the chasm down below. I couldn't even recognise it! All of that flared your neck into a few painful rings of angst. The sheet split in two. With a thrust of air through your teeth, you ripped it apart with both sets of fingers - again and again - until it scattered into tiny beige pieces.

You squirmed out just now that you wished to go home. It sounded like wailing as your head twisted around in a fit of panic. You called out for any soul, which echoed through all spaces. Bats flew out again and brushed past your crooked body. We were all scaling all over the walls, watching as you struggled to notice me and the other men. You could only walk around with very little supplies to spare.

After an hour on that trek, a rock ran through with a particular texture between your digits. It was dry. Your pinky pulled the ring up. It creaked and can knock just by lifting it. I could imagine the rust on my dead fingers through some patches of the otherwise glossy parts. With your head hovering next to the panel, you reached for it. It turned, pulling the guard up. It opened.

With a spot of hope, you lit the entire place with your tiny object. There, a bed. You fell onto it and snoozed. It was soft, despite rigid down below to the worn mattress. Still softer than the whole flooring.

*

A few knocks rattled through the room. Bursts of heat crawled up across the walls. Though an icy draft had sent shivers through your skin without the protection of a blanket. Not even the mattress helped; it featured tatters and stains, and it was broken beyond repair.

You crept up, pale faced with a twisted mouth, fearing for any nasty surprises that lie behind the doorway. It was pitch black. You stormed over to slam it shut, before you laid your back over the door's surface. Laboured breaths went up into the groggy air, brushing against the stone ceiling. It all howled as if it was about to crush you with their phantom fangs.

Your heart clutched. Mists left between your teeth. The fear of the approaching unknown waiting behind the woods, striding closer to break in and rip your hapless body out. It was only natural for any of us to fear monsters, most of which would have lived inside your head.

You muttered to say as if nothing matters anymore in this world. Any source of belief, with a spark of hope for a more prosperous life. I would have hoped a lot more people would visit this mine again, but too many of them have left it into a dusted, barren wasteland. They have deserted all of us alone in that deep void.

A bunch of chopped wood in a carved out place looked like it could be used for a warm fire. You grabbed a lighter from your backpack and brought it over. With a few clicks and sparks, a fire lit, spreading over their dusty grooves. It revealed an unusual room, which was burrowed out from nothing but rock. I think I recognised that from a miner's mad attempt to build his place of rest.

The knocking returned. They rattled like a stampede of cattle, panicking for their lives. You covered your ears, grinding your teeth together. You had to cough out a lot. There was no hole in the room to suck the smoke out from the fire, which instead crawled under the ceiling. Your sleeve rolled over your hand, and you used it to cough into.

Everything became thick with a lot of carbonated air, all swirled into an inhabitable zone. You spun off balance and headed for the exit. You shook on that ring so hard, it broke! The door opened on just one hinge. You escaped, leaving behind your backpack.

You rushed through the tunnel on your own. It all whirled into a continuous pathway, with your head swooning into a stronger state of dizziness. Your palms landed on the blob of rugged rock, brushed with laboured breaths. After so much running in your damp shoes, you gave up in this godforsaken environment. You dropped by the rough floor, with your mouth drooped. I saw saliva drooling down from your lips, prompting me to assume your head still throbbed in piercing pain.

Hot breaths left through your lips into an invisible heat arising from the grounds. It mixed in with the chills, upsetting your balance. Your heart raced out from varied emotions; confused and distressed. All of that sapped the warmth from your body and replaced it with numbness. Your eyes rolled around in different directions.

You lulled down to your sleep. No sight of blue, despite a few discoveries of cracks within the rock walls. Those tears were peered towards the chasms of running water, pouring through into flowing streams. Cool currents from the hills, so fresh you didn't care what parasites lie within. You could feel the cleansing, bubbling pool right in your dying dreams.

Your body struggled. You hissed at your mum and dad to get away from you, trying to flee to some odd place. You said you wanted freedom. I was only guessing from the words you have muttered in your sleep, but my overall reaction to your apparent nightmare was nothing but pity.

Knock, knock.

The knocks returned, echoing into a linear pattern. They rumbled over to a chamber, or so you thought. You tried to snooze again and rest with all the vivid colours in your mind, with grass brushing under the winds of the Cornish coast.

The knocking got worse, banging from the same spot. With your eyes popped wide open, they refused to stay closed. Your hand planted on the wall. With a gentle push, your knees lifted off the floor. A serious groan left out of your limping body.

You cried out to them to stop knocking. You begged them to just give a better sign than having to hear those piercing noises. Your feet marched through a stable path. Your joints ached after sleeping on the stone cold bed of rock.

There was light. You entered it.

I saw a steep room, with a heavenly hole of silvery clouds many feet away. So bright, your eyes constricted, which were shielded by your hand. There was foliage near to the top, with green leaves dripping with a veil of mist and smells of fresh dew. It was too far up to escape through.

You cried out to the heavens, pleading for help. No

response. You continued to shout. Some of my friends have been doing it for years, turning it into an echo chamber. I still haven't known the true nature of this place.

After a few moments, you checked around the wide room. The half landings featured a few skeletons, with their old clothes tattered and covering their broken bones. You covered your mouth, trying to push down the sickening pressure from your throat. You tried to look elsewhere for a better escape.

There were two exits out of three holes in this immense area. Which way did you arrive from? The knock came from your right. It echoed like a morse code, which you didn't recognise without any knowledge of its patterns. The next knock channeled like a stone smacking on a solid floor. It pierced through your ear drum, like a knife to your nerves.

All too much for you, I guess? You cared more about the issues of knocking than the treasures buried inside the mine. Instead of fulfilling your reason to visit that damn place, you wanted to flee from there as painlessly as possible, and you began by turning left.

You were no miner, but a spoilt freeloader longing for a get-rich scheme. Working in the mines had left workers with bruises on their hands and rashes across their entire body. A mixture of heat and mist was troublesome, which contrasted from the damp, miserable weather Cornwall had suffered for years.

Your senses have weakened, ignoring the warning signs left behind by those who tried to escape. You kept yelling out to them, demanding them to stop.

A new sound arrived. It differed from the hammering

of fists, a stream of water pouring nearby. The knocking subsided. The thrusts of cold air shot through your inner nostrils. You charged for it, stumbling on your crying feet.

You could sense the waves brushing against the rocks. The sea layered with turquoise, blue and purple. The taste of rubbery salt healing your dry throat, washing away all the scrapes off your skin. There was so much of it, we have forgotten the beauty of it.

The stream roared louder, nearing to the source of life. Oxygen surging up from the vents below like the sniff of clean seas. You could fall face flat over the water, quelling the heat from your shoulders. Those sounds were the only ones you could grasp, soothing and crashing down.

There it was, the waterfall. I'll be damned. Clear blue like the sky, the stream with clean streaks. The pacing increased as you ignored the aches in your feet, catching the cold air breezing through a wider opening. Your arms crawled to support balance, wobbled like a stick rattling through the pathway.

The knocks rumbled from behind you, like a wave of a phantom earthquake. They flew to catch up with you.

Your knee smacked on the ledge. You rolled past where the waterfall ended. You screamed out of panic and distress, where the eyes had deceived you. Your belly lobbed around like a weight, sickened by the sheer velocity of a drop.

Thud!

That sting must have been the worst pain you have ever experienced; it covered your entire bones. Your senses faded out of defeat, overwhelmed by the horrors fed within the rocky stone, dry as the bedrock of hell.

Your nerves retreated to your eyes, the last active organs in your body. They pointed to a tiny dot in the ceiling. The light at the end of the tunnel; the heavens to escape to from the constant tide of suffering. You could sense the light given from the covering clouds, offering peace to your pains.

Your breathing stopped. Strands of heavenly light vanished. The heat thinned into cold strands of ice attached to your fibres, as blessed by the mine's unforgiving environment.

Fade to black.

Botanical Microscope

by Felicity Tattersall

The gift

My heart pounded in my throat.

Overwhelmed by the unknown territories ahead. Wild poppies lightly stained my cheeks as I gazed in awe at this gift. A thing of absolute beauty; its aura made me fearful to touch it.

A pristine new microscope.

I suppressed my childish joy and embarrassed gratefulness. 'I just don't know what to say, Mr Enys.' He nodded. 'You don't know what this means to me,' I tried again, using my awkward words to convey the magnitude of his offering. Quiet smile. He knew. His hands clasped my clammy ones, squeezing them briefly with intention. The look in his eye meant, 'use it well'. Mr Enys could see the man within the boy before him and his natural benevolence wanted to expedite my journey.

I loved plants. I had wanted to be a botanist before I knew what the word 'botanist' meant. My feverish excitement was almost too much to bear. A working boy of humble origin given a chance to be a real scientist, and escape the daytime drudge in the arsenic and gun-powder works by devoting the rest of his time to the mysterious study and wonder of botany.

I was fifteen years old, itching to get out and gasp fresh air. Eager to start my new botanical cataloguing work, I would look for toadflax, wallflower cabbage, dog violet, blue starred borage, and blue eyed Mary; and all of the other plants my father had told me about. My love of plant-lore was an extension of my love for my father. But, first, I must take you back to my childhood.

Focusing mechanism

I was born in a dusty, working Cornish village into a large family with a loving mother and father in 1868. Like many within our local community, our downfall was ill health, not uncommon for our times. During the good times, fanciful elders of the village would lean wheezily on their walls, and tell whimsical stories to the youngsters playing in the new grass. They would say they believed that ants were fairies scampering through woodland glades. We would gasp and wonder, and think they were silly and then their stories would seed themselves and become cultivated in our own young minds.

It was only when I was older that I realised that this act of telling stories brought joy, solace and whimsy into their otherwise exhausted lives. Witnessing our innocent faces spark up helped them escape from their backbreaking experience at work producing copper, arsenic and gunpowder.

Eyepiece lens

Disease was never far from the village. Many ailments were common at that time and, as such, I came to note down many plants which were purported to relieve various conditions and especially eye trouble. It will become clear why.

In all truthfulness, I can't even say the medical qualities of plants are what started it. From the earliest age, I had an inexplicable preexisting fascination with plants. Their form fascinated me, there is nothing so perfect to me as the curve of the frond of a fern or the perfect symmetry of a leaf.

After I had 'the gift' in my possession, the wonder of that borrowed eye allowed me to look inside every flower. I saw the stamen, the anther, the filament, the ovary. My own weak eyes revelled in the affinity and proximity that the extension of the superior eye gave me.

*

Until one day when I saw something else. Something which can only be described as a translucent sort of wing, the venation and veins of a tiny arm and torso inside the actual flower. I pulled away, shocked and startled. No one else must ever use my microscope. It told too much truth.

Body tube

Almost as potent as my love for plants, was my rampaging illness. It started when I was just five years old. The onset was a fever. Burning feathers clawing at my throat like brambles slowly setting on fire. As the fire died back, my wrists started to ache like they were tied up with rough sailor's rope, then my ankles and knees and elbows, until it felt like the whole of me was dragged down beneath the deepest wave. I was just pain and tears and sweat. As my gentle mother nursed me I gradually ached less, but my recovery was painfully slow. The doctor said I must convalesce, which seemed to mean sitting indoors while all of my friends played games out in the fields and roamed the lanes looking for sticks. I watched them longingly as they swarmed past my window. How I longed for my body to work properly so I could play too.

It made me angry that I could hear their laughter, when there was no laughter inside me.

But I had the window, and I was grateful for it, my imperfect gateway to other worlds. I would recover and then relapse. Gradually I got used to this cycle. Inevitably with each bout of rheumatic fever I watched the children less, and the plants more.

All the shapes and hues of the different greens fascinated me. I watched their changing colours and daily struggles. I watched them bud and flower, proud of their offspring like any other parents. I saw them die back in autumn and fade to nothingness in the winter, ready to emerge the next spring as if nothing had ever happened. This endless cycle was comforting to me, because it chimed with my own cycle of wellness and illness, wellness and illness. However unwell I became, I could still observe from the confines of our lowly cottage on Higher Terrace.

Observation had always been my gift. Had I not been so sickly, I would have been out working all of the time, so my potent illness enabled my plant passion to develop. I was consumed, both body and soul.

I left school very young, and faced up to the necessity of a life of manual labour, to earn enough money for my family. Working at Bissoe and Kennall Vale works, I was exposed to extremes of heat and cold. Constant running between points, and responding to incessant demands to keep the operation flowing. But oh, those aching limbs which hardly felt like my own by the time I came home. Father was my salvation and his love (of botany) became my own love. It provided my father with the diversion he needed from the smells, noises and weights to be carried around the industrial wasteland he faced at work every day. It provided me with another world to inhabit, like those village elders telling their stories, creating new places for my imagination to roam. My stories were plant catalogues, a new kind of telling a plant's story.

To rebuild my strength after each bout of illness, I started to roam the local lanes, reclaiming nature's healing messages with each limp. As children, we knew the fields and lanes better than the backs of our own hands. Every stone in every wall, every pennywort growing in every gap where the mortar had come loose. We knew the fabric because we were a moving part within its picture. The streams became rivers in our imaginations, the leaves our umbrellas and eyepatches. We made tunnels in the long grass and constructed dens in the ferns. We knew where the daffodils would flower first and where the fox sets were, just by the smell of musk. We could sense the change in seasons just from the touch of the wind, and the silken brush of an early catkin. We were children of the air and wind and rain.

It didn't take long for creatures to enter our make believe worlds, gleefully encouraged by the village elders. My neighbour told me that a 'love lorn maiden' would dream of her future husband if she performed a ceremony on midsummer's eve, enacting the sowing and harvesting of hemp seed young ears. Ancient whispers would suggest ways in which plants would help impact upon our lives. They were all around to those who would listen. I always had ears for their stories.

*

Objective lens

Whenever I was well, I enjoyed playing with other children outside but I quickly found that I wasn't like them any more. I enjoyed their diversions, yes, but as I grew older, I started to tire that they didn't share the same intensity of feeling for plants. Over time, I started to head out of the village after work, more often alone. I would tirelessly comb the fields for specimens, meticulously organising the hedgerows in my head. Some even said I talked to the plants. Plants became my friends as the local children faded out of view.

Stage

I'm now one of those ancient voices whispering into your young ears, only I fancy you already know this story.

As a young man, on a heady day steeped with the scents of tobacco and meadowsweet, I had wandered alone up into the fields and trackways above the village. It was dry and the dust swirled like a murmuration of starlings. I could just see the china clay mountains in the distance. My forehead was burning, my eyesight blurred as perspiration stung my eyes. I lay down, my head cradled by the soft maternal grass. That is when it happened.

I can't even find the words.

Something very small discovered me. My sore eyes met its

tiny inquisitive ones. Shocked and startled, as I remembered to carry on breathing, I saw the delicate gossamer wing. With a thud, I recollected with the same shock I had had from 'the gift'. Could I be delirious or dreaming?

The fairy cooled my brow with feverfew in a very matter-of-fact manner. I slowly regained my senses. At this stage I started to notice that there were hundreds of them all around me. They drew me on my clumsy giant's legs through a mighty moss and lichen forest and a curtain of diamond waterfall, deep underground below the earth. They started to decorate me with flowers. They dangled Betony behind my ears, lodging Soapwort and Ragged Robin into the seams of my clothing. I sat stupefied in wonder. I was more flowers than man. As they worked they chattered away. I learnt their names, Toadflax, Wallflower Cabbage, Dog Violet, Blue Starred Borage, Blue Eyed Mary. I learnt their ways and customs. I was Gulliver and they my lilliputians. We spoke the same language, the language of plant-lore. They had lured me with their plants and I had spent my whole life looking for them. 'If you follow the path the plants lead you, you will find gold' the fairies told me. The floribunda festival to cement our friendship was eventually over when the last primrose was placed on my eyebrow. Regrettably they had run out of space using me as their canvas. Farewells were given and understood and I wandered back home trying to make sense of this extraordinary occurrence. I trailed my feet, flower after flower slowly dropping from my body. By the time I arrived home, my floral robes were shed. I was just man and flower no more.

*

I felt like a spent match. Of course I couldn't tell anyone what had happened. Who could I tell? With a heavy weight, I already knew that I would never rise above my family roots to become a respected botanist if I started talking about having seen fairies. So I kept (shamefully) quiet, and the poppies gave a greater crimson stain to my cheeks.

Substage mirror

The rheumatic fever returned, this time affecting my eyesight. I had little interest in anything within the material world. Without my eyesight my future was crumbling before me. Without my eyes I had nothing. I started to lose hope.

The fairies, however, had not forgotten me. Toadflax started making a night time vigil lit only by fireflies to my cottage to come into my bedroom to offer healing fairy tinctures in minute bottles. He came because he knew my roots were somehow intertwined with those of the fairies. I saw him every night and as he healed me, he shared his knowledge. He told me tales about where to find the rarest orchids, how to find the most perfect type, and variations of each plant and how to delicately cut each plant specimen. Toadflax kept repeating what the fairies had already told me, that if I followed the path the plants led me along, I would eventually reach gold. He was patient and kind and taught me all of the elements of what I now know to be botany. The more knowledge I absorbed from him, the more my eyesight improved. The second great gift perhaps: fairy-sight.

Drawer

The fairies knew that I always kept the next flower to be examined under the microscope in the little drawer at its base. So that day I opened it, as I did every few days. But something was entirely different this time, and I knew it from the first moment my eyes caught sight of the inside of the drawer. This drawer was about to make the single greatest revelation that the gifted microscope could possibly ever bestow upon me.

I heard my sharp intake of breath as I saw him. There I watched the transformation.

All of the fairies congregated around my window with their firefly torches. Toadflax, ashen faced. Lying solemnly in the drawer. Helplessly I watched him wilting. I watched transfixed. His face grew paler until it was the colour of a snowdrop. He became still. There was nothing I could do, and it pained me to see a fairy's life slipping away when they had ensured my own recovery. I had no tools to help. He had told me every aspect of plant-lore, apart from how to save a dying fairy. At the moment he died, I promised myself I would learn every bit more I could possibly learn.

And then the wider truth dawned on me as I watched Toadflax fade and transform into a flower. Lights went out all over the village as the other fairies outside the window all started to fade too, like a gushing river of sadness, until there were no more left. Outside on the road by my house there lay bodies of faded flowers.

The truth always comes too late. The flowers I had found in the hedgerows weren't fairy spells. They were fairies, wilted into the ground, they were fairy gravestones. I wasn't a plant recorder, I was memorialising the fairies.

They had given me enough knowledge to carry on their work, but imagine my utter desolation when I realised I must continue without them. Afterwards, I wandered the lanes grieving, with the sickening sense of my new understanding. Slowly the stars in the grass and jewels in the hedgerow started captivating me in a new way, singing their soothing lullabies. They chanted to me from another realm.

I could see why people thought they saw fairies in nature, particularly those who lived in towns and cities where smog and industrials spoils consumed every aspect of their lives. The reason they thought they saw fairies was because, they actually did ... see fairies.

Every time you see a flower, a fairy has died, I learned.

'If you follow the path the plants lead you towards, you will find gold,' the fairies always told me.

They were right, of course. As I grew older, I made a considerable fortune and reputation from listing and cataloguing fairy deaths. I was one of the first and most celebrated botanists of Cornwall.

As a symbol of my lifelong friendship and devotion to the fairies, I decorate myself with a wildflower in my buttonhole as a memorial. I carry a fairy with me wherever I go. I keep a fairy near my heart always.

When my study of the Flora of Cornwall was finally published, I owed my life's work and achievement to Toadflax and his kin. I was rewarded with the gold. I was grateful. But no amount of gold in the world can make up for the profound loss of the fairies.

My greatest distress is to report to you that I never saw the fairies again. It wounded me every single day. The graves could only comfort me to a point.

And so I believed that they were all gone, wiped out, lost forever and I never knew why.

Until I met you...

Time at the Bar

by Ben French

SETTING

Traditional Cornish village pub bar, Saturday night. Imagine the low beams and soft clink of glasses being set down. The log fire crackles, there's background chat and easy-listening music set low. Three pairs of drinkers prop up the bar. The barman circulates between them, serving drinks, wiping the top down and occasionally being brought into a conversation.

CAST

DENNY: *Retired builder, ex-local rugby star, big hands and no neck*

CAROL: *Miss Cornwall 1978, Denny's partner, lacks confidence, works in the village shop*

CYRIL: *Elderly gentleman, tall and slim, wears a cravat*

JACK: *Retired farmer, salt of the earth, always has a smile,*

Cyril's drinking partner
MICHELLE: *Young lady, studying, slightly frustrated with rural life, wants to move up in the world*
ROSIE: *Gardener, same age as Michelle but looks older due to her weathered complexion. Happy with her lot in life, Michelle's best friend*
JAY: *Young barman and student*

SCENE 1
(Spotlight on DENNY and CAROL. JAY is pouring a pint)

DENNY: Hey! Tom Cruise – where's that drink? C'mon ... s'not as if we got all night – gonna be Sunday in a minute!
(JAY sets the pint down, DENNY studies the picture in the froth)
Call that a shamrock? And you're at art college!
JAY: Environmental Science actu-
DENNY: And I'd like a whole pint please - should offer a flake with that!
(CAROL examines it)
CAROL: Looks more like a pasty. *(Pause)* So is Tex not comin' out for a drink? Not like him.
DENNY: I did ring him, he said it's a bit urr ... frosty up there.
CAROL: Ah, well he did stay out late last night, p'robly in the dog house. You know who wears the trousers there.
DENNY: Yeh, he said it's like Colditz. *(Glances at the top of the pint again, and says under his breath)* Looks more like your Mother...

(Long pause. Spotlight moves to CYRIL and JACK)
CYRIL: ...No Jay, the Goodies are not the same people as

Monty Python, two completely separate programmes! You can borrow them – I have them on VHS. Here endeth the lesson.

JACK: Youngsters hey?

CYRIL: Well Jack, surprisingly the old gal passed her MOT, she is vintage after all – and my Sunbeam's doing well too! (*Guffaws from CYRIL and JACK*) ...the front suspension was a bit saggy – no Jack – I know what you're going to say! (*More chortles*)

JACK: Yur Sunbeam be no good up farm – got 'oles in the track that would swallow a bus.

CYRIL: Quite. Care for another? My round. (*JAY collects their empties*) Ah thank you Jay, sherry for me, and a pint for my father here. One for yourself too. On a serious note the chap said there's a bit of corrosion underneath, I told him I keep her in the garage, only take her out on special occasions -

JACK: Yeh but whadabout yer CAR!!

(*Hysterical guffaws again, coughing fits.*)

(*Long pause. Spotlight moves to MICHELLE and ROSIE*)

MICHELLE: Steve, the other night, got to be three in the morning, (*MICHELLE hogs the crisps*) he rings the doorbell like five times, doesn't give me a chance to get downstairs -

ROSIE: What, *your* Steve? Pass the crisps.

MICHELLE: Yeh - what other Steve would it be? Anyway I open the door and he's standing there with the key in his hand, like this, pointing it at the door, swaying side to side with this stupid look on his face. He's got to buck his ideas up ... 'coz I've got plans.

ROSIE: Woz he on snakebite or somin'? Pass the crisps

Chelle.

MICHELLE: ...And then I couldn't get back to sleep 'coz I was worried about college. I get my results next week. Hey did I tell you I phoned that company in Plymouth? They seem interested.

ROSIE: Yeh you did, but no offices down 'ere? What 'bout yer Mum, what she say?

MICHELLE: Nearest branch is Plymouth, Rose, not that far away. Maybe I'll commute, or get a flat or ... not sure. I'll cross that bridge.

ROSIE: Well you'll have to cross that bridge to get into Devon girl, get your passport stamped. (*ROSIE finishes her pint and starts rummaging in her gardening bag, putting tools and gloves on the bar in an attempt to get at the bottom*) 'Nother Chelle? I think I got enough here ... got paid in apples again by Mrs Trefusis ... Two ciders please Jay, *and a pack of cheese'n onion for me...*

JAY: Sure. You look as if you've earnt it. Nice to have all that fresh air I guess...

ROSIE: Well I won't lie, sometimes in the middle of winter, and it's peeing down with rain, I sometimes dream of a cushy desk job – like what Chelle's after, all typing away with your Britney Spears headset – 'how may I facilitate your call Madam..', but nah, couldn't cope with being cooped-up like that.

JAY: What got you into gardening?

ROSIE: My older sister.

JAY: Ah how nice, so she's a gardener as well? And inspired you to follow in her footsteps?

ROSIE: No, I bleddy hated her – but footsteps come into it. When we were young we didn't get on, she was a right bee with an itch, just usual sister stuff; scrappin', head-locks, y'know - she stole my board-wax and then stole Kevin Roskear from me but before that, when we were little, I found a way to get back at her. I used to go out nice an' early, before anyone was awake, and hunt round the garden-

MICHELLE: Oh I've heard this one – and her sister still doesn't know!

ROSIE: Hunting for snails, or anythin' slimy, but usually snails as you could hear the crunch. Well, we had a small porch which was crammed with wellies and coats an' all. My sister could never work out how the snails got in, and why they favoured her wellies. Thas what I mean about the crunch. Didn't tell Mum, didn't tell anyone, only Chelle, and now you. I did it a couple of times and she started checking her boots, so I'd leave it a few months, just long enough for her to forget, and then CRUNCH I'd start doing it again. Didn't stop any arguing or fighting but I just remember her screaming from the porch – Mum used to run in thinkin' she was being murdered! I reckon it was me rooting through the flowers and bushes snail-hunting that first got me interested in gardening...

JAY: Remind me not to cross you!

ROSIE: Speaking of which Jay – c'mon take these apples, and turn 'em into cider.

(*Long pause. Lights and sound fade out*)

SCENE 2

(*Lights and sound fade in. It's a week later. Spotlight on DENNY who enters the stage, removes his coat and shakes the rain from it. He joins CAROL at the bar and pours a load of coins on the top.*)

JAY points an empty glass at him)

JAY: Raining?

DENNY: 'Liquid sunshine'. Saw plenty of it on the building site. Ever worked on a building site Jay? It's a battle I can tell you, you're battling the elements all the time – imagine halfway through pourin' a pint, then you gotta run and grab a tarp and throw it all over the bar quick as you can. Soon as you weighed it down the sun would be back out, tarp off, back to work, just like Wimbledon! Well no more of that for me. Balls to that I say! But if Eskimos know two hundred words for snow, then I can match that for rain (*DENNY notices JAY is waiting, poised*) – ah yes please Jay m'boy, and fill 'im up this time.

JAY: Actually, I've been considering signing up to this project for my gap year, it's a charity that builds schools in third-world countries.

DENNY: That'll put hairs on your chest for sure, good on ya. Now pour some liquid sunshine into that glass.

CAROL: 'Cornish sweat' Mother used to say.

DENNY: What *didn't* your Mother say? ... She not sayin' anything any more, thank God...

CAROL: What was that? And anyway, where you bin? S'pose you had a couple in the clubhouse ... a good game?

DENNY: Yeh not bad, we won, just. Stupid blimin' hooker swung for his opposite number. Back in my day a bitta handbags was all part of it, but you can't do things like that these days and expect to stay on the pitch. We all get the red mist sometimes I s'pose ... (*JAY sets down DENNY'S pint, who theatrically inspects the top, then the side, before taking a large gulp*) Ah, thas better. I remember I was playin' for 'druth – we were losing badly to Penzance and at the time they were bottom of the league. Anyway, we were losing badly, and there wasn't much time left. It seemed like the rest of my team just didn't turn up, y'know? You don't play rugby do ya Jay?

JAY: No, I run – I'm a member of the local running club, we usually meet up on Thurs-

DENNY: Pfft! – couldn't think of anythin' worse! Anyway – so I thought to myself, 'I'm not walking off with you buggers,' I was that embarrassed about the score. I thought, 'I'm definitely not walking off with you lot'. Y'know what I did? (*Pause*) Well, my job was to nail their fly-half every time he got the ball. Well I nailed him alright – I went SMACK!! (*DENNY acts out an imaginery punch to the face*) Right in his mouth I got him! SMACK, like that. Right in front of the Ref. Well I got sent off, but I thought t'myself, 'Hah – I ain't walking off with you buggers after all'. (*DENNY chuckles, then downs his drink*) Fill her up Jay, and put one in for Yoko 'ere, I'm off furra Jimmy Riddle... (*DENNY gets off the stool, grabs his knee in pain, then limps off stage*)

CAROL: That'll be it after thiz one Jay, and then you can call uz a limmo if you wouldn't mind.

(*Long pause. Spotlight moves to CYRIL and JACK*)

CYRIL: ...so you're off to see the Doctor you say?

JACK: Yeh, no, I dunno. Don't wanna cause a fuzz, besides I got too much to do! Had a problem with a calf the other day, should've asked the Vet if he 'ad any cream for me!

CYRIL: Do you mind me asking?...

JACK: Well, it's urr ... difficult to explain, urr...

CYRIL: Does Betty know?

JACK: Betty? Ha - yeh she knows alright ... it's to do with

me... (*JACK glances down to his belt area*) ... to do with me ... me ... me an' her, if you get my meanin'?

CYRIL: Oh! I see, right!

JACK: Stoopid woman asked if I gone off her. Worra silly thing to say, I said 'I bin with ya for nearly forty year!'

CYRIL: Yes, well, I shouldn't have stuck my nose in...

JACK: Less jus' say, when a Ram is no good for ... y'know ... what a Ram's menna do ... he's off to the abbatoir, quick as you could say 'roll me over, in the clover'.

CYRIL: (*Keen to change the subject*) Care for a drink Jack? I might treat myself to a sherry...

JACK: Yeh, brown-split please Jay – you know what that is? Half pint bitter, in a pint glass, with a bottle of Mann's brown ale. Just give it me by the neck and I'll pour 'im in (*JAY presents the drink, stands back, and waits for approval. JACK takes a long sip, then finally nods at JAY. Pause*) Yeh, I might go doctors, but I ain't tellin' Betty. (*Pause*) 'Course I got problems with me Land-rover too, s'off the road. The steering – ball joint – track-rod – thingummy – something like that the garage said. Piston broke too. (*JACK suddenly explodes into laughter*) HAH!! Thas me that is!! Oh yes, that jus' sums me up completely!!

CYRIL: Sorry, I don't quite follow-

JACK: Piston broke! PISTON BROKE! PIST – N – BROKE!! (*The two chaps laugh, nearly spilling their drinks, JACK has a coughing fit.*)

(*Long pause. Spotlight moves to MICHELLE and ROSIE*)

MICHELLE: ...Then I said, 'Well, do you love me?'

ROSIE: Yeh, what did he say?

MICHELLE: Well that's it – he didn't really say anything,

just gimme a weird smile and then tried to hug me. Three years I've been with him, I put up with a lot, he always seems to be out with the lads, and I'm left looking after his kids more often than not ... I don't know what I'm tryin' to say. I don't know what to do...

ROSIE: The way I see it I think you do know what to do Chelle. To be honest it sounds like - whas that song by urr ... Boyz to Men? 'End of the Road', thas it. (*ROSIE empties her glass*) 'Nother? One for the road?

MICHELLE: Yeh Rose, one for the end of the road...

(*Long pause. Lights and sound fade*)

SCENE 3

(*Lights and sound fade in. A week later. Spotlight on DENNY and CAROL mid-argument*)

CAROL: Excuse me! I'm stone - cold - sober I am!

DENNY: Stone cold sober when you walked in woman!

CAROL: Las' weekend I want feelin' too well, and besides, it's Satday night-

DENNY: Jus' sayin – if ya can't handle it then have a shandy or somin'. Fill it up Jay, an' better get one for 'er as well. Tex might be in later, he owes me a pint – I covered for 'im the other night – told his missus he was with me playin' backgammon. He was playin' a different type of backgammon...

(*CAROL starts to sway and dance*)

CAROL: ...Ooh, I like this one. Turn it up Jay! Reminds me of the seventies...

DENNY: Eighteen seventies...

(*Pause*)

CAROL: Why do they call him Tex?

DENNY: Tex? The 'Texas Longhorn'? Well urr … it's a rugby thing…

CAROL: He ain't American.

DENNY: Right – gonna' water the hanging basket.

(*DENNY exits stage*)

CAROL: Saw you out runnin' today Jay.

JAY: Oldest form of transport. (*JAY lowers his tone a bit*) Can I ask you something? Why have you never learnt to drive?

CAROL: Well … and this is 'tween me an' you… (*tapping her nose and leaning forward*) If you can't drive, then you can't get done for drink-driving. That's the sorry truth. But this is 'tween me an' you, right? I don't want him to know how bad … you know wot I mean?

JAY: Sure

CAROL: I 'ate the way he takes the mickey, 'specially when I've had a drink. Y'know wot I mean? He can be a bit of a bully. Do urr … you think I gotta problem?

JAY: Well you're not recommended to drink more than fourteen units per week … but it's down to the individual, you know - whatever you're comfortable with, and whatever your body is fine with. We're all adults.

CAROL: Thanks Jay, not everyone sees it like that. Now my first husband, Tony – don't s'pose you met him, he died in ninety-one…

JAY: I was born in two thousand and two … in Derbyshire –

CAROL: …was a fair bit older than me. Now he was a secret drinker, if y'know what I mean, except everyone knew. I think it damaged his pride, and he was a very proud man. And a gentleman – he would always drive and always got out to hold the door open for me, things like that. One of the reasons I never learnt to drive – he always said I look prettier in the passenger seat. I did ask him to teach me but... (*CAROL takes a sip*) 'Course he wasn't always a gentleman. Depends on what he drank – if it was whiskey then I had to watch wot I said, y'know what I mean? He had a white Jaguar...

JAY: I generally walk, or take the bus, but it's never too late to learn Carol.

CAROL: No ... I don't think so, I don't think I could do it... (*DENNY rejoins the bar.*)

(*Long pause. Spotlight moves to CYRIL and JACK*)

JACK: Think I'll 'ave a brown-split please Jay. S'pose you want a sherry...

CYRIL: Fancy a glass of wine actually. What wine have you got Jay?

JAY: (*Checks the shelf behind him, then says with a smirk*) We have red ... *and* white...

CYRIL: Oh very droll ... do you have any Chilean?

JACK: He's too young for kids!!

JAY: You two - it's like serving drinks to a couple of comedians-

CYRIL: What, like Tommy Cooper, and Ken Dodd?

JACK: Except we don't wear silly hats

CYRIL: And we pay our taxes - well one of us does... (*sniggers and chortles from CYRIL and JACK*) I'll just stick to a sherry. (*JAY sets the drinks down, JACK takes a long, noisy slurp*)

JACK: Well, I urr ... did go an' see the doctor.

CYRIL: Ah excellent, everything ... tickety-boo?

JACK: Well, he gimme some of these 'ere special pills...

CYRIL: Oh right!

JACK: Yeh – you could say everythin's on the up, if ya get my meanin'!

CYRIL: Well that's jolly good news indeed! I'll drink to that! (*CYRIL changes the subject*) What do you drive Jay? Bet a young flash like you has a GTI or something like that ... bit of backseat bingo ... burning the clutch waiting for the lights to go green, that sort of hi-jinx – hey?

JAY: I don't drive, I walk or catch the bus - trying to do my bit for the environment. You're probably fed up with us youngsters going on about it, but it's important to me.

CYRIL: Admirable

JAY: Yeh I try and only eat local produce wherever possible-

JACK: I got a chicken for ya if you want – I only live up the lane!

JAY: Thanks but I don't eat meat-

JACK: No meat? Well thas up to you, all the more for us...

CYRIL: Ooh, no meat ... that would mean no liver and onion

JACK: No bangers n' mash

CYRIL: No fried kippers on a Sunday morning...

CYRIL/JACK: No ... no ... PASTIES!!

(*They shake their heads in dismay and look at JAY pitifully.*)

(*Long pause. Spotlight moves to MICHELLE and ROSIE*)

ROSIE: As I said Chelle – you can stay as long as you want, s'no bother.

MICHELLE: Thanks, but I don't want to be a burden. It's only for a few weeks, then I'm up to my Aunt's.

ROSIE: The one that lives just outside of Plymouth?

MICHELLE: Yeh that's right. If I get that job then I can stay with her for a while before I settle somewhere, too far to commute. Hey, you could always come up and flat-share – plenty of gardens up there for you I reckon!

ROSIE: Maybe... (*MICHELLE and ROSIE share a bag of crisps*) So, what about Steve then – kicked 'im into touch at last?

MICHELLE: Oh yeh – kicked him out of the park Rose!

(*Long pause. Spotlight moves to DENNY mid-anecdote*)

DENNY: ...and then I kicked 'im into touch. Then Tex, Cap'n at the time, said, 'You stupid flanker!' Or words to that effect, 'forwards don't kick the ball!' He was gettin' on my nerves, too big for 'is boots. An' I said 'Well I could always kick you instead!' - and I did too!!

(*DENNY laughing, acts out a comical, swinging kick*) Jus' like that! I got him! Well, I was on the bench the week after, but it was worth it. 'Course we're all friends now, but good times... (*Pause*) Fill 'em up Jay! – I'm off to shake 'ands with the Vicar... (*DENNY exits stage, chuckling to himself*)

(*JAY pours the two drinks, checks his watch, then rings the brass bell above his head*)

JAY: Right – that's Time at the bar!!

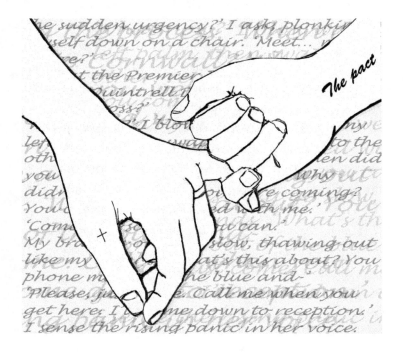

The Pact

by Angela Linney

Collecting wood from the log store at the bottom of the garden is not one of my favourite chores. The sky is clear blue above me, but snow clouds sit in the distance. It's a sharp, chilly morning and smoke dances out of the chimneys across the village. It's a comforting sight as I make my way back to the cottage.

As I step onto the porch, the solo violin, beginning the orchestral arrangement of Poldark's theme tune, alerts me. I shudder and drop the logs into the worn wicker basket, which creaks its protest. I yank off my boots, almost tripping over, and rush inside to grab the handset lying upon the old farmhouse table.

'Hello,' I puff, not registering the caller's identity, wondering if it's another nuisance call, selling something or other.

'Tank God, you kept the same number. I'm after just

changing mine. Look, I need to see you.'

'Bernie?'

'We've to meet... urgently.'

'What's wrong? I've not heard from you in ages, Bernie... years even. Why the sudden urgency?' I ask, plonking myself down on a chair. 'Meet... meet where?'

'I'm at the Premier Inn, in a place called Quintrell Downs. Would you come across?'

'What now?' I blow warm air into my left palm, then swap the handset to the other, repeating the process. 'When did you come down to Cornwall? Why didn't you tell me you were coming? You could have stayed with me.'

'Come... as soon as you can.'

My brain is on a go slow, thawing out like my hands. 'What's this about? You phone me out of the blue and-'

'Please, just come. Call me when you get here. I'll come down to reception.'

I sense the rising panic in her voice.

'Are you in trouble?'

'I'll explain then.'

'Bernie, you can't expect me to just drop everything.' Not that I'm busy. My life isn't exactly full. In fact, my only company these days is Elliott, my rescue cat. 'At least give me a clue.' Why this sudden demand? Birmingham is miles away; a distant memory for me. My addled brain suddenly gifts me a plausible explanation. 'You're not hurt, are you? Has Brendan done something?'

'No, like I said, I'll explain when you come.'

'I'm worried now. If you're not in trouble, and you're not hurt, then what's this about?'

'The Pact.'

The line disconnects, and I sit in stunned silence, forgetting the chill penetrating my bones. My task of building a fire is a distant memory. I rise and fill the kettle while trying to process the last few minutes and set about making myself a coffee. The hot comforting mug thaws my hands as I stare unseeingly into space.

The Pact... We've carried the secret for as long as I remember.

My brain is swarming with questions. What has brought this up? The pact was years ago, and my lips remained sealed. As for Bernie, hers, too. After all, she's the one who has everything to lose.

An hour later, I'm in Newquay, entering the hotel's reception through the automatic doors. Bernie is already waiting, scanning tourism leaflets. She turns on my approach.

'You don't look too good,' I blurt without thinking. Her face is pinched, and the pallor has nothing to do with her natural Irish skin tone.

'Well tanks, Tish. Say it as it is, why don't you.'

I haven't heard that name in years; I'm Patricia in Cornwall.

'Sorry, Bernie. I didn't mean to... it's good to see you.' A need to hug her fills me, like old times, but I hold back.

'I know. Well, you look great anyhow, all nutty brown and tanned, and in winter, too. Anyone would tink you were Cornish.'

'I'll always be an Emmet.'

'A what?' Bernie's brow creases, adding emphasis to her ageing features. The years haven't been kind to her.

'An Emmet. That's what the Cornish call us if you are non-Cornish. They use other names, too, like grockles and incomers, and woe betide you if you're from Devon.'

'That's divisive, considering it's the same country.' Bernie's eyebrows meet in a frown. 'Sure, it couldn't be as bad as when we moved over from Dublin? I prefer to forget those times. If not for the kindness of the church, well.'

'Gosh, no! In fact, there are loads of incomers down here,' I tell her, miming inverted commas in the air. 'I think they're getting used to us. There's quite a few Brummies, Mancs and Londoners down here. Mind you, some locals still grumble about the visitors, despite needing the revenue. Still, I understand now I live here,' I say, retrieving keys from my pocket. 'Come on, my car's outside, I'll drive us to the beach, and we can have a stroll if you'd like.'

Her lips curl into a smile. 'That would be nice.'

It is a quiet journey to Porth; the roads don't have the high volume of vehicles out of season. Bernie takes in the view, chatting only catch-up talk. After a ten-minute ride, I drive into the car park of the Mermaid Inn and we get out, slipping on hats and gloves. I pull up the collar of my Regatta and turn my back on the strong sea breeze.

'Fresh, isn't it?' The wind blows hair strands across my lips as I speak. I tuck them beneath my hat. 'Good for blowing the cobwebs away, though.'

'Ah, it's much colder back home. We've-' Bernie flinches mid-sentence as a cheeky seagull swoops down beside her. He lands on one of the pub's outdoor tables next to the car park and gobbles up leftovers from a plate. 'Gosh, he made me jump out me skin! Would you look at him with them chips? What a gannet.'

I chuckle. 'You should have seen your face!'

She grins. 'As I was saying, we've had snow. I worried about the drive and all, but sure it was fine, until I reached the moor at least.'

'Bodmin's beautiful, whatever the weather, though it can be bleak.'

Winter is my favourite time of the year in Cornwall. The beaches hold mainly dog walkers and surfers. To walk across the sand, without dodging dozens of people sitting behind windbreakers, is a rare treat, and one I cherish. The serenity nurtures my soul. Tasting the salt upon my lips, and watching the ebb and flow of the tides, gives me pleasure. I will never leave Cornwall.

As we walk, the crosswind bites, whipping up grains of sand. I steal a sidelong glance at Bernie. She's disturbed. Bernie isn't one to stress over problems, so this must be bad. Why else would she arrive here unannounced? I still can't get my head around it. She stares ahead, focusing on the sea. The tip of her nose and her cheeks have already turned pink.

'Beautiful, isn't it? You're lucky to live here. Just the place to escape.' I watch breath clouds leave her lips as she speaks.

'Escape?' She hasn't mentioned the phone call, or our pact and I want her to volunteer the information. I don't see what good it will do to press her. I need to tread with care.

'He came to see me.'

I stop in my tracks.

'Who?'

'You know who.' Bernie stares at the sand and her foot plays with a clump of seaweed.

'Are you talking about Dermot?' I step in front of her and tilt my head to gain her attention.

'Yes, Dermot, who else?'

'After all this time? Why?'

'Because... because of Finn.'

Her eyes brim, and it isn't from the biting wind.

'Come on, let's get warm and we can chat about it over a hot chocolate.' I link her arm, and we make our way back to the car in silence.

I drive to Lewinnick Lodge on Pentire Headland; one of my favourite places. At the bar, I order drinks, then choose comfy seats near the crackling log fire, and adjust my chair to gaze out of the floor-to-ceiling glass window.

'What a stunning view,' Bernie says, looking out across the Atlantic. She turns and gives me the first genuine smile since her arrival.

'What?'

'You have cream on your nose.'

Laughing, I pick up the serviette from my saucer and dab my face. Bernie leans forward and spoons marshmallows into her mouth.

I nod at the spoon. 'Since when were you such a lady?'

'I'm savouring the treat. It reminds me of when we were kids and I stayed at yours. Your mammy would froth up hot chocolate with a whisk and add white chocolate shavings on top. Mmm.'

It draws wonderful memories. A snapshot of my mother, standing over the stove, pouring milk from a glass pint bottle into a saucepan that sat over a small flame. She had her own unique ways of making our stay-overs a special treat. Bernie's home lacked such comforts. She was one of ten children who lived hand to mouth. Her father's taste for Guinness didn't help.

'Where have all the years gone?'

'Oh, to be a child again.' Bernie sighs. 'You were the sensible one, though. I remember you having private bible lessons from a Jehovah's witness and your Da had a fit!' Another smile. 'Your curiosity got you in big trouble, but brave to explore your faith so young.'

'I remember. He chased the poor woman out of the house, and he marched me straight to confession.'

'At least your Da took notice. D'ya still go to mass?'

'Not for a long time.' I realise church worship for me belongs to the past. I lost my faith years ago, along with my parents. And, thanks to the headline news of the car accident, I can never banish the distressing image from my mind. I seldom step inside a church these days, aside from weddings and funerals. 'How about you?'

'Well, I can hardly say I'm a good Catholic now, can I?'

Her mood changes, her expression now sombre.

'Bernie, isn't it about time you stopped punishing yourself? It's the past and-'

'The past's come back to haunt me, Tish,' she says, staring hard into my eyes. 'I don't have to punish myself because I'm being punished... by God. And now Finn will be, too, and it's not his fault. None of this is his fault.' She turns, pushes her drink aside, and folds her arms across her chest.

'You're not making sense. Punished? How?'

'Dermot heard Finn was getting married, so he came to see me. Just turned up. I was shocked.'

'Married? Already? Time flies. But what's this have to do with Dermot? Has Finn asked for Dermot to marry them? Oh God, no!' I hear a sharp breath being drawn in and stifle my mouth with my hand. 'That will be so awkward.' I realise I can't be at Finn's wedding, and sorrow sinks into my stomach. My barren womb means I can only ever experience godmother status, anyway.

'If only it was as simple.'

My pulse steps up its pace as I wait for her to continue. I remain silent, giving her the space to talk, stifling the urgency of my questions. I watch Bernie's thumb twisting her wedding ring around her finger. She catches my gaze and stops, setting her hands in her lap.

'Brendan was out when he came - tank the Lord for small mercies. But Finn was home, and he called over my shoulder at the door, "Hello Father Dermot. Will I get the kettle on?" I was speechless. "Come on inside, out of the cold," he said, and he did.'

'Oh no!'

'He has his eyes, you know. Every time I look at Finn's eyes, I'm reminded of Dermot.' She drifts into private thoughts; thoughts obviously tormenting her. 'Why was I so foolish?'

I reach out and stroke her hand. 'He was supposed to be a man of God.'

'And I was married! It was my fault.'

'It's deceit.'

'And what about the rest of this? We're all guilty of deceit, even you!'

She's right. I can't argue, but my reasoning is to protect the innocent.

'Dermot helped me through some dark moments, and you know what living with Brendan was like - though that's no excuse. I wonder why he doesn't take his bed to that pub; spends most of his time there. He's just like me Da.'

'He hasn't changed then?'

Her deep sigh reflects her defeat.

'He's worse than ever.' Bernie shakes her head and stares at the fire, her eyes fixed upon the dancing flames as she continues to speak. 'Dermot lifted my spirit. He would come into the kitchen while I prepared supper for the priests. Dermot never judged. He was kind, a good listener... my saviour. I didn't believe for one moment I would fall for a man about to take a vow of celibacy.'

'Regardless, he was a man of the cloth, and he took advantage of you. He should never have taken his vows after that.' I swallow down my frustration, not wanting to get into a dispute. Not this time, not now we are reunited.

She turns and faces me with wide eyes. 'He was in placement, not ordained,' she says, making excuses for him. 'Don't persecute him! Don't you think he suffered, too? Tormented, questioning his faith? None of us expected it. It just happened. It shouldn't have, but it did. And then... and then we moved on with our destined lives... loveless lives to serve others.'

Her tone sounds despondent. And who am I to question? I got divorced, and divorce was forbidden.

Get off your high horse!

'So, what happened?'

'We couldn't talk because Finn was there. But I

noticed Dermot's hand shaking when he lifted his cup, and when he walked to the door on his way out, he seemed to struggle a bit.'

My heart jolts. 'Is he ill?'

'You should see him, Tish.'

'Let's not go there.'

'He's your brother!'

'He gave up that title when he made you pregnant.' All my past hurts bubble to the surface and my barriers are up. My brother no longer exists to me. But fear dries up my mouth. Fear of impending doom. Is this the reason she has come, trying to reunite us? 'Carry on, what happened?'

'He asked me to meet him. Said it was important. I tried to protest, and he pleaded, so I agreed.'

'And?' I lean forward, hungry for the answer, yet apprehensive at the same time.

'He told me we have to tell Finn that he is his father.'

'No way! You can't! Not after all this time. It will destroy him!' I glance around and lower my voice, despite there only being a few customers sitting at distant tables. 'When you confided in me, we agreed on a pact that only we would ever know. You're not going to, are you?'

Her silence answers my question.

'And what about Brendan? Have you considered the implications? My God, Bernie, you can't. They'll never forgive you!'

'Like you've never forgiven us, d'you mean? Because you never have, have you?'

Resentment sits behind her steel eyes, and I feel ashamed. In truth, I've missed having Bernie and Finn in my life. I can't say the same about Brendan, and I don't know if I'll ever forgive Dermot. His sins have torn us apart, and I'm thankful our parents weren't alive to witness his immorality.

'I'm sorry. I never meant to shut you out, too. I guess my pride has robbed me.'

'It's not too late to make amends.'

'Why now, after all this time? There's too much water under the bridge. And why tell Finn?'

'Because I have no choice, Tish. Finn has to know.'

'But why?'

She draws a deep breath and sighs, the heavy burden clear in her body language. Something has changed. Still, I see no reason to reveal the truth. Not ever.

'Please, just tell me.'

Bernie swallows and bites her lip as tears threaten, causing my stomach to churn with anticipatory dread.

'Dermot has motor neurone disease.'

'What? What does that mean? Is it genetic or something? Is Dermot going to die? I... I don't understand.'

'I'm sorry, Tish. Dermot carries the gene that makes it possible, yes,' she tells me in almost a whisper. 'I'm so sorry, Tish. I'm sorry for us all.' Her shoulders hunch up, and she bows her head, struggling to hold back the tidal force of grief.

Her words have stunned me into silence and shock reverberates through me. Time stills along with my body until I feel my jaw drop in disbelief. Would this be my fate, too? I battle with internal terror. I can find no voice. Instead, I cover Bernie's trembling hand with my palm, willing the loud thudding of my heart to stop.

I suppress my fear; for now, at least, because Bernie

needs me, and I have an overwhelming instinct to support them all. So, I force back my devastating grief for the sake of them all. We will get through this cruel blow of fate, somehow ... together.

The Cabin

by Anita D Hunt

Aimee walked past the bus driver, found a double seat that was unoccupied and dropped down onto it. Holding her school bag on her lap, she put her headphones in her ears and pressed play on the app on her mobile phone. The banter on the school bus annoyed her. The boys seemed to think it was the perfect time to let off all that pent up energy they had been holding onto all through the long afternoon sitting behind their desks, listening to their teachers droning on.

'Oi! Catch!'

Aimee ducked and turned to watch a brown half-eaten apple core sail past her towards the back of the bus. The target of the throw wasn't quick enough to react and the core slapped into his shoulder before bouncing off and dropping to the floor. He tried to wipe it away but only managed to make it worse.

'What d'ya do that for?' he yelled, as the first boy started to laugh and perform a series of chopping actions with his hands.

'Ha, ha, you need to work on your ninja reactions. Hi-ya!'

Aimee increased the volume of her music to drown out their voices and turned to face the window, absentmindedly fiddling with the piskie keyring that dangled from the zip of her bag. The school car park was filled with teenagers, all laughing and joking, discussing the latest gossip and their plans for the evening as they made their way onto the waiting transport. Aimee had been that carefree once, chatting with her mates and making plans for the weekend. Trips into town for window shopping and a McDonald's for lunch. She couldn't do any of that anymore. She had grown up quicker than her friends and the juvenile boys that surrounded her. There was more reason to be wary, keep her wits about her.

Her stop was one of the last ones on the route. A walk up the long, rutted path led to a large clearing which had individual paths leading off it to the garages, the house and the woods. Slowly, she turned towards the house and took a deep breath as she tried to gather the courage to go inside. She wished she didn't have to go in yet, wished there was something, anything that she could do apart from having to go in there.

The house looked as cold as she felt. In the mizzle and the fading February light, the windows were dark and foreboding. She knew she wouldn't find any comfort inside. Mum wouldn't be home for a couple of hours and her father's form of comfort wasn't the kind she wanted.

A small flash of light caught Aimee's eye and she turned again to see where it came from. Another light multiplied into two and then four. Dancing fireflies began to cavort along the path, away from the house and into the wood. Intrigued, Aimee followed them. Turning her music off, she pulled the headphones from her ears and heard the whistling of the breeze through the foliage.

The fireflies turned down a smaller path. Their movements alternated between flying towards her and then darting away, encouraging her to follow like Lassie did in those old films she loved to watch, snuggled up on the sofa with Mum. It was a habit from childhood that had continued into her teenage years, she hoped it would continue as she got older too. Just the two of them, watching old movies in front of the fire.

Ducking her head, she pushed her way through the tangled undergrowth. More sparkling orbs joined the throng until a myriad of shining lights coalesced, almost blinding her with their brightness. She raised her hand to shield her eyes and tiny pinpoints of pressure gently pushed it away, pulsating and warming her hand as they supported it to point her forward. The orbs were surrounding her, moving behind her and urging her to continue where they led.

The path gradually opened out into a clearing. An old wooden cabin with a weather-beaten pitched roof and a lop-sided chimney stood forlornly in the centre, surrounded by patches of muddy puddles and yellow-topped gorse. It reminded her of the large Wendy house her father had built for her in the garden when she was little. Before it became her teenage hang out and he came in there with her and ruined it. Shaking her head, she turned back to look at the path behind her, wondering why she had never noticed it before. It looked well-trodden and it led directly from her home, yet this was all new to her.

The memories of the Wendy house rose in her mind. She didn't want to think of that. She never liked to think of that. She didn't like the Wendy house anymore.

Some of the lights swarmed to the path, blocking her way and then started to float towards her, pushing her forward through the cabin's open door.

I should be scared, she thought, but the warmth that was emanating around her settled her wariness. The room was barely furnished, the windows barred against the outside world by haphazard planks nailed where the panes should have been. Several rust-spattered mirrors lined the walls while a small square wooden table and a solitary hardback chair were placed along the far wall next to an old, battered wood burner. The door of the fire hung limply from the one remaining hinge revealing the unlit ashes inside, and yet heat still radiated from it. The scent of woodsmoke hung in the air and she sniffed appreciatively. A dirty threadbare rug lay forlornly in the middle of the floor. Relics of someone's attempt to make the room seem homelier, now abandoned to the mice who'd nibbled holes in the fabric to line their own tiny beds.

Aimee dropped her coat and bag on the table, no longer feeling the chill of the late afternoon. The soft metallic click of the battered door closing behind her seeming incongruent with its surroundings, making her feel safer than she had for months.

Music slowly filled the space around her as the orbs

restarted their dance. The melody continued; white lights shone while the dancing pulsated in time to the beat. Pure voices echoed from the centre of each sphere and entered her soul.

Her feet began to move. Swaying in time to the music she lost herself in the haunting harmonies and the twirling, flickering stars that were all around her. She was freer than she had been since those early days in the Wendy house when life wasn't as complicated as it was now. When she had loved her father, not feared him.

The lights began to glow. The music grew louder, words became clearer, faces began to appear. Tiny replicas of those she saw in her dreams when she needed to escape the pain. Blue eyes shone into hers, miniscule noses and cherry red lips mouthed the words she danced to. Bodies appeared, then arms and legs, multicoloured, shimmering dresses flowing around them. Hands reaching out to each other as they formed a circle around her.

The kaleidoscope of colour merged into one. Gossamer thin wings appeared, fluttering, continuing their merry-go-round jitterbug with Aimee at its axis, laughing and throwing her hands above her head in free abandon, spinning and dancing, round and round.

The fairies stopped.

Stood still as one. Only their wings subtly moving to keep them in flight. In the silence she heard the crunch of a footstep breaking a rotten twig. One of the fairies held her forefinger to her lips.

'What? Where did this come from? Aimee! Aimee! Where the hell are you?'

His voice stilled her. Fear took hold in the pit of her

stomach, dispelling her joy. She broke out of the circle and shrank back against the wall. Sliding down to form a ball and holding her knees tight within her folded arms. Ethereal fingers entwined with hers. Opening her eyes, she saw a fairy holding her right hand. Another reached out for the left. More came, forming a semi-circle in front of her, guarding her. She watched in silence as the rest flew to the door. They came together, wings touching to form a barrier that shone so bright she was sure it could be seen for miles around.

'You'd better get out here girl, it'll be worse if you hide!'

The footsteps came closer, stopping at the door. The handle rattled. She bit back a scream as she saw it move. Tiny hands crossed over the metal latch, holding it firm. She jumped as his thump on the door shook the wood, but it held firm.

'Aimee!'

His footsteps crunched around the building, thumping the walls as he went, trying to find a way in, his voice shouting her name. There was a loud thud followed by a string of curse words as he slid about in the mud. The thumping on the ramshackle wood was harder and louder but the slats held firm, never budging from the rusty nails that held them there. The fairies' calming hands helping to blunt the shards of fear that pierced her heart.

They raised their arms towards the walls and Aimee heard a new song, a high-pitched reverberation which seemed to make the air shimmer around her. Slowly, the mirrors began to brighten and clear. A circle of light formed in the centre of each one, slowly revealing the clearing outside and the woods beyond. She saw her father in the largest window, his face puce with rage as he made his way up and down the building.

A figure emerged from the trees, as fantastical as the fairies who surrounded her. He was just a couple of feet tall with a brown leather waistcoat, beige britches, a felted woollen hat perched between unmistakable pointed ears. She tensed and started to shrink back against the wall again, but the fairies continued to hold her safe and calm her nerves, whispering and nodding that she had nothing to be scared of. He smiled at her and placed his finger to his lips in the age-old sign for silence.

The piskie picked up a fallen branch and, as her father continued to make his way along the wall, his concentration focused on thumping the wood, the tiny being poked the stick in front of her father's foot, tripping him neatly to the floor.

'What the...?'

His words were cut off as he became surrounded by seven more of the piskies who arrived in a flurry of different coloured waistcoats: blue, red, yellow, green, black, orange and purple and carrying old gnarled sticks with bulbous ends. They seemed to be dancing around her father while he twisted and turned, unable to raise himself from the floor although nothing appeared to be holding him down. She walked closer to the mirrored wall and watched breathlessly as the curious performance continued. Red coat would move in, Blue coat would come in from the other side to meet him and they would raise their sticks, clashing them together above the writhing body. As Red coat moved back Yellow coat would make his move towards the man and Green coat opposite would come in to meet him, repeating the actions of their brethren. The eight beings acted in unison like a bizarre cross between Morris dancing and a Mexican wave.

Black coat stopped. He raised his stick above her father's head while all the other piskies stood still, watching intently as the sound of the wind intensified. Aimee could hear it howling around the cabin, yet the leaves of the trees were motionless, as still as on the sunniest high summer day. She felt a gentle breeze across her cheek as the fairies flew closer, their wings causing her fringe to flutter and she raised her hand to sweep it back out of her eyes and tuck it behind her ear. A pure soprano began to echo around the room as the piskies held still, her father motionless, seemingly unable to move or utter a sound.

'The piskies' dance has one last beat,
Their revenge almost accomplished.
The end however is yours to choose,
Your heart's desire, executed.'

Aimee looked from the fairies to her father and then to the piskies. Black coat looked up and held her gaze as she wrestled with the decision, she knew she had to make. Images of the Wendy house whirled around her mind, the atrocities he had subjected her to inside its brightly painted walls. Memories of touches where she didn't want him to touch, words she didn't want to hear and secrets she didn't want to keep but was too scared to utter for fear of his painful retaliation. She tugged her cardigan tighter around her chest and her skirt straighter to cover her knees. The shame of her developing body always uppermost whenever he was around. It was her fault. All her fault.

She closed her eyes as Black coat brought the stick down, slowly encircling her father's head with its tip. The other piskies began to move again, running their sticks over his body barely an inch from his clothing but, not quite touching. A shimmering light emanated from them, joining to form a silvery haze that slowly grew and encompassed the body of the man on the floor.

A flash made her jolt back in alarm and she covered her eyes, not wanting to see anymore, and yet, she knew she had to see what they had done to him, what his punishment would be. As the piskies started to move back from the body, she let out the breath she didn't realise she had been holding as she saw him take a ragged gasp. He started trying to sit up, but, although he could move his arms, his legs were immobile. She heard him shout as he raised his hands and rubbed his eyes, heard him shout that he couldn't see, couldn't move. Heard him begging for help, for someone to do something.

> 'No more is he able to cause you harm,
> The piskies have served your sentence.
> His death would have been too easy,
> To suffer will be his penance.'

*

Climbing on the school bus, Aimee found her usual seat and plonked herself down upon it. Turning, she beckoned for her best friend, Jackie, to sit beside her.

'So, jam or cream first?' Aimee asked.

'What a stupid question, we're Cornish aren't we? It's gotta be jam first!' Jackie replied and laughed.

'That's alright then, Mum'll love you as much as I do when you say that to her. She's been baking the scones today, so they'll still be warm when we get home.'

'Perfect, I'm so looking forward to our sleepover tonight. Are you sure it's ok with your dad the way he is?'

'Oh, don't worry,' Aimee replied, 'We can have an all-girls night watching old films. We've got *Lassie* if you fancy it?'

'As long as you don't mind when I cry? I love that film.'

Aimee absentmindedly twiddled the piskie keyring, dangling from the bag zip.

'That's fine. I don't mind anything anymore.'

Aimee never visited him in the nursing home.

Nobody believed his stories about piskies attacking him.

They thought he had fallen from a tree and broken his back.

They thought the fall had caused his blindness.

They thought he had received such a blow to the head that his mental capacity could never be recovered.

They thought he was delusional and the hallucinations and disabilities meant he could never live at home again.

But Aimee knew the truth.

And it made Aimee smile.

Moonshard

by Stephen Baird

Nan's Cornish cottage seemed smaller than I remembered. Four years is a long time and Nan's hug was tight as ever. I had to steel myself. At fifteen, I wanted to show that I was in control. I wasn't. My world was shattered and I was broken and empty.

Dad had had his big plans to be the next big 'something' in London and I was taken along as a scrawny eleven-year-old with a reedy voice and somebody else's hairstyle choice. I'd felt unimportant, like an object that you don't particularly want but take with you anyway. London was tough, but I eventually began to feel the person I wanted to be. And now I was back where I'd never wanted to leave, uprooted again. I had left Cornwall angry and I was angry with my parents still. I was ashamed that I felt like this, because they had gone forever and nothing could bring them back. But the anger still boiled.

Nan showed me to the spare bedroom with its twin beds, mine for the next few months at least, while all the legal issues were sorted. Adults making my decisions again. I'd never slept here before. Why would I when we'd lived so close in the village for all those years? It felt odd.

This had been my favourite place on earth, my Cornish village by the sea that didn't get too busy in the summer because it was overlooked, wedged between two honeypot tourist centres. I'd loved that. I felt it belonged to me. I told myself I didn't care what I would find when I came back, but it wasn't true.

Jen would be in the village, of course. Jen. I hadn't understood about soulmates back then but now I recognised the deep friendship we'd shared. She could help me through all this mess but, if she didn't want to see me ever again, I wouldn't blame her. It was my fault we'd parted badly and not spoken since. I think I was pretending to be my dad. Trash it all. Burn bridges. Trouble is, a kid of eleven doesn't get what that means. I hurt Jen. I knew I was doing it and had gone ahead anyway. Our bond had been unbreakable, but I proved that wrong.

I decided to go out and clear my head. I was tired and didn't want to chat with Nan in case I became angry. Awkward silences would be as bad. Did I hope I might see Jen? Possibly. But I didn't feel ready for that. Not yet.

As soon as I stepped through the gate and onto the road, I knew where I was going. I wanted to be somewhere that was special to Jen and me. She might feel differently about it now, but it would still mean a lot to me.

I passed our old cottage. Most of the lights were on as if to prove people lived there, in case I wanted it back.

I didn't. It wasn't my home. Not now. Turning left after the old church, I headed down Beach Road. It was better being out. The summer evening was warm with a gentle breeze carrying the tang of salt. I inhaled, then blew out heavily. Tears weren't far away again, and I didn't want to be seen looking like the gibbering wreck of someone nearer boyhood than manhood – as if that mattered. My mind was just messed up with everything and my place in it.

At the end of the road, I branched right, away from the main beach and towards the little-known cove. The locals' cove. Darkness was falling all around me but, so long as I took the path down to the cove and didn't stray onto the old cliff path where the dangers of the mineshafts were, I'd be fine. Unless something had changed. I doubted that. Things never changed much around here.

I heard the sea before I saw it and listened to the rhythmic sound I'd so longed to hear again. Jen and I had loved it. Listening with only smiles shared between us in the silences. Could we get back to that? I remembered this beach as magical. I needed some magic now. For my anger. My helplessness. Something flickered in my heart. This was a beautiful evening, so beautiful I could almost believe anything could happen.

The sound of the sea was the same, the outlines of the rocks were the same, the beach was the same. Everything was the same, except it wasn't. Some of my happiest times had been here but, at this moment, happiness was for others. Not me. Not anymore. That's a stage of grief, they would tell you.

The moon had dusted everything with silver. I loved

nights like these. A movement caught my eye and I watched the shooting star sweep down across the sky. I hadn't seen one of those since I left Cornwall. London has light, lots of it, but not from stars.

I stopped. Something was different. Something new on the beach.

Curious, I wandered nearer. It looked like a cross, a silver cross, stuck upright in the sand near to where the water's edge flowed gently to and fro. I narrowed my eyes. It was not a dissimilar height to me and – I froze. It was a person.

He had his arms held out at right angles from his body like a crucifixion. As I approached, he remained motionless, staring out to sea. The moonlight had washed his body silver like everything else. The fact he wore not a stitch of clothing was less of a surprise than the fact he was here at all, caught in some moment of wonder. All silvered. Like a piece broken off the moon.

I felt calm, almost enchanted. My brain told me not to get involved and creep away before I was noticed. But my heart drew me to stay and be part of this scene. This moment. I wanted to prolong the magic, not break it. I could think of nothing to say, so I sat down and scanned the cove slowly from right to left and back again. What on earth was I doing? I had no answer and I didn't care. I felt peaceful for the first time since they came to tell me about the crash.

As my eyes returned, I saw he'd turned and was facing me. He seemed my age, maybe a bit younger. Maybe older. It was difficult to tell. My mouth felt dry. He was beautiful. Not like I was attracted to him. Not in that way. But he was just perfect. A work of art. He wasn't adding to the beauty around him; he was part of it.

'You ok?' I asked. Pathetic.

He nodded and said nothing.

Perhaps I should go. This felt – weird? No, not weird. Unusual was a better word.

He watched me, smiling.

'Can I get you some clothes?' Something to say. I didn't care if he wanted to wander around starkers. He'd probably left his clothes somewhere nearby.

'Thank you,' he said softly. 'That's very kind.' He smiled a silver smile.

'You a visitor?'

He nodded.

'Here for the summer?'

'Perhaps not that long.'

'Where are you staying?'

He was silent but I sensed no discomfort from him. And I felt none either.

'You need somewhere to stay?' My question tumbled out, surprising me but not him, apparently. What would Nan say? But the question had been asked and I couldn't drag it back.

He nodded gently and smiled. I nodded. Nothing about the strangeness of the situation seemed to matter. I felt at ease. It was a long time since that had happened.

'I'm Nat.'

He nodded as if in confirmation. 'You can call me Artem.'

'Artem.' An unusual name for an unusual situation.

I stood up and we wandered back along the edge of

the sea in companionable silence. Speech wasn't needed.

A flicker of movement in the rock shadows ahead made me alert.

'Long time no see, Nat.'

My heart stopped. My brain stopped. My breathing stopped. Then my heart started picking up speed till it was racing. From the first syllable, I knew the voice. The voice I'd wanted to hear for so long.

'Jen,' was all I could say.

She stepped out of the shadow of the rock. Our rock.

'That's a long speech after four years.'

'I –'

She held a finger to her lips. 'I was so sorry to hea –'

'Yeah.' I cut her off. Too raw.

After an awkward pause, Jen looked Artem up and down several times without any suggestion of embarrassment or shyness. Typical Jen.

'Who's your friend?'

'Er, this is Artem.' I coughed. 'We just met.'

Another movement in the shadows.

'So, still buzzing around, Gnat?'

My heart dropped. Another voice from my past. Leon. With the same old jibe. Positive thoughts were swamped as blackness pressed down in my mind. I hadn't given him a thought since leaving. Hadn't wanted to.

'Bringing your London habits down to Cornwall, eh?' said Leon. I said nothing. 'Doubt it'll go down well in the village, picking up naked boys in the local beauty spot. People might wish you hadn't come back at all.'

Red replaced black. Distorted images crashed and splintered through my molten mind – my parents, the crash, Jen from four years ago, friends from London, Nan and ... and ... Artem. I took a step forward, fists clenched at my side but ready to use them. I was losing it. Fast.

Then two things happened. Two hands. Jen's forcing Leon back a step and the lightest touch from Artem on my arm. Immediately, my anger drained. I sighed.

'Idiot!' said Jen, but not to me. Leon swore under his breath and stomped away.

'I'm sorry,' she said.

I nodded.

'Leon can be such a pain.'

'What's new? But are you and he together?' My tone was more accusing than intended.

She nodded then shrugged. 'Four years with no word from you. Life moves on, Nat. We're older.' She glanced away.

I kept my eyes on the ground. Jen, my soulmate, hooked up with Leon. He'd always enjoyed upsetting me as we grew up. Names, sly kicks and trips, spite, unkindness. Just an unpleasant guy. How could she have chosen him? But who was I to judge? Jen must have felt I didn't care and had gone for ever.

'I'd better get after him,' said Jen, 'but I think you and I ought to meet up – if you like.'

I nodded. 'Yeah, I'd like that. I want to – '

'Save it till then.'

She turned, her raven hair melting into the darkness.

Artem was watching me.

'We'd better be going,' I said. 'You can stay at Nan's tonight. I'm sure that'll be fine.' I wasn't sure. He smiled.

*

I woke and gazed at the ceiling while my fuzzy mind trawled around, working out where I was. A frown tightened as the previous evening surfaced in my memory. It had ended better than I could have hoped. We met nobody on the way to the cottage. Artem seemed unconcerned about his nakedness, but I was thankful not to attract more attention. I slipped in to get Artem a pair of my jeans and a t-shirt. He was a little taller than me, but it worked. If Nan was surprised to have a visitor, she didn't show it and gave Artem a warm welcome, although she looked tired. With all the shock and emotions of the last few weeks, maybe this was the least of her worries. I wasn't awake for long, despite the mess of images whirlpooling around my head.

I looked over to Artem's bed. He lay face towards me, catching the sunshine pouring through a gap in the curtains. What was it about this guy? He seemed to attract light, like he was part of it. Even the source of it.

As I showered, I thought about how secretive Artem was. No, that wasn't right. He was a secret. I felt I'd known him for much longer than half a day. Returning to our bedroom, I found Artem dressed and kneeling on the bed looking out of the window. I'd left him some more of my clothes and they suited him.

Nan had breakfast all laid out and ready, as only nans can.

'So, Artem, do you have family?' Nan was determined to get through her list of questions.

Artem gave the slightest of nods and smiled. Nan beamed back as if he'd given her the complete details of his family tree. I could tell she liked him.

'How long will you be staying with us?' she asked.

I turned my head towards Artem. He couldn't answer that one with just a nod and a smile.

He looked at me and said, 'I wish I could stay longer.'

Nan nodded again. Couldn't she see she hadn't been given a proper answer? I kept studying Artem. I wanted to know him better but wasn't sure I ever would. Perhaps somebody who appeared without warning in your life, could disappear the same way.

Artem looked up. 'We should be going, Nat.'

'Where?'

'Into the village.'

I nodded like it was a plan.

Artem stood up. 'Thank you for breakfast.' Nan would love that. 'It's going to be a good day, Anne. A really good day.'

I saw the smile on Nan's face crumple for just a second. Her guard dropped. She looked drawn, then the smile was back.

Artem held out his hand and she took it. He laid his other over hers too. 'It is going to be a good day,' he repeated. 'I know it.'

Nan nodded and smiled. I still had a half-eaten piece of toast in my hand, transfixed by what was playing out before me. I had so many questions, but I knew, if I pursued them when we left the cottage, I would get lots of smiles and little more.

How had Artem known Nan's name was Anne? When he repeated it was going to be a good day, Nan believed it. I felt I believed it. It was so easy to trust Artem. Nan had looked discomforted and then at peace. I didn't know what had caused the momentary change in her, but Artem had reassured her.

'Thanks, Nan,' I said as I pushed the toast into my mouth. 'You're the best.' She smiled.

We headed into the village.

'Where are we going?' I asked.

'There's someone I want to see.'

'You know someone in the village? I thought you only arrived last night.'

A smile and another bypassed question.

'Then you should be getting to your meeting with Jen,' said Artem.

'I'll need to drop by her house to arrange that.'

'I think she'll be waiting for you shortly.'

'Waiting for me? Where?'

He stopped and touched me on the arm. 'I think you know, Nat.'

And I did. I really did. It was the only place she would be. At that moment I believed it. She'd be there as Artem said, yet it hadn't been arranged. Or had it? I couldn't quite recall.

And then I surprised myself. As he took his hand off my arm, I smiled. And said nothing. He smiled back. He knew I understood.

'Now we must move or I'll be late.'

He turned left onto Beach Road.

'Are we going to the beach?'

He shook his head. A pregnant woman was leaving the garden of a house that stood out for its turquoise window frames and door, bright against the white render. She walked along the pavement towards us. I stepped off the pavement to let her pass, but Artem didn't.

'I know it will go well for you today, Sandra.' He glanced at her belly.

She blinked then smiled. 'Another few weeks for me yet.'

Artem smiled. 'If you say so.'

He offered his hand and Sandra took it. 'I wish you well, Sandra, and it will be a good day for you and the baby. Take care.'

Her smile broadened and she went on her way.

'What was that all about?' I asked.

Artem turned to look at me. 'I wanted to wish her well.' He smiled. 'You had better go to Jen. It's important.'

I nodded. He held out his hand and I took it. 'Is it going to be a good day for me too?'

Artem's smile widened. 'You're learning.' Then he looked more serious. 'It will end up being a very good day.' He paused. 'You know that grief and hurt can heal.'

I hadn't even intimated to him what had happened to me in recent weeks but I found I wasn't surprised. 'Is this a time-will-heal-all lesson?'

He looked at me. 'I feel your pain, Nat. It won't always be like this.'

'Why are you here, Artem?'

He was silent for a moment. Was I going to get a proper answer at last?

'I do what needs to be done.'

An answer that only prompted more questions.

'You remind me so much of Peter Kellow,' said Artem. I stared. 'Who's Peter Kellow?'

He smiled. 'I'll see you later. Now go. You mustn't be late.'

I walked back up Beach Road and turned into the churchyard, heading for the old oak tree in the far corner. Another of our special places. As I approached, Jen stepped from behind the tree and smiled. Smiles everywhere. Was Artem the cause of this outbreak of smiling in a scowling world?

Jen and I talked and talked, then talked some more. It was easier than I'd expected. We were such good friends, we picked up from where we had left off all those years ago. I said my piece early on because it needed to be said. I thought she would hit me, scream at me, but she cried and smiled all at once. I told her about my parents. Why I was back here. The crash. The hospital visits. The unreality of that final visit. The overwhelming loneliness and anger. She cried again. I cried. We hugged and hugged, then kissed. In an instant, I was lying on the ground and Leon was there, fists clenched.

There was shouting, much of it mine. A sharp pain in my side set me rolling down the shallow grassy slope onto the gravel path. Face down. Another kick and my body lurched, and I felt the gravel tearing at my cheek. I turned but there was no time to escape before Leon was straddling me and fists came hard and relentless. I put up my hands to shield my face, but a punch found its way through, and flashing stars and blinding colours filled my vision.

I managed to push Leon off and could hear Jen shouting and hitting him. She swore then ran off. And of course, Leon followed her.

'Jen, wait up!' I heard him call as the sounds subsided.

I continued to lie there, gasping and staring at the cloudless blue. An arm touched mine and Artem's face appeared.

'Let me help you up,' he said.

'That thug's made a right mess of me.' I stood but felt unsteady.

'You need to get after Jen. She needs you.'

'Leon wouldn't dare hurt her.'

'She still needs you.'

'Ok.'

Looking up, I saw his face. One eye was closing and the surrounding skin was turning darker. His cheeks had rough grazes down them with bits of gravel.

'Did Leon do...?' My voice faded as I felt my own face. No grazes and no tenderness around the eye. I gaped. 'What have you done, Artem?'

'What I do.'

'But how?'

'You must go now.'

'Where will you be? Are you coming with me?'

He shook his head. 'I will be with you. Always.'

I nodded and the smile lit up his damaged face. I clasped him in a hug. Unexpected for both of us, I think.

After a moment he said, 'Go!'

'Which way?'

'Towards the beach. You'll know.'

I turned and ran. As I left the churchyard, I looked back but there was nobody to be seen. I ran down Beach Road and took the path towards the cove.

I stopped at the narrow way down to the beach. 'You'll know.' I could almost hear Artem speaking to me. I closed my eyes for a moment. No. Not the cove. That's what Leon might expect. Straight on along the old cliff path. I was certain. The route to the mineshaft openings. All at once, a freezing dread began creeping through me. Known mineshaft openings were fenced and marked but other openings could appear at any moment. This was not a good place to come. I hoped I was wrong but I knew I wasn't. I edged forward.

'Jen! Jen!' No reply. 'Jen!'

What was that?

'Jen?'

I was bellowing now and being less cautious. Foolish, but I didn't care. My parents were gone and Artem was going. Jen was the here and now, the future, and I wanted to get to her to tell her just that. I heard her voice and my heart soared.

The next minutes were frantic as images careered through my head. A crumbling edge to a dark hole, a ledge that could give way at any moment, and the rush of adrenaline as Jen clasped one of my wrists and then the other. I was aware of danger, but nothing was going to stop me. As Jen's shaky grin appeared above the surface, I became even more determined. We threw ourselves on our backs and shouted and yelled, our minds empty of anything but a piercing joy to scream at the sky. Jen had been lucky. It could all have gone so wrong.

We walked to Jen's home holding hands all the way. Her parents immediately reported the new mineshaft opening, while Jen and I arranged to meet up later. There was so much to catch up and we were both impatient to do so.

I opened the gate to Nan's cottage. The fragrance of

summer flowers played around my nostrils in the late afternoon sunshine. The side door into the kitchen was open. I decided not to worry Nan with all that had just happened. I didn't want to add to her worries.

'Hi, Nan.'

Nan appeared, all smiles.

'Have you had a good day?' I asked. She looked ten years younger.

'One of the best,' she said, her face shining. 'A miraculous day.'

She sat with me in the kitchen and explained that she'd been diagnosed with cancer six months previously and the prognosis hadn't been good. Treatment didn't seem to have made much difference. She'd had some test results back today and there was no trace of the cancer. No trace at all. The medics were stunned.

Pictures flicked through my mind of Artem holding Nan's hand, holding Sandra's hand, touching my arm, holding my hand. I hugged Nan and made us cups of tea.

'Where's Artem?' asked Nan.

'He had to go. He wasn't staying long. Had to be elsewhere.' My memory prodded. 'Do you know Peter Kellow?'

'Yes, of course, dear,' said Nan. 'He was your great-great grandfather.'

The silence thrummed.

'Have you a photograph?'

'Yes, of course.'

Nan took me through to the study, opened a box of very old photographs and rifled through them. 'Here we are.'

I looked at the figure of a man, unsmiling at the camera.

'You've a look of him,' said Nan.

There was a roaring in my ears as if I had large conches pressed to them.

'He almost fell off the cliffs in a heavy fog. He always said a blonde boy pulled him back from the edge at the last moment. But he never saw him again. Must've looked something like your friend. Young Artem had very blonde hair, didn't he? So blonde. Lovely.'

Nan didn't make the connection. Why would she? I couldn't make any sense of it, but I knew he'd come to help me and save Jen. Just as he saved Peter Kellow so long ago. Artem could've saved Jen himself, but he knew I needed to do it.

Later, Jen and I strolled down Beach Road. It was a sultry evening and very calm. I stopped at the turquoise gate and said, 'I must see how Sandra's day has been. I won't be a moment.'

Jen looked askance at me. I started to open the gate when I heard the cry of a baby through the open windows. I smiled and closed the gate again.

'Doesn't matter after all.'

We walked on and clambered down to the cove.

'So, you don't know where Artem has gone?'

I shook my head. 'He was only passing through.'

'It seemed like you and he had known each other for a long time.'

I nodded.

'You were so easy in each other's company.'

I smiled.

'Funny though. Someone of his age just wandering around on his own.'

'Oh, I think he was older than he looked.'

I nudged Jen and pointed to a shooting star. We gazed in wonder until it passed out of sight behind the moon.

'Goodbye,' I said in a dry whisper. 'And thank you.'

The tiniest splinter of darkness fell away from my heart.

I smiled.

The Giant of Gull Rocks
by Samuel Crosby

The herring gulls are nesting under his eyebrow again, scraping and chattering at his skull. He begs for quiet, thumping at his face with the heel of his hand, and lichen-mottled shale showers down a hundred feet. The flocks grow louder, screeches drowning out his thoughts, drowning out the scents of the world, drowning out the taste of the sea and the gorse flowers. He sits. Closes his eyes. Waits. Not because he expects the waiting to bring a sudden kind of change, but because he'd never known a companion more loyal than patience. He could feel the balance of it in his body.

He had lived since the beginning, even before the human men called him 'giant'. And the lonely years had shifted like the waves, erratic and frothing in short bursts, but always finding a greater rhythm. Some of the world's shifts were swift, others slow and humourless, but there was always balance. He'd seen snapping, snarling food-chain creatures, clouds at rage and forests at flame. In days of ruin, he'd seen the air turn to ash and bodies rot down into his layers. With enough time, even the most powerful things had withered and died. Balance.

Gulls flap around his eyes and shout at their nests. He forces his anger back down his throat. He sets his jaw and waits. At last, in the night, after the moon paints edges on things and the cold offers a blanket, the final herring gull chick is found by its mother and falls quiet.

He is snatched from sleep at first light. The little birds cry out for breakfast, echoing in his crevices. The adults wheel and squawk and skim the water, opening fierce beaks and fierce bowels. In his morning fever he shakes his body, quaking the birds into fretful, scrabbling quiet. But the silence isn't stuffed up for long. One bird tries a fractured cackle and the rest add their calls. He aches, his body forgetting patience, and he finds himself crunching a trail up the headland, grabbing chunks of cliffside to haul himself along. He traces the human train tracks to a mine, the gulls wailing in a midday froth around him, louder even than the squealing, steaming rail machines, louder than the cries of the humans fleeing at his sight, abandoning buckets and dull metal tools and chains at the mouth of the yawning mine. He swats at the birds and reaches down for one of the miner's tools, a splinter between his barrel-thick fingers. Eyes going wide, he stabs it into the gap below his eyebrow, scraping, scraping, scraping. Silence. The nests gone. A trail of feathers and blood streaked across his forehead.

Mouth pinched in concentration, he waits to hear the

sea breeze. For a time, he hears it, revels in it. He closes his eyes to savour the sounds between sounds. But there is a building, flapping rush. A newly energised clamour. In his scraping fever he has torn great chunks away from his face, widening the gap, opening his face for more birds, more herring gulls and common gulls now, gannets and terns, jackdaws and kittiwakes. Harrying, jostling, clattering in his face. Scratching, squabbling, rattling in his soul. He stumbles across the mainland, thumping his hands into his head, following the iron tracks to the towns of the human men, crying out to them for help.

The land underneath unfurls beneath him like a familiar garden he once tended. It is scarred and torn, criss-crossed with tracks and roads and stacks of bricks, but the shape is the same to him. He remembers this valley *... There, the shaft where they dug, going deeper under the hills to pull shining rocks out of the ground. Here, with plans and machines they stood sweating and scheming and waving. And here, the crater I left when I woke like a dead thing from an ancient grave, roused from a thousand-thousand years of sleep. Where I stood, my eyes weeping at the smoke and the splitting ground. We screamed at first, them and me, but I went on cautious and asked them questions, bowed low, put my chin to the ground. We struck a deal. I dug for them. And for me, they began to turn off their black-spewing machines. I emptied armfuls of dirt and minerals into their carts for weeks, tearing chunks out of the land with my hands. And they made sure the last of their steam engines were made silent and the smoke cleared.*

The birds have stopped calling so loudly, murmuring and whimpering now. He joins his voice to the lament. The land is full of smoke again, thick darkness and blackened earth. The men have returned to their machines. The birds fly from his face in mobs, rushing on an instinct to disappear. The chicks die in their nests. He catches one as it falls from his face, cradles the speck on his great palm. All is quiet. He is awash in smoke and nostalgia, wishing for the flocking cacophony, just to hear some other living creatures here to remind these humans how to feel. He blunders on, reaching a thicket of stone buildings, metal and built things sticking out of doorways like poisonous thorns. Humans emerge, ruddy, defiant. The crowds point and murmur, shout, rally together, send runners to fetch and messengers to call. Soon, he is face-to-face with a man he recognises, a tiny soot-blackened face peering into his eye from the top of a slanted roof. *This same one who betrayed our deal. This human man who dug into my face as I slept, tried to pull out my eyes, left me with this bird-perch under my eyebrow. Set me to running and hiding.*

He grips the train-building the man is standing on and lifts it, snapping beams and foundations, rails and sleepers hoisted up into the air like lures on a line. The miner's man stumbles to his knees as he is lifted to the giant's face, and stares into the glinting, raging eyes. The miner's man remembers. He mirrors the sorrow and the shame of the giant in his silent pleading. In that instant, his greed is chased away like the gulls in the smoke.

He signals to the others on the ground with the flap of an arm, makes a cutting motion across his throat. When the last of the engines are quiet, the giant sets the platform to the ground, and the miner's man slips away into the buildings.

In the clearing smoke, the giant turns wordlessly to

his part of the deal, digging the open mine deeper, filling the waiting carts. Men, women and children skip under his legs as he works and pull the carts away to the town. As the sun slips behind the far horizon, he lies down to rest.

In his dream he is human. He rides along a track on a human machine and stamps his boots off at the door and eats freshly baked bread. Family faces hover around him like happy cook fires. They eat and eat, take and take. Outside, their broken things are strewn on the streets, they fight easily, they let the animals die easily and choke the land with black poisons. He swings his fists. Their teeth turn to slate and slip out of their heads and shining, beaked rocks unfurl and flutter from their eyes.

It is still dark when he wakes. The birds are a raucous chorus again, screaming and clawing at his head with beaks, talons, hands, tools. No, not birds. Human men. He twists. Ropes snap from his neck, body, arms, legs. Cracks echo across the hillside. A new kind of men are standing around him in a crowded crescent of patterned blue and gold and white, feathered hats and golden buckles, smoke rising from the end of dark tubes between them. Shining welts open across his body, glittering wetly in the moonlight, waterfalls of shingle gurgling from his shoulder, back, legs, face. A small cloud of birds take to the wing, adding their cries to the cannon fire, adding their silhouettes to the ghostly figures in the blaze. He runs, drunk on the din, eyes wide, smashing through buildings and carts. He sends an engine tumbling over a cliff edge, stumbles backwards, a crowd of horses shying from his earth-shaking steps, and thuds across the countryside, sinking craters into the turf with every lurch. The dark tubes flash again, a cracking boom across the landscape. In the orange light he sees the shape of the miner's man waving his arms. A frantic, distant speck.

He staggers across hillsides, running on, on, down, down to a stream between dunes, one hand steadying between rocks, the other swiping at the feverish birds. One more step. On to a beach. Another step. Another. Then, wild waves hammering his legs, he falls into the sea.

Blissfully free. He rolls onto his back. Ears beneath the water to dull the ache of calling gulls, lichen flanks sucked at by curious fish. *I'll lie here and let the water soften my edges. I'll sing with the birds when the wind blows.*

In the sea's muted moments and massaging swash, the aches ease in his body. He listens. Whales call and dolphins click. Kelp sways in eternal song. Crabs and seals investigate, scraping gently at his granite skin. Years pass. New sounds start to impose themselves on the songs of the bay. Sounds without imagination. Motors whirring in dreadful consistency. Rigid metal machines flying unceasingly overhead, searing white lines by day and blinking away at night. He imagines the grandchildren of the grandchildren of the miner's man, all of them desperately pointing and shouting at shining rocks through lifetimes of greed. He urges himself to stand, to force a different word in the human story, to rage at the thickening smoke.

Instead, he waits. Not because he expects the waiting to bring a sudden kind of change but because patience is his oldest companion, and it reminds him there is balance to all things.

Pure of Heart

by T J Dockree

Marie traced the upright pen strokes on the notepaper with her forefinger: *ich weiß, wo du bist* (*I know where you are*). A tear splashed, puddling the ink.

She looked out across the grassy, stone wall next to her foster parents' home. Below, barbed wire barricades and landmine warnings crisscrossed Perranporth beach. The grey sea beyond was restless but empty. No U-boats yet.

The wind tugged at the paper. She scrunched it up and tucked it in her pocket, then stared at the other envelope. It was embossed with the insignia of the Royal Veterinary College. Taking a deep breath, she tore it open.

Abe's breath was warm on her neck as he came up behind her and nibbled her cardigan. She stroked his velvet nose and leant on his muzzle.

'Du weißt immer …' She hesitated. 'You always know

when I need comforting.' She screwed her face up to stop the tears. It was too late. His love unlocked them. She buried her head in his mane.

Abe wrapped a leathery wing around her and waited.

'Being a vet is my dream. I've wanted this forever but now it's happening, I don't want to leave! What will happen to our little zoo? What if Mumie Nankivell forgets me?'

A hedgehog on Abe's back stirred and looked at her, then yawned and settled back to sleep.

'Dreams need courage, child. You have hidden away here so long you've forgotten how to fly.' Abe's voice was gentle but that only made the tears fall more freely. He held her closer.

'He used to call me "liebe Marie."' She hiccupped on subsiding sobs. 'We were inseparable at school. Then the pogroms began. He joined Nazi Youth. My parents died and I had to run away because he gave them our names. He betrayed us!' She pulled the note from her pocket and thrust it in front of Abe. 'And now he's hunting me. How did he find me?'

Abe snorted at the note, then stuck out his tongue, sucked it into his mouth and swallowed. Marie stared at him, then laughed.

'Do you trust me, Marie?' Abe asked.

She nodded and threw her arms around his neck.

'Come, child. I have people I want you to meet.' Abe lowered his wing to lift her up onto his back.

'But people can't see you. They never see you.'

'They will today. Come.' Abe lifted her up and set her on his back with their travelling menagerie.

Marie sniffed and wiped her face. She smiled at the

chicks in their nest, urging their parents to return quickly with food. The young hedgehog lay on his back, four limbs outstretched in abandonment while he snored. Abe did not seem to notice hedgehog spines digging into his back. Marie marvelled at how skin, so soft to the touch, could be so impervious to damage.

Abe bounded along the cliff path then launched into the air. Marie hugged down into the well of Abe's back between his wings. The journey was quick, a few flaps high above the beach and soldiers eating their dinner outside Droskyn Hotel. They landed at their secret place, the smugglers' caves.

Abe snaked into the largest entrance and the length of his body filled most of the chamber, even with his tail curled up to his nose.

Within minutes, a fox ran down the path towards them. He slowed to listen, ran a little further, then stopped and sniffed the air. His ears flattened.

Abe called out to him: 'Do not be afraid. I will protect you from those who hunt you.'

The fox dashed into the cave and Abe lifted it up to nestle in with the others.

A pack of dogs appeared, barking in excitement. The lead dog stopped and growled.

Abe's head seemed to grow out of the cave, his salivating gums revealing long, sharp teeth. 'Go!' Abe warned.

The dogs ran back up the hill, tails between their legs.

Marie watched the fox as it panted nearby. She opened her water bottle and poured a little into a small bowl. She placed it next to the fox, who stared at it while his panting slowed. After a while, he approached the bowl and drank. He flinched slightly, when she started to stroke him, but kept on drinking. When he'd had enough, he stretched then crawled into Marie's lap.

'You have a wonderful gift with animals, Marie.' Abe was still watching the path, but Marie suspected he had eyes hidden somewhere on the back of his head.

A rabbit hopped by.

'Why do some animals see you and some not? Aren't all animals rein von herz ... um, pure of heart?'

'Animals are like people. They can all see me until darker desires start to rule them. For some, it's killing for the sake of killing rather than for food. For others, it's taking what they want from others, even if they don't need it. It's rare for magpies to see me. Once they get the horde-lust, that's all they see.'

'Will I always see you?' Marie stroked the fox and fixed her gaze on its bushy tail.

'No, my child. But I hope you will see me again, later.'

She picked the fox up and buried her face in its fur. 'What do I do that stops me seeing you?'

'It's not what you do, child, it's what you don't do and what you allow to take root in your heart. Your fear of the unknown and the new pushes me out.' Abe turned and looked into her eyes. 'In perfect love, there is no fear. When you are afraid, remember me.'

'I'm afraid,' she admitted, 'I don't want to be, but I am. I'm afraid Hans will find me. I'm afraid of leaving everyone I love. So why can I see you now?'

'You believe in me. And my love for you.'

Uncomfortable, the fox wriggled in Marie's arms. She let it go. It started to settle back in her lap then froze and stared at the top of the path.

Marie wiped the tears from her face. 'You're very alert, Mr Fox. Is that what being hunted does to us?'

A child of about seven appeared, knees streaked with blood and a muddy face streaked with tears.

Abe blew at him. The child gasped, then ran into the cave. Abe covered him with a wing and held him close.

Two teenage boys scrambled into view.

'Where did that little emmet go?' The scrawny teen searched behind the rocks. 'He was here just now.'

'You know what, Phil, I'm tired of all this,' his brother huffed. He bent over and rested his hands on his knees. 'I'm off.' He stood up and started to walk away.

'He must have run further up. Come on, Ben!' Phil

lifted his arms up in despair. 'If we don't get him, the old man will lash us instead!'

Ben paused and turned back to look at his brother. 'No, I'm leaving. Going to join up. Did you not hear how many died when the Nazis bombed Truro Hospital last night? I'm not going to hide with our coward father while the enemy destroys our home.'

Ben looked at the cave and saw the runaway. Child and chaser looked at each other. Ben smiled and shrugged. Then he noticed Marie. He nodded before walking quickly off, with Phil in pursuit, protesting his cause.

'He saw me,' Marie spoke softly and blushed.

'He did notice you, didn't he?' Abe chuckled. 'He's had a change of heart. He's starting to see the world and his place in it.'

'But he didn't see you,' Marie teased.

'I'm a black dragon in a dark cave and I had my eyes and mouth shut.'

The child peeked up at Marie and she smiled. 'Would you like to meet a fox?'

He nodded and when Abe lifted him up, Marie noticed his swollen eye.

'You need to come home with me. My foster parents are very kind. They'll look after you. You don't have to stay with those ... tyrannen.' She held out her hand. 'I'm Marie.'

'Charlie.' Charlie shook her hand. 'Ben's okay. It's just his dad who hits me.'

There was a click of flint on metal and a waft of nicotine filled the air. Marie lifted her finger to her mouth to caution Charlie to be silent.

'Put that thing out.' A man's voice. Marie recognised

it as belonging to one of the soldiers patrolling the coast path. Jack.

They heard a dying hiss and another soldier's voice: 'Hey! You owe me for that.' Harry, Marie thought. Jack usually had a shift with Harry.

'If you want to light yourself up like a beacon at target practice, do it in your own time, not when you're on watch with me.'

The soldiers walked closer to the cave. Jack prodded the grass with a rifle butt and bent down to pick something up.

Harry walked past the cave entrance and tripped. 'What the ...!' He looked around for the offending obstacle.

Jack laughed. 'Take more water with it, mate.'

'There's something here.' Harry lifted a rifle from his shoulder and started to circle the cave opening. 'It might be a weapon with some clever camouflage device that stops us seeing it.'

'Yeah,' Jack snorted, 'or it might be an invisible dragon with critters and kids on its back laughing their heads off at you.'

'What? Are you on something?' Harry pushed at the air before him like a blind man and moved towards Abe with tentative steps.

'Time to go!' Abe twisted around and exited the cave from the other entrance.

As he launched up into the air, Marie watched Harry go inside. 'You did that on purpose.'

Abe chuckled. 'I love how oblivious people are of what's right in front of them.' He sighed. 'But at the same time, I do so want them to see.'

Marie looked at Jack, watching them. 'He saw us.'

'Jack's been a good and faithful servant for a while.'

Abe hovered over the cliffs near Marie's house. 'Introduce Charlie to your foster parents then lock yourselves inside the house.'

'What? Why?' Marie looked down and scanned the sea. 'Is Hans here?'

Abe circled the house and landed in the garden. Charlie and Marie slid down onto the grass.

Abe wrapped Marie in his wings and blew into her hair. 'Remember, when you're afraid, think of me.' And then, he was gone.

It was getting dark. Marie led Charlie into the house, locked the door, then introduced him to her foster mum.

'Welcome, Charlie.' Mrs Nankivell gently held him by the shoulders. 'I'll send a message to the billeting officer in the morning, but you're welcome to stay here tonight. I think one look at your eye should be enough to persuade him to let you stay here.'

Charlie smiled. 'Thank you, Miss.'

Mrs Nankivell looked at Marie, twiddling her hair. 'So, Marie, what's going on?'

'Well, Mumie, do you want the good news or the bad news?'

'Let's deal with the bad news first, shall we? Then we're free to celebrate the good news.'

'Well ... I had a letter from Hans,' she started slowly, 'He knows where I am and ...' then the words rushed out, 'he wants to kill me.'

Charlie looked up at Marie. 'Why would he want to kill you?'

She sighed. 'He is tyrannen.'

'Does Abe know?' asked Mrs Nankivell.

'You too? Who else knows about him? I thought he was my secret.'

'Abe's too special to stay a secret.' Mrs Nankivell chuckled. 'He'll look after you. He always has. Who do you think helped find you in Germany and bring you here?'

A loud banging on the door startled them.

'Who is it?' Marie hissed in a whisper.

Mrs Nankivell killed the lamp and went to the window. 'I think it's Jack and Harry. Harry looks ... like he's seen a ghost. Guess Abe's introduced himself.'

Marie rushed to the window. 'Abe said to lock all the doors. He didn't say how long for.'

'Let's wait, shall we? I think you'll know when it's okay to unlock them.' Mrs Nankivell drew Marie away from the window.

'Now I know how that fox felt.'

They waited. Marie hadn't noticed how loudly the clock on the mantel ticked before. Or how many trees scratched the windows.

Remember, when you're afraid, think of me. Marie closed her eyes. It was as though Abe was in the room with her, holding her close, blowing his warm breath around her, keeping her safe. Her heartbeat slowed.

There was a shout outside and a clatter of rifles and ammunition fell into the yard. Trucks pulled up at the gate and a floodlight lit up the house and garden. Marie peeked through the blackouts to see five men in scuba gear, bound hand and foot, with their backs to each other. She went to the door and opened it.

Jack was on the doorstep and nodded at her. Harry kept looking up at the sky as though expecting a pterodactyl to swoop in and carry him off.

Marie walked across the yard and stood in front of Hans, but he refused to look at her. Military police ran into the garden, pulled the captives up and dragged them away. Not running off with their tails between their legs but Marie was liking how it was all turning out.

Jack ambled over. 'I found this by the smugglers' caves where you were hiding out with Abe.'

Marie looked at the soggy scrunched up note. 'You know Abe swallowed that earlier so he must have ... you know ...'

Jack held it a little further away with fewer fingers.

'Where did you find the Germans?' Marie asked.

'They were climbing the cliffs near Penhale. Abe spotted them and dropped them here for us.'

'So, the decoy airfield is still working then. Keeping the real airfield secret and safe,' Marie mused.

'How do you know about the decoy airfield? It's supposed to be classified,' Jack whispered.

'It's like Abe, the best kept secret but everyone seems to know.'

'Sorry Abe, I think she's jealous of us.' Jack chuckled at the garden.

Marie looked around. 'Is he ...? Oh.' She sighed. 'I didn't think it would be this soon.'

'He says you did good in there and you'll see him again soon. We'll hang around tonight and guard the house, just to be safe.' Jack nodded and returned to his post next to Harry.

Mrs Nankivell walked across the garden and put her arm around Marie's shoulders. 'So, the bad news is dealt with. What good news are we celebrating?'

'I have a place at the Royal Veterinary College. I can start in September, but I haven't decided whether to go yet.'

'But this has been your dream!' Mrs Nankivell searched Marie's face. 'If you don't go, you will always regret it. And being a qualified vet will enable you to do so much. Travel the world. Look after countless animals. It's perfect for you.'

'I know. But I don't want to lose all this.'

'This time is just for now. Even if you stay, it will all change at some point. And you can always come home to us, whenever you want.'

'I think it's already changing.' Marie sniffled. 'I can't see him.'

'Why? Why can't you see him?'

'Because I'm afraid to leave.'

'It's okay to be afraid.' Mrs Nankivell laughed. 'But it's not okay to let it stop you from doing what you know is right.'

Marie looked at the ground and closed her eyes. *Remember, when you're afraid, think of me.* 'Okay! I'll do it. For the animals. But I'll be back here every holiday.'

Mrs Nankivell hugged her close. 'I'll always be here for you.'

Marie heard a rustle and looked up to see the fox jump down from Abe's back. Together they watched the fox trot off, tail high, through the front gate and up the cliff path.

Up Frogs

by Ross James

'Where are you going?' Mum used to shout.
'Up Frogs,' I'd shout back.

That's how it got to be known as Up Frogs. I'm starting secondary school at the end of summer, so Mum doesn't ask now.

I don't like going near the shed, but I've got to so I can climb the hedge, and follow the Red River up the valley. Up Frogs is my favourite place. Nobody goes there except me, and the frogs. I take a stick because the path is overgrown. The brambles swipe at my arms, unzipping my skin, and I see the red below the surface. I clear a path through, but tomorrow it'll be grown over again and the scratches on my arms will have healed.

The Red River cuts through the green grass of the valley, and I follow it to Up Frogs where the leats and lagoons are. Dad said it was an Old Tailings Works. He was a miner and knew all about Tin and Metal and things like that. There are settling tanks where the clean rainwater collects in ponds. It's all concrete, but the frogs and butterflies don't care, so I don't either. It's cleaner than the water in the Red River. Dad said it bubbled up from the mines full of Red Ochre and was poisonous. It's no good for frogs.

There are concrete walls to walk along with water on each side. I've got good balance because Mum gives me hell when I get my shoes wet. By the oblong pond there are circles of smooth concrete like an upside-down stack of plates. They are big enough so that when I lie in the middle, I can only just reach the edges. I don't know what they're for. I used to think they were rocket launchers, but I was a pretty stupid kid. On sunny days, the concrete gets warm and I just lie there feeling the warmth of it, watching the frogs in the ponds. The butterflies do the same thing, so they must like it too. I think they like the warmth, not the frog-watching, but who knows? I wish there was a job where you could spend all day watching frogs.

The frogs don't make a ripple when they come up to the surface. Their eyes are gold when the sun catches them. They're toads really, well, some of them are. You can tell because toads are warty, but when I was little, I didn't know the difference and now I can't get used to saying Up Toads, so I just keep to saying Up Frogs. Sometimes you see newts too, so it would be stupid to call it Up Frogs But Mainly Toads And The Odd Newt.

Aunty Jan gave me a toad made of solid brass; you could feel by how heavy it was. Dad said brass was made from Copper and Zinc. It was about the same weight as a real toad, and it felt cold like a real one too. Its back was warty but under the chin was smooth. I would rub his chin so hard that it shone like gold, well, brass really. It was just the right size to fit in your pocket so you could rub it with your thumb, and nobody would guess you had a brass toad in your pocket which you could rub with your thumb if you wanted to. I always carried it in my pocket.

A couple of years ago, when I was little, Dad took me down Crofty. Everyone knew Dad. Whenever we were in Camborne or even down Portreath beach, people would recognise him and shout out, 'Hey, Janner!' or 'Alright, Dyno?' Nobody ever called him Daniel. The only person I ever heard call him that was the vicar, and I don't think he'd ever even met him.

Anyway, it was the same at Crofty, everyone we passed in the mine knew him and I felt proud. He acted different when we were at Crofty, comfortable, like he was meant to be there as much as a frog is meant to be in water. There were tunnels everywhere, and it was pretty dark, but I wasn't scared, or not much anyway. The mine smelled like Dad, or I suppose Dad smelled like the mine, it was earthy and bit sort of spicy like metal and matches. Dad kept talking about which bits of the tunnel he'd worked on. He had names for different parts of the mine just like we have names for places on the surface, it was like a whole other world - Dad's underground world. And the other one, 'Grass' he called it, he shared with Mum and me.

Dad's job was to set the explosives, that's why he got the nickname Dyno. He told me all about the fuses, detonators, primers, everything. I was too young to understand it all, but I knew it was important and dangerous work. I think that's why everyone knew him.

One tunnel he took me to went right under my school. We sat down on a ledge and Dad told me how he'd blasted it only a few months before. And then I remembered what happened in the playground. We were all out mucking around, playing tap-tap-in, when all of a sudden half of the kids in the playground fell over at the exact same time. I didn't hear a bang, or even feel anything really, except we all fell over. Even Mrs Pengelly, the dinner lady, fell over, and she was sturdy on her feet like a rugby player. Dad said she used to play for Redruth, but I think he was joking. Anyway, after we fell over, we sat quietly for a second, wondering what had happened and then Mrs Pengelly farted, or maybe it was someone else, but we all heard it because it was so quiet in the playground. Even the birds had stopped singing. When she got up, her tights were laddered, and she was teasy as an adder, so she rang the bell and made us all line up five minutes early.

Dad laughed when I told him about Mrs Pengelly farting and getting ladders in her tights and the kids falling over at the same time. He had a loud laugh that came up from his belly and made him shake. It echoed through the tunnel. I laughed too. We laughed so much my face and stomach hurt, but it was worth it because it felt brilliant, like I was one of his workmates at Crofty, having a good laugh.

Then bam! I tripped. Knees on rock, hands skidding in dirt, palms stinging like they were on fire. Gravel stuck under my skin and blood oozing out black in the darkness.

Dad picked me up off the floor. 'Come on, let's get you back up to grass,' he said, but he was too kind and I wanted to cry because all of a sudden I was his little kid again, and not one of his workmates and my hands really stung.

When we got back up top, Dad cleaned the grit and dirt out of my cuts and bandaged my hands. After, without thinking, I put my hand in my pocket to stroke Toad's chin, but he was gone. My pocket was torn and empty. I felt sort of nervous and empty inside, like somebody had scooped out all the happiness from my belly with a cold spoon. It was the first time I remember having the hollowed-out-cold-spoon feeling. I hate that feeling.

I really missed Toad and having his smooth chin to rub with my thumb. Everything changed after that. Toad was lucky; when I lost him, I lost my luck.

We used to go camping in the summer, or we'd have days out down the beach. Sometimes we'd go down Falmouth for fish and chips or go crabbing on the harbour wall. We went up to London once and saw the pigeons at Trafalgar Square. We always used to have good times. Mum and Dad used to laugh all the time, but after I lost Toad, they seemed to run out of laughs. I got home from school one day and Dad was sitting in the front room looking like he had the hollowed-out-cold-spoon feeling. Dad never sat in the front room during the day. Nobody sat in the front room during the day, or at all come to that. Mum saved it for best. Mum said Crofty was closed, and Dad lost his job. Everyone lost their jobs. Just like that.

The wheels in the headgear over Crofty were still. The gates chained up. Someone wrote graffiti on the wall by the road, '*Cornish lads are fishermen, and Cornish lads are miners too. But when the fish and tin are gone, what are the Cornish boys to do?*' I was going to ask Mum what the Cornish boys would do, but she was staring straight ahead at the road.

After Crofty shut, we didn't go for holidays or days out, and Dad hardly ever came out of the house. He shrivelled up like a plant without water. The mine must have given him something me and Mum couldn't. I think it was the same for Dad's friends too. We never saw them in Camborne. There were never the shouts of 'hey, Janner!', no belly laughs.

Mum said we had to Cut Our Cloth which I didn't understand, but then she explained it meant we had to shop in Norman's supermarket because it was cheapest. On our way around the shop, she kept adding up the price of everything in the trolley to make sure she could pay for it when she got to the checkout. Her face was tight, like a wrung-out rag. One day when we got home from Norman's, Dad wasn't in the living room. He didn't come and help unpack the shopping. It was me that found him in the shed, but he was already empty and gone.

Sometimes I dream that I'm Toad, lost in the mine. The mine is flooding, water rising around me, pitch black. I can't see the water, but I know it's red and poisonous, then I realise I'm not down the mine, and I'm not Toad, but I'm in the shed, and the floor is red and oozing. That's when I wake up.

That dream always makes me scared, but I tell myself to imagine a happy place, somewhere warm, somewhere safe. I walk out of the shed, climb the hedge, and follow the Red River up the valley. Up Frogs is my favourite place. Nobody goes there except me, and the frogs. I take a stick because the path is overgrown. The brambles swipe at my arms, unzipping my skin, and I see the red below the surface. I clear a path through, but tomorrow it'll be grown over again and the scratches on my arms will have healed.

Biographies

David Allkins has worked for Waterstones, United Response, and is currently working in administration. He has written book reviews for *horrifiedmagazine.co.uk*, which celebrates British horror, and is currently dealing with researching various projects, books to be read, a garden being reclaimed by wilderness and two demanding black cats. Twitter: AllkinsDavid, Goodreads: David Allkins, Instagram: davidallkins.

Stephen Baird, after a career in education, is writing a YA (Young Adult) historical fantasy set in Renaissance Italy. His first novel was *Fire in the Straw*. He has written three plays and a rock musical for 8-13 year-olds. Stephen's wife correctly predicted that all three sons would reach adolescence before their dad. Stephen and Liz live in Truro with Mustard the Whippet. Genres: Young Adult, Historical, Fantasy, Adventure. Twitter: sbairdauthor Facebook: Stephen Baird Author www.stephenbairdwriter. wixsite.com

Kate Barden: Living in Cornwall all her life, Kate works with care-experienced young people. Along with published poems, she has co-written and performed shows with her company, Blabbermouth, including at the Edinburgh Fringe. Kate is currently rehearsing with the RSC, Hall for Cornwall and Carnon Downs Drama Group. She writes and performs spoken word and is collaborating on a poetry anthology about women who sea-swim in Cornwall. Kate sings in an 80s covers band, collects tattoos, and rides pillion on a Harley www.katebarden.co.uk

Sam Crosby is a storyteller and wild walker living on the edge of Langarrow, Cornwall's buried city. He journeys in folklore, myth and place, bringing the wisdom of old stories and oral traditions back to the campfires and hearth-sides of our contemporary crises. What can Tregeagle teach us of compassion? How do mermaids speak to the human condition? What did our ancestors hide in their stories? Join him at the fire: www.samuelcrosby.com

TJ Dockree is creator and editor of the *Ethical Rebel* zine and a fashion designer at Truro's Sewing & Design Studio. She mainly writes fantasy and historical dramas and is currently working on the novels: *Timeline 67, Dream Walkers, Bait* and *Mine the Light*. Previous short stories are *Knights on a Train* and *Little Bear*. Her poem, *The Maiden*, won first prize at *Poetry Today – Beyond the Horizon* in 1997. Find out more at: cornwallwriters.co.uk/t-j-dockree, Instagram: tjdockree Twitter: DockreeTj Facebook: TJ Dockree

Ulrike Duran Bravo is German-Chilean, now living in beautiful Cornwall. With an MA in Creative Writing, she has various stories published in anthologies and a short play performed. When not writing, she might be busy teaching, tour-guiding or story-telling. Most of her stories are inspired by her heritage and quirky historical facts. Her favourite days are spent with her two children by the beach looking for sea-glass. Facebook: Ulrike Duran - Writer

Angela Linney is passionate about many things, including writing, and wishes for more hours to hone her craft. She also writes under the name Angela Evron. Her passion for natural health inspired her current project, a non-fiction book on Homeopathy. Her first novel, *Bitter Pill*, is soon to be published. Angela has three beautiful children and six lively grandchildren. She lives with her husband near Perranporth, where the Atlantic Ocean and stunning golden sands are her inspiration. cornwallwriters.co.uk/angela-linney/

Rachel Fitch moved from North-East England to Cornwall to develop her career in the education sector, where she spends her time nurturing and caring for the wellbeing of children throughout Cornwall. When she isn't scribbling down her latest short story, she is creating art and getting crafty ... and the surf is so much warmer down here! www.stardustmagicandeternaldreams.home.blog

Ben French enjoys creating - words on paper, bedtime stories for his children, noises on guitar, and dodgy DIY. Loving all things literary he studied English at Falmouth College of Arts and went on to teach. On the weekends he can be seen dragging his family around country walks but always stops for a second-hand book sale. He divides his time between his home near Falmouth and his ranch in Montana. He wishes.

Jo Grande has an interest in local history. Her friend Heather Cox determined the site of Saint Wenappa's Well in Gwennap and asked Jo to research and write about the life of the Saint. Sadly, Heather died in October 2018. This story is the fulfilment of a promise. In 2017 she saw a course advertised at Falmouth University. Delighted when accepted, she thoroughly enjoyed her studies which resulted in an MA in Professional Writing and a load of ideas about what she might do next.

Anita Hunt has an MA in Creative Writing and she is a published poet, theatre reviewer and author. Hobbies include walking her dogs, being crafty, anything to do with the theatre and singing with the Rock Choir. When asked how she fits everything in, she shrugs her shoulders, gives you that I don't know look and is heard to mutter: 'sleep is for wimps.' She can be found at: www.piskiedreams.com

Lamorna Ireland is a Cornish maid with a Cornish heritage, taking inspiration from her county at a young age. In April 2020, she released her debut novel *Unexpected Beginnings* – a contemporary romance set on a Cornish cider farm. In April 2021, Lamorna released another feel-good romance *Unexpected Truths*, this time set in Mevagissey. In December 2021, Lamorna's readers returned to Trengrouse Cider Farm in her first festive short story *A Merry Trengrouse Christmas*. Follow her on social media: lamornairelandauthor

Ross James grew up on the north Cornish coast and now lives in the Falkland Islands with his wife and children. Obsessed by the sea and the things that live in it, his first book, *111 Days - Tales of a Fisheries Observer*, is a firsthand account of life on a trawler. Ross is working on a series of mystery books set in the Falkland Islands and South Georgia. Find him at www.rbjames.com Facebook: rossjameswrites

Emma Lamerton is a Cornish writer, artist and daydreamer. Having recently completed an MA in Creative Writing, she is now working on her first novel. When she's not attempting to convert made-up places and people into words, she enjoys walks in the woods, dancing to live music and being on the lookout for bats. She can be found on Twitter: mayhemtwine

Catherine Leyshon is a geographer, corgi-wrangler and runner. She has published widely in academic journals and books on non-fictional topics as diverse as climate change, film, landscape, volunteering and care, but also likes to have a crack at fiction from time to time. She has her best ideas for short stories when walking the dog, who now wants co-author credits and to be paid in gravy bones.

Claudia Loveland gets excited by words and music and has a happy history of combining the two. Since moving to Cornwall in 2008, she has written short fiction, often exploring the experiences of newcomers and returners to the county: those who may want to lose a bleak backstory or move into a re-furnished future. She loves surprises and humour – and enjoys singing, playing table tennis and walking the Cornish carns and coves. Facebook: ClaudiaLovelandWriter   www.cornwallwriters.co.uk/claudia-loveland

Abigail Ottley writes poetry and short fiction. Her work has appeared in numerous outlets including The Lake, Poetry Wivenhoe, Ink, Sweat & Tears and The Survivor. A Pushcart nominee in 2013 and shortlisted for the

Cinnamon and Three Trees awards in 2021, Abigail was a contributor to *Invisible Borders: New Women's Writing From Cornwall* (2020). She is the author of *Old Soldiers, Old Bones & Other Stories* and is writing her first novel. Abigail lives in Penzance. Abigail Elizabeth Ottley on Facebook and Instagram.

Emily Charlotte Ould is a freelance writer, editor, and proofreader from Cornwall. She studied Creative Writing at Falmouth University before completing a Masters in Writing for Young People at Bath Spa. She is proud to be a founder of *PaperBound Magazine*, an online publication celebrating children's and young adult fiction, and is an enthusiastic lover of country music. Find her on Twitter: emilyocharlotte Instagram @emilycharlotteeditorial and visit her website: emilycharlotteedit.wixsite.com/website

Caroline Palmer wrote the films: *The Secret, The Candlestick, John Harris, Some Scenes from The the Life of John Harris* (won Best Documentary at Buxton Film Festival), also short stories including *Barnacle Bill*. Her books are *The Cats of Tregoyne, What the Cats of Tregoyne Did Next, Porthtowan and Towan Cross* and *More about Porthtowan and Towan Cross*. (FB page Porthtowan and Towan Cross). Her plays are *The Turning of the Tide, Taxi* and *We Have to Ask Some Questions*. She's currently editing her novel *The Time of the Cuckoo*.

Anne Rainbow Ha-Ha retired, Anne wears three hats: writer, mentor and teacher. Her extensive publishing career of textbooks in Mathematics and IT/Computing under the name Jenny Lawson is listed here: www.linkedin.

com/in/anne-rainbow-69b3945/. In *EDITING The Red Pen Way*, she explains her tried-and-tested approach to self-editing and makes it sound fun. Her blog www.scrivenervirgin.com encourages writers to use Scrivener and opens the door to her RedPen Training and Mentoring schemes. In her spare time, she writes novels.

Jennie Rawling is a writer, actor and puppeteer based in Falmouth. She has written for *in Falmouth* magazine, is Assistant Editor of British UNIMA's *Puppet Notebook*, and worked in marketing communications for nearly 10 years. Jennie's first published short story, *Emily*, appears in *Day of the Dead: Tales of Death and Dying* by Portsmouth Writers' Hub, published by Life is Amazing. She writes about her relationship to nature at muddyscribbles.com. Find out more about her work at www.jennierawling.com.

Greg Richards is a proud Cornishman who likes to spend his time writing about things he finds interesting. Most of his stories lie in a drawer marked 'unfinished' so he is always glad when one gets to see the light of day. As a husband he has a wife who encourages this sort of thing. As a Daddy he's not slept in two years, but is grateful for every moment. Bespectacled, with long hair and a beard he would make an excellent Guess Who character. He can be found on Twitter: writechards

Philip S Rollason writes from his home in South Cornwall. With one foot in literary fiction and a toe or two from the other dipped in the surreal, Philip's stories deal with class, love, loss and tales of reconciliation, and of things once broken that never quite fit together as they used to. Find more of his work, and links to social media at philipsrollason.com

Felicity Tattersall is an author illustrator and has lived in Cornwall for over a decade. She completed her MA Illustration at Falmouth University in 2017 and her first picture book *Cornish Mice and the Treasure Garden* was published by Tor Mark in 2021. She writes short stories, plays and children's books. She creates illustrations for cultural organisations and museum clients. If left to her own devices, she would probably just draw plants and flowers, and fill notebooks with nonsense.

Alice Thomas has lived in Cornwall for most of her life and studied to achieve two Master's degrees. She now practises in digital art and writing, currently drafting a few books in a new series, where it's set in a sci-fi fantasy universe she daydreamt about for many years. She has written many short stories and a few winning drafts for the National Novel Writing Month, as well as writing for a few websites as a freelance journalist. Her website will be set up soon, but she can be found on her Instagram as ProperNeko.

Ella Walsworth-Bell is a speech therapist and writer based in Falmouth. She creates short stories and poetry about myth, motherhood and mental health within rural communities in Cornwall. This is her first foray into the intriguing world of sci-fi, and she suspects it won't be her last. Twitter: BellWalsworth